MILWAUKEE NOIR

EDITED BY TIM HENNESSY

BROOKLYN, NEW YORK, USA
BALLYDEHOB, CO. CORK, IRELAND

Published by Akashic Books
©2019 Akashic Books

Series concept by Tim McLoughlin and Johnny Temple
Milwaukee map by Sohrab Habibion

ISBN: 978-1-61775-701-3
Library of Congress Control Number: 2018960606

Akashic Books
Brooklyn, New York, USA
Ballydehob, Co. Cork, Ireland
Twitter: @AkashicBooks
Facebook: AkashicBooks
E-mail: info@akashicbooks.com
Website: www.akashicbooks.com

For my mom Karen and my sister Lori.

*In memory of my grandmother Dolores Biemann
and my dad Ed Hennessy.*

And for Carrie and Jack, with love.

ALSO IN THE AKASHIC NOIR SERIES

MOSCOW NOIR (RUSSIA),
edited by NATALIA SMIRNOVA & JULIA GOUMEN

MUMBAI NOIR (INDIA), edited by ALTAF TYREWALA

NEW HAVEN NOIR, edited by AMY BLOOM

NEW JERSEY NOIR, edited by JOYCE CAROL OATES

NEW ORLEANS NOIR, edited by JULIE SMITH

NEW ORLEANS NOIR: THE CLASSICS,
edited by JULIE SMITH

OAKLAND NOIR, edited by JERRY THOMPSON
& EDDIE MULLER

ORANGE COUNTY NOIR, edited by GARY PHILLIPS

PARIS NOIR (FRANCE), edited by AURÉLIEN MASSON

PHILADELPHIA NOIR, edited by CARLIN ROMANO

PHOENIX NOIR, edited by PATRICK MILLIKIN

PITTSBURGH NOIR, edited by KATHLEEN GEORGE

PORTLAND NOIR, edited by KEVIN SAMPSELL

PRAGUE NOIR (CZECH REPUBLIC),
edited by PAVEL MANDYS

PRISON NOIR, edited by JOYCE CAROL OATES

PROVIDENCE NOIR, edited by ANN HOOD

QUEENS NOIR, edited by ROBERT KNIGHTLY

RICHMOND NOIR, edited by ANDREW BLOSSOM,
BRIAN CASTLEBERRY & TOM DE HAVEN

RIO NOIR (BRAZIL), edited by TONY BELLOTTO

ROME NOIR (ITALY), edited by CHIARA STANGALINO
& MAXIM JAKUBOWSKI

SAN DIEGO NOIR, edited by MARYELIZABETH HART

SAN FRANCISCO NOIR, edited by PETER MARAVELIS

SAN FRANCISCO NOIR 2: THE CLASSICS,
edited by PETER MARAVELIS

SAN JUAN NOIR (PUERTO RICO),
edited by MAYRA SANTOS-FEBRES

SANTA CRUZ NOIR, edited by SUSIE BRIGHT

SÃO PAULO NOIR (BRAZIL),
edited by TONY BELLOTTO

SEATTLE NOIR, edited by CURT COLBERT

SINGAPORE NOIR, edited by CHERYL LU-LIEN TAN

STATEN ISLAND NOIR, edited by PATRICIA SMITH

ST. LOUIS NOIR, edited by SCOTT PHILLIPS

STOCKHOLM NOIR (SWEDEN), edited by
NATHAN LARSON & CARL-MICHAEL EDENBORG

ST. PETERSBURG NOIR (RUSSIA), edited by
NATALIA SMIRNOVA & JULIA GOUMEN

SYDNEY NOIR (AUSTRALIA), edited by JOHN DALE

TEHRAN NOIR (IRAN), edited by SALAR ABDOH

TEL AVIV NOIR (ISRAEL), edited by ETGAR KERET
& ASSAF GAVRON

TORONTO NOIR (CANADA), edited by JANINE ARMIN
& NATHANIEL G. MOORE

TRINIDAD NOIR (TRINIDAD & TOBAGO), edited by
LISA ALLEN-AGOSTINI & JEANNE MASON

TRINIDAD NOIR: THE CLASSICS
(TRINIDAD & TOBAGO), edited by EARL LOVELACE
& ROBERT ANTONI

TWIN CITIES NOIR, edited by JULIE SCHAPER
& STEVEN HORWITZ

USA NOIR, edited by JOHNNY TEMPLE

VANCOUVER NOIR (CANADA), edited by SAM WIEBE

VENICE NOIR (ITALY), edited by MAXIM JAKUBOWSKI

WALL STREET NOIR, edited by PETER SPIEGELMAN

ZAGREB NOIR (CROATIA), edited by IVAN SRŠEN

FORTHCOMING

ACCRA NOIR (GHANA),
edited by NANA-AMA DANQUAH

ADDIS ABABA NOIR (ETHIOPIA),
edited by MAAZA MENGISTE

ALABAMA NOIR, edited by DON NOBLE

BERKELEY NOIR, edited by JERRY THOMPSON
& OWEN HILL

BELGRADE NOIR (SERBIA),
edited by MILORAD IVANOVIC

BOGOTÁ NOIR (COLOMBIA),
edited by ANDREA MONTEJO

COLUMBUS NOIR,
edited by ANDREW WELSH-HUGGINS

JERUSALEM NOIR, edited by DROR MISHANI

NAIROBI NOIR (KENYA), edited by PETER KIMANI

PARIS NOIR: THE SUBURBS (FRANCE),
edited by HERVÉ DELOUCHE

SANTA FE NOIR, edited by ARIEL GORE

TAMPA BAY NOIR, edited by COLETTE BANCROFT

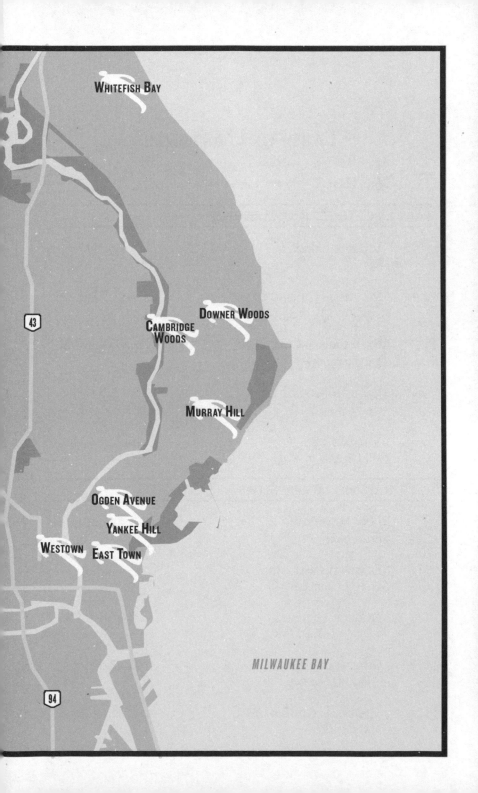

TABLE OF CONTENTS

PART III: WHAT MADE MILWAUKEE FAMOUS

INTRODUCTION
DISTURBING REVERBERATIONS

A few years ago, an ad campaign featured Wisconsin native Willem Dafoe sitting in a Greyhound station, in front of him two buses: one departing for New York, the other for Milwaukee. His destiny hanging in the balance, he tells us: "Life boils down to a series of choices. Before long, the choices you make and the ones you don't become you."

Dafoe's vampiric, underfed gremlin face is transposed on a regretful, hardworking wrinkled old man cleaning up after circus animals, while overhead his confident, athletic composite swings on the trapeze. The voice-over is damning.

"Whether you're good enough, strong enough. All choices lead you somewhere." Be that a CEO flying in on a private plane, a bored, pencil-pushing shop foreman, a chess champion outthinking his opponent, or a sumo wrestler. It's a minute and a half doubling down on an infamous throwaway joke Dafoe made about himself and Houdini. Both shared the same hometown, and their greatest escape was leaving Wisconsin.

Poking fun at the stoic simplemindedness, the gleeful love Midwesterners have for low-paying, blue-collar existences because we're too practical to make bold choices. Dafoe's ad presents the problem facing Midwesterners: how do you move into the future and hold onto what you love about the past?

When you grow up in or around the city once known

as "The Machine Shop of the World," the expectation isn't that you'd have the wherewithal for creative pursuits. I didn't grow up knowing any writers. Teachers, machinists, insurance salesmen, store clerks, office workers, greenkeepers, civil servants; but not writers. People did that somewhere else. Our stories weren't important enough. We were too bland. Few books take place in Milwaukee, and from the time I could read I gravitated toward any faint mention of Milwaukee or Wisconsin in pop culture. Turns out Milwaukee has more of a literary legacy than imagined.

Robert Bloch's family moved here from Chicago in 1929, and he lived here until 1953. An avid reader at a young age, Bloch bought copies of *Weird Tales* from local tobacco and magazine stores with his hard-won allowance. He fell in love with the pulp and wrote a fan letter to H.P. Lovecraft, with whom he struck up a regular correspondence. Lovecraft encouraged Bloch to write and introduced him to a circle of pulp authors who would go on to shape contemporary fiction. Bloch lived on Brady Street above Glorioso's deli during that time. He began publishing regularly and worked writing ad copy until he got a job as a speechwriter for future mayor Carl Zeidler's campaign. It wasn't until he and his wife moved from the city to a small northwestern Wisconsin town that he wrote *Psycho*, inspired by events in nearby Plainfield.

Fredric Brown worked as a proofreader and typesetter for the *Milwaukee Journal*. Among his odd jobs, Brown copy-edited pulp magazines, which led him to submit his work because in his mind, he couldn't do any worse than what he was editing. A heavy drinker, his career grew slowly as he ground out science fiction and mystery paperbacks to keep the bill collectors at bay.

Before he became a major force in publishing and entwined himself in pop culture, Robert Beck, better known as

Iceberg Slim, grew up here. Disturbing reverberations of the themes in Beck's work can still be felt in Milwaukee today, as it's known nationally as a major hub for sex trafficking. While here, he became enamored with street life despite his mother's efforts to educate and raise him in a middle-class lifestyle. Beck's writing career didn't start until after a stint in jail, but years of hustling on the streets of Milwaukee and in much of the Rust Belt provided the backdrop for his books.

One of the authors who was a gateway into crime fiction for me was John D. MacDonald, the prolific detective story and thriller writer who died in St. Mary's Hospital. He came here for a heart bypass surgery and is buried in Holy Cross Cemetery. A legendary writer who didn't reside here while alive, but now spends eternity in the glacial clay soil of Milwaukee, coincidentally in the same cemetery as Dolores Biemann, my grandmother—a woman who appreciated great crime fiction.

Milwaukee is also the hometown of crime writer and Academy Award winner John Ridley, as well as crime/horror legend Peter Straub, whose formative years here left such a deep impact that they continue to haunt his work. Millhaven, Straub's stand-in for Milwaukee, is the kind of place where a character wonders, *What happened to the Millhaven where a guy could go out for a beer an' bratwurst without stumbling over a severed head?*

Straub's industrial city rampant with crime proved the inspirational fodder for Nick Cave's song "Do You Love Me? (Part 2)" and more directly "The Curse of Millhaven."

And it's small and it's mean and it's cold
But if you come around just as the sun goes down
You can watch the whole thing turn to gold . . .

That's as accurate a description as you're likely to find. Milwaukee, like so many cities in the Rust Belt, built its identity as a home to manufacturers, a growing immigrant community, and booze. Over the last half-century, as jobs disappeared so did the dreams that came with them. The chance to make an honest living eroded the blue-collar families' quest for upward mobility.

Presently, Milwaukee is going through a renaissance—abandoned factories being converted to condos, craft breweries and distilleries pushing out corner taverns—yet at the same time it is among the most segregated and impoverished big cities in the country. The gentrification of neighborhoods outside of downtown bear the impact of twentieth-century redlining efforts, forcing residents out due to housing demand, adding fuel to the affordable-housing crisis. Such an environment and atmosphere make excellent fodder for noir fiction—an outlook out of step with the romanticized nostalgia that *Happy Days* and *Laverne & Shirley* created of Milwaukee.

Near the end of Willem Dafoe's ad, he boards a bus headed for New York. "Bold choices take you where you need to be." In a recent interview, Dafoe explained that the path he took led him to Milwaukee, where he studied and performed with other passionate, supportive performers. Living in Milwaukee exposed him to diversity and different social classes outside of his experience. It lit a fire in him.

The book you're holding is the first of its kind—a short fiction collection about Milwaukee, by writers who've experienced life here. The crime/noir genre at its best can be one of the purest forms of social commentary. I've gathered contributors who can tell not just a fine story, but who can write about the struggles and resilience of the people who live here. Maybe you picked up this book because you recognized an author's name, like Jane Hamilton or Reed Farrel Coleman. You'll also find Matthew J. Prigge and Jennifer Morales, among others, whose stories you won't soon forget. Or maybe you were intrigued by the word *Milwaukee* in the title. Whatever the reason, I'm honored to compile a body of work that represents what I love, and fear, about Milwaukee. I love my city's lack of pretension; its stubbornness and pride in the unpolished corners. I fear that my city faces an uncertain future—that as it becomes more divided it may push our best and brightest to find somewhere else to shine.

Tim Hennessy
Milwaukee, Wisconsin
February 2019

PART I

Schlemiels & Schlimazels

RUNOFF

BY VALERIE LAKEN
Downer Woods

We shouldn't have been there in the first place. That's the problem with telling you anything real. We should have been tucked into soft little beds, dreaming of algebra or homecoming or whatever. We shouldn't have been creeping through the sewers under your city. I know that much. We shouldn't have been hunched up like rodents, sweeping our flashlights along the damp, scratchy walls, trying not to hit our heads while we searched for those metal rungs that lead up to manholes. Don't worry, I'm not talking about your real sewer system, Mr. Mayor, that deep channel of shitty dishwater that flows down to Jones Island and fills up Lake Michigan. I'm talking about the old spider-web of pipes that runs closer to the surface, under the East Side. Maybe you don't even know it exists, but we do. Me, Diego, and JJ, we drop down into it at night, because some of those manholes don't open onto streets or alleys like you'd expect—they open up into the garages of people like you. And people like you store all kinds of pawnable shit in your garages—so much that you forget you ever even had it. I bet nine out of ten people we hit don't even know they've been robbed. So how bad am I really supposed to feel about it?

Friday night, the three of us wormed our way through the tunnels for at least a half hour before we found anyplace new. We try to be careful. We leave spare lights hanging like torches at forks in the pipelines, and we stay together, in boots and gloves, and I trust these guys, Diego and JJ, they look out for me like I'm their sister. A cousin, at least. But that night, I started losing my bearings down there, I got all wobbly and sick, like maybe the tunnel was a throat that could tighten and swallow us. Trailing last, I stopped to get a grip and let some air open up between me and Diego. He's a big guy, heavy and slow, and the whole backside of him nearly blocked my view of the route ahead, so I shone my light backward, to where we had been, and I was about to break down and beg them to turn back when finally JJ stopped and said, "Shazam." He found one.

If a manhole opens onto the world, and you press your face up to its little finger holes, you can see the glow of streetlights and hear cars rolling over. If it opens into a building, though, you get nothing but dark silence, like we got then. So JJ heaved open the lid and shoved it aside with a loud scrape, and we waited. When we first started doing this, that part used to scare me, till JJ explained: "If you were sitting around your garage at night—and why would you, when you have a whole house right there—you'd have the lights on, right? And we'd see those lights, and we wouldn't go up. But let's say for whatever reason you *are* sitting around in your old, cold garage with the lights off, and you hear this heavy scrape in the floor, and whoa, look, here's three sewer rats climbing up out of nowhere?"

I like picturing it, the look somebody like you might get on your face seeing us. Before you could even find your voice or the light switch, we'd have closed up that porthole and scrambled, disappeared. JJ said, "Nobody with a house like that would ever follow us down these holes." So, we figured the risks were slim.

Anyway, this garage, like all the other dark ones, was empty of people, and goddamn, it was a good one. Not just a garage, but a big old carriage house, they call it, with three cars and a snowblower and some kind of chicken coop thing up in the middle of the ceiling, with four little windows up there letting in street light. All the walls were lined with hooks and shelves, sagging under the weight of a thousand hardly used tools. Drills and drill bits, wrench sets, saws. A brand-new Bosch nail gun. More than we could carry, for sure, so we started picking through them, thinking *gold mine*, when suddenly a nasty scraping sound and a whimper rose up from the back corner of the room. Good God.

Diego and JJ killed their flashlights, but I was closer to that noise, and my light went straight to it. So I saw.

"Girl!" JJ whispered at me, and I turned my flashlight against my jeans to dim it.

Fast as rats, Diego and JJ scrambled back down that hole, gone. But I stood there like some dumb, frozen homeowner staring through the blue glow at that thing in the cage. I even stepped closer. It was curled up and twisting its face toward me, searching left and right under its blindfold. And I saw it was a man.

The cement floors of those old garages slope down toward the hole to drain, and as I backed away from that rattling cage, I trusted the slant of that floor to lead me back down where I belonged.

Once I was in the pipeline again, I wrestled the heavy lid back into place over my head. But Diego and JJ's lights were nowhere around.

"You guys!" I hissed, panicking. Then off to my left, half a block away, they turned on their lights and burst out laughing.

"Come *on*!" they called out, waving.

When I reached them, Diego said, "What the hell *was*

that?" But I have to admit I just shoved them forward. I had to get out of there.

JJ's contact, Tommy, was having a party that night, some weird situation in a house near campus where everyone was wearing pajamas for no reason I could figure out. They were all older than us, in college, but they looked like little kids cleaned up for bed, holding their red Solos to their faces like sippy cups. JJ pointed at Tommy's bunny slippers and said, "Should I read you a fuckin' story, man?"

"You smell like swamp," Tommy responded, but once we took off our boots and coats, he let us in.

We went upstairs to his bedroom, where we traded him what we'd found for a bag of pills and forty dollars. None of us had the right ID to pawn things.

"You look kinda spooked, Lucy," Tommy said to me. He had shaggy hair and a slanting, tweaked-out smile that I liked but knew not to trust.

"She's fine," JJ said.

"She's always fine." Diego threw a hamhock arm over my shoulders. I felt like a can being crushed in his armpit, but I waited a few secs before pulling away.

"I guess I got a chill," was all I said.

"You see something down there?" Tommy asked.

JJ had already told us not to talk about it. Down in the tunnels, that made sense. I was too spooked to stick around and try to argue with him in the dark. But now that we were aboveground, the regular rules of life trickled back to me, and my brain kept playing a video of that guy, tied up and contorted, blindfolded, gagged, straining to figure out what kind of monster was making the noises we had made. I'd seen dogs in cages bigger than that.

"Let's go downstairs and drink some beers," JJ said, end of discussion. Down in the front room, the stereo was blasting Kanye, and more kids in slippers and flannel pants had arrived and were dancing and stumbling around like drugged monkeys. While JJ made his rounds with the pills, Diego and I sat slumped on the broken-down couch for a while, just watching.

I was tired, and Diego said, "Man, I could go for a sandwich." The college kids made a point of ignoring us. After a while, Diego passed out, and I waited till no one was noticing me and went back upstairs and took a shower. My skin was still cold, like a slab of meat stinging when the hot water hit it. Then I put my dirty clothes back on, with my underwear inside out.

On the staircase, a girl with pigtails and a teddy bear reached out to touch my wet hair, like it was some kind of new fashion statement she might want to copy. Diego and JJ were nowhere—they must have left. Aside from some boys playing cards in the kitchen, most people were slowing down. I let one of Tommy's housemates mack on me until he passed out, so I could sleep in his bed.

The trick about crashing with people for free is not to bug them when they're sleeping and to get out of their sight before they open their eyes. I failed on both counts, flopping around all night with terrible dreams. The guy in the cage kept rattling back to me. Wherever I went in dreamland, there was his body, curled up, knees to armpits, wrists tied to ankles. And it was bad enough if he lay still and I thought he was dead, but then he would squirm, and I'd jolt back, thinking, *Do something, Lucy. Do something.*

So at dawn when I should have been sneaking out, I was just getting trapped in the black tar of sleep. I was too slow, and Tommy's housemate woke up groggy and gave me a squeeze. In his T-shirt and straining boxers he took a good look at me, and I braced myself, but he just said, "Jesus, how old are you, anyway?" So I scattered.

Luckily, my boots and coat were still on the porch, though cold and stiff. It was drizzling outside, like the air itself was wet. I walked down Kenwood in the hard gray light to the nasty apartment building on Oakland where lately JJ'd been camping out in the basement. I found him curled up on an old crib mattress behind some boxes in the boiler room, his long bony ankles sticking out of some Hello Kitty pants he must've taken off someone at the party. I squeezed his grubby sock and waited, squeezed again.

He startled awake with a gasp, then saw it was me. "Girl." He reached an arm out. "Just sleep awhile." So I leaned against him and tried, I did. But it didn't work.

"I think we have to go help that guy," I whispered.

He just groaned and rolled over to face the wall, all flaky with mold. So I scratched his back the way he likes, first through his T-shirt, then under it. This calmed him down, so I said, "I'm serious. That guy's gonna haunt me."

"I don't even know what you think you saw," JJ said.

"I saw a guy, cuffed and gagged. Hardly any clothes on."

"Leather?" he said.

I shrugged. "So?"

JJ rolled back to face me and smiled. "Little Lucy, you found yourself a gimp."

I twisted my face up. "I've seen the movie. I don't think that was it."

"You know," he said, "some people do bad shit because they *like* it. Rich fuckers get bored. They play weird games in those houses. You know."

"It was the garage," I replied, a dumb clarification. "It wasn't even heated."

JJ patted my hair. "He's gonna be just fine, girl. You don't have to worry one bit about that guy." Then he closed his eyes and was gone; there was no more reaching him.

Outside, it looked like it was going to rain all day, so I went to school.

In government class, Mrs. W said, "Nice of you to join us," so I gave her my wounded, sad-sack look, and she seemed to regret it. She asked us to turn in our Call to Action letters, but mine was of course not done, as this was the first I heard of the assignment. We could pick the mayor, the governor, or the president—all tools.

I decided to pick you, Mayor Barrett, because in your picture your face looks like somebody's kindly, barely-there grandpa. I sat down and wrote to you about the giant sinkhole that opened up in the street outside my Aunt Tina's house last spring, because a) that freaked me out, and b) what kind of city is it if the streets can just open up and take you? Plus, c) Aunt Tina said that wasn't even the first time. Apparently, a few years back, North Avenue cracked open after a long rain and swallowed a whole SUV that was just driving down the street. It's the stuff of nightmares, Mr. Mayor, I hope you know. JJ says Milwaukee's built on swampland, with rivers running under it, and that the system keeping the wet away from the dry is always breaking down. I don't know about that, but it sure feels true.

In the seat next to me, Lexi Hunter flipped her yellow hair through the airwaves and whispered, "You smell like ass."

So I slid my cruddy boots over to touch her backpack on the floor, and told her, "Thank you."

I brought my Call to Action up to Mrs. W, and she read through it, clenching and unclenching the muscles around her eyes. Then she flipped it over, looking for the rest of it. "A good strong complaint," she said, "is not the same as a Call to Action." She handed it back to me. "To be a *citizen* means not just to complain but to think of solutions, and then to plan and act and get others to act *with* you. A *Call* to *Action*. We went over this."

Oh God. Plus, what am I supposed to ask for, seriously? The sinkhole's already been filled. Mr. Mayor, could you maybe up and move this whole city to some more stable terrain? And stop the water falling from the sky?

"And I need you to type it," Mrs. W said. "Can you type it?"

The bell rang, so I nodded and fumed off through the crowded halls toward the library, dragging Lexi's insult behind me like a lame dog. I was almost positive I smelled okay, after that shower, but my whole way through the halls kids seemed to step back and clear a path for me, and suddenly all I could smell was shit and rot. But there, in the dim back corner of the library, I saw Diego in his bulky brown coat hunched over a desk, a giant turd sleeping. Ms. Himler let us rest there if we were quiet and no teachers could see us. I went over and touched his red hat to wake him. "We gotta get out of here," I said. One look at me and he knew not to ask why.

Outside, the rain had stopped. Diego fished a pack of Nutty Bars out of his coat pocket and gave me one. We walked without talking for a long time, and I led him toward the alley behind the hookah café, which is where we started out the night before. He slowed his steps, and when I squatted on top of the manhole cover to untie and retie my shoelaces, he stepped away from me and said, "We're not going down without JJ."

"I know." Anyway, through the finger holes of the manhole cover I could see the water flowing fast down there. Every trickle of rain on the street is just one of a hundred thousand sources draining down to these pipelines, even the defunct ones. And there's a ton of dead ends down there, locked grates and sudden drop-offs—a million ways for the city to swallow you.

"I mean, it's like JJ's territory," Diego said.

"I *know*," I said. "I would never burn him. Or you."

"What is it about this guy you saw, anyway?" he asked.

I sighed. "I was just thinking if we started from here, we could figure out where we went last night. We could find that guy's garage from aboveground." I told Diego about the chicken coop thing on the top of the garage, the little upraised section of the roofline with its tiny windows.

"Yeah, but find the garage and do *what* exactly, in broad daylight?"

"Just leave if you're not gonna help me."

He turned away, looked up and down the alley, and I braced myself for that feeling you get when somebody gives up on you. But then he started moving a finger along his palm, and I could see he was charting out the neighborhood, trying to diagram the pipeline below our feet.

"It had to be east of Downer," I said. "The garages over here are too small."

"Yeah. But you're gonna get tangled up in this for a stranger?"

Diego has one of those big flat faces that holds you like a mirror, and he's known me longer than anyone I trust. He was just trying to help me, I know. But I turned and headed east down Locust, toward the lake. That area between Downer and Lake Park is really only a few blocks wide. I could probably cover all of it before dark, on my own.

Diego caught up and fell into step next to me, and we walked down Locust a few blocks without talking. When the red light stopped us at Downer, he put his hand on my arm and said, "I'm just trying to say—that guy, in the cage? You know nothing like that is going to happen to you again, right? You know that."

"I know," I said. "I know."

Mr. Mayor, I'm not going to drag you through some long sob story about my past. It's a conversation stopper. Anyway, I'm sure it's all in a file somewhere if you really want to know. So look it up.

A few years ago I told Diego my story, and he said, "Well, then the rest of your life is gonna be easy. It's like you got the bad part over with." He's sweet that way; his imagination only goes so far. And I know that's a good thing, a thing you have to protect.

When we crossed Downer, the houses went from rentals to single-family, and they got big fast. Brick and stone, with steep slate roofs and green copper gutters, they're the kind of houses the word *stately* was invented for. The streets were wide and empty, lined with big craggy trees that looked down on you like security guards. There were no more alleys, just straight, skinny driveways cut through the narrow space between houses, so the garages were tucked way at the back, almost out of sight. We had to slow down as we passed to get a good look at them. It was hard not to feel suspicious. But when we walked past an old man being dragged by two wiener dogs, it was like he didn't even see us at all. We were just too far outside his picture of this place.

The rain started up again, harder now, and I could feel Diego getting tired beside me, though he would never say so. He's got issues with his lungs, and I could hear these little shrieks escaping his throat with each breath.

"You okay?" I stopped.

"Sure thing."

The thing you learn in this kind of life is that you have to pay your way all the time, pay ahead if you can, so when it comes down to the really low, dark times, you have somebody still willing to help you, someplace you can go. So I said, "I can finish this myself. You should go warm up someplace, get out of the rain." I fished in my pocket for coins. "I can meet you in the laundromat. Go dry your coat." I could feel the rain seeping through my sleeves.

He shook his head and kept walking. His knit Badgers hat was deflating under the weight of the rainwater. And then behind him, behind this house, I saw it—the chicken coop in the sky. "There it is," I said, turning Diego around.

He squinted at it. "You think?"

"I know."

He studied the house in front of the garage, a pale stone monster of a house with eight huge black windows, symmetrical across its face. The wide flat roof had a cement banister all around it, like you could put snipers up there. A hundred years ago somebody built this place, thinking he'd rule the world from it. And back behind it, a wide, tall carriage house, with three fancy wooden garage doors, and there at the top of the roof, the chicken coop.

I tugged Diego down the driveway before he could bail.

"You kids need something?" A lady came out of the house next door, pulling her long gray cardigan across her chest in a hurry.

Diego froze, like a kid who thinks it'll make him invisible.

I said, "I lost my cat. We're out looking for her. A little black cat named Tina."

The woman peered up at the rain. I could see her face film over with regret at coming outside. She did not want to get tangled up, she did not want to help us in this weather. And she did not want to be the kind of lady who sees kids like us and feels suspicious instead of helpful.

"You live around here?" she asked, holding a hand over her hair.

I nodded and pointed vaguely back toward Downer. "I saw her run this way. You mind if we just take a quick look, and then we'll get out of here? She has leukemia, she needs her—"

The woman waved us on and went back inside. I had to tug Diego into motion. I crouched down, saying, "Tina? Kitty, kitty, kitty. Tina?"

We got back near the carriage house, and I crept around the side of it. There were a few empty planters and a wheelbarrow turned upside down against the side of the building. "Are you in there?" I called. "It's okay. It's me, Lucy. We're gonna help you."

I reached up and tapped on a window. I wanted to make some noise that he could hear. Diego and I jumped up and down, trying to get a look in the window, but we saw nothing. We went around the back of the garage, though it was all scrub and rotting firewood—we could hardly pick our way through it—but finally, around on the other side of the building, we saw a black door, so I tried the handle.

That's when the alarm went off. The door was locked, anyway; the handle wouldn't turn. Diego took off. I'm sure he wasn't trying to abandon me. He probably assumed I'd be right behind him. But in that minute, with the noise of the alarm so strong, I figured, *What the hell, we're already in trouble, and I probably have a minute or two before the cops get here.* So I stepped back and kicked at that door, I kicked and kicked. I got into it, it felt good. And then when I heard the siren approaching, I kicked even harder. I figured the only way to explain myself would be to show them what was inside this garage. And if I didn't open it myself, I just knew no cop was going to.

In the movies, strong men kick through doors like this on the first try. They do, it's so easy. But me, I was still there kicking and kicking, bruises on the bottom of my foot, and I didn't even dent that door. I barely even scuffed it. I can't even claim any kind of lasting damage.

When the cops got there, it was a guy I already knew, a guy who used to date a foster mom I once had. That was a bit of luck, really, 'cause God knows how they might've treated me otherwise.

So I'm writing this now, Mr. Mayor, from inside your system, where they have me again. The cops did not believe me, big surprise. We sat in the squad car in the rain out front of that monster house, waiting till it was dark, while the cops knocked on all the doors and called all the phone numbers they could find for the owner. They weren't going to break into anybody's garage on the say of a girl like me. And so we drove off.

So my Call to Action, Mr. Mayor, if you ever even get this, is I'm asking you, I'm asking you just to send somebody over to that house. The address must be in my file. You can look it up. Just have a peek in the garage, in the back corner. Maybe it's nothing. Maybe it was a sick game. But even if it was, maybe it went bad along the way. You know, sometimes your imagination fails you, you can't see as far ahead as the person you're with, you can't picture the foul fantasies that might come to them midstream. And so you find yourself trapped somewhere bad, even though you know it was *your* leg that stepped into that trap. I'm asking you to consider this, Mr. Mayor.

I knew a girl once, back in a group home, who told me

that when she was little she lived for a while in a house where the dad got a fighting spirit some nights, and when her mom saw that spirit coming she would take the girl and hide her in the cupboard under the stairs. She meant well, that mom, when she turned the lock on those cupboards and hid the key, she meant well. Obviously, she meant well.

3RD STREET WALTZ

BY MATTHEW J. PRIGGE

Westown

The roar of the industrial vacuum cleaner tore through my bottom shelf–whiskey stupor like a chainsaw into a rotting pumpkin. I pulled myself upright in the wooden theater seat as the light and noise and movement of the morning revealed itself. The house lights shone full force, and the messy din of the cleaning crew's once-a-week visit echoed through the auditorium. I leaned forward over the balcony rail. Four figures dressed all in blue moved about the aisles and rows, tidying the frayed carpets and beaten-down seats.

I had, once again, passed out during the late show.

One of the figures noticed me. "You the manager, right?"

I croaked that I was.

"Mr. Bradlee said you got the check for this week."

I went into a coughing fit and felt a dry heave—I hoped—coming up on me. I put my head into my hands and tried to maintain.

"You okay?"

I pulled myself up, knock-kneed and cotton-headed. "Yeah," I said as loudly as I could. "Cash all right?" I didn't even hear the reply as I dragged myself up the few stairs to the exit and down a cold hallway to the theater's office. I took three ten-dollar bills from the petty cash box and folded them into an envelope. It was mid-April 1973. I was the manager of the Princess Theater, Milwaukee's dead-end stop for adult entertainment. About a week earlier, word had come down from on high that the theater was closing at the end of the month. The checking account was empty. Debts were to be settled from the safe.

I left the cash on the glass candy counter as I made my labored way to the front doors. The white glow of the morning sun stung my eyes, and I squinted hard as I stepped out onto 3rd Street and lit a cigarette. A few doors down from the theater, a beat cop roused a bum from the sidewalk and told him to move along. Across the street, a pair of hookers sat slumped at the lunch counter of the Royal Diner, their wigs sitting in the chair between them. A few civilians dotted the sidewalks, busily making their way to wherever they were headed. My eyes finally focused on a red shape in the gutter. I kneeled and picked it up. It was a metal letter *L*, coated in chipped paint. I looked over my shoulder at the marquee and raised a hand to shield my eyes from the wicked sun. *DOUBLE FEATURE / RATED X*, it blared. *COUNTRY LOVE & COME ONE, COME AL*.

The early show that afternoon was at 12:30, the "businessman's special" that we held every weekday to cater to the downtown pencil-pushers with vacationing supervisors or the stray prairie-bred conventioneer looking for something they couldn't get at home. The 5:30 show was mostly for the bachelor set, the hip-flask crowd looking for a charge before heading out to cruise the bars. The 10:30 show was strictly dead end—johns, drunks, and jerkers. I was still stiff from my overnight in the balcony when the customers began to trickle in.

There wasn't much sense in breaking the news to the staff as a whole. We had about a dozen people on and off the payroll at any given time. Most were transients who drifted over from one of the legit Bradlee hotels: janitors who couldn't stay sober, housekeepers who were pilfering wallets, hotel desk men who'd been caught skimming. A stretch at the Princess was a punishment, an attempt to reform a person through humiliation. They usually stayed just as drunk and crooked under my watch but went back to the honest world with a bit more perspective.

The Bradlees had once owned a swath of Westown so mighty you could damn near walk from the river to 10th Street without leaving the shadow of one of their properties. Hotels, theaters, steak houses—they played to travelers and locals both, and you'd be hard-pressed to have any kind of honest fun downtown without passing them at least a few dollars. But those days were long gone. George Bradlee, who was gifted his first hotel by his father at age twenty-two, had dropped dead on Christmas Day, 1949. Beverly, his widow, took over the business and managed to steer the sinking ship until 1960, when Dick, their only son, took over.

Dick put me in charge of the Princess a few months later, plucking me from the management staff of the last Bradlee neighborhood theater to go dark. Over the next decade, with Mother Bradlee slipping into a haze of dementia, he ran a dozen or more Bradlee properties into the ground, bleeding them until they couldn't turn a dime and then leaving them to rot. When Beverly was still lucid enough to leave the mansion, she'd ask questions like, "Dickie, why is the marquee empty at the Empire Room? Why aren't you watching after our Empire Room?" He'd pat her leg and tell her that Pop had never owned the Empire Room. He'd do the same when she asked indignantly about the filth shown at the Princess.

The only other regular left at the place was Earl, a union projectionist who had been on 3rd Street even longer than me. He had been around since the first nudist camp grinders showed up in the city in the mid-1950s. When a house was forced to go blue and chased away the old staff, Earl got the call. Through the sixties, when the city censor board was cracking down hard, keeping any hint of tits, ass, or bush from the screen, Earl became a smut picture surgeon, snipping out offending material before the board even knew what to be offended by. And when the board was satisfied and had lost interest in the picture, he'd slip the skin back in for a few nights of big business before the print was hustled out of the town and the censors came sniffing for whatever picture was scheduled next.

Earl was an outlaw in town for the taking. He came to the Princess in 1962 and played the same game here. Each house he worked had a code for the marquee to indicate if the show was "hot." At the Empress, an old burlesque across the street, an exclamation point was added to the title when the breasts were bare. At the Palace, just around the corner on Wisconsin Avenue, a line of running lights was left dark to signify a blue reel. And at the Princess, floodlights that showed off the architectural majesty of the original 1909 façade were lit when Earl was doing his dirty work. On those nights, the box office was instructed to call the booth immediately if any of the censor board's checkers showed their city-issued pass. Earl could turn a hot reel cold in a matter of minutes, with hands quicker than Henry Aaron's.

But Earl was the master of a dead game. The dam broke in 1969 when the operators finally pushed back against the board and secured a court ruling in favor of smut and against the bluenoses. By the time the axe was falling toward the Princess's neck, a half-dozen other theaters were running X-rated pictures full-time with two others already having gone full-on hardcore. The houses that survived the rush were those that leaped into bed with the Mob. The Milwaukee families had locked up distribution of the best softcore in the city, and the Chicago outfit ran hardcore all across the Midwest. Dick might have been a cad, but he had his limits on what he could lie about to Mother. And so, we were left with five-year-old scraps while other houses got all the newest pictures with all the bustiest girls. From that point, it had only been a matter of time.

There was a funereal air in the office as I caught up on the balance book while Earl sat across from me, using a small screwdriver to adjust a film splicer. "A letter fell off the marquee," he said without looking up. "Did you see?"

"Yeah."

"It says, *Come One, Come Al.*" He went on, looking down his nose through low-slung spectacles at the device. "We're gonna have every guy named Al in town beatin' down the door."

I ran down the end column of the ledger. Another losing day.

"And then beatin' off when they get here."

I snickered. Earl was as crude a man as I'd ever known, but he carried it with a weird kind of refinement that seemed appropriate for a silent-era palace lingering on softcore life-support. He was nearing seventy, with salt-and-pepper hair and a round, lumpy face. He spoke of almost nothing seriously and had no convictions.

"Why do you even bother with the books?" he asked, tightening a tiny screw. "This place is fully fucked. You're only wasting the ink in old lady Bradlee's pen."

I finished my entries and closed the book. "Why do you

bother fixing that thing?" I asked. "How many splices do you think you've got left here, old man?"

Earl kept looking down. "Yes, you're right. I'm just wearing out the old lady's screws."

Earl and I were the only employees who had no clear next move. The doghouse lobby workers were strictly low-dollar cogs, easily movable back into other compartments of the sputtering Bradlee machine. The two part-time projectionists both had side gigs at a handful of other city theaters. The cleaning crew wouldn't miss the spare work we threw them. The pavement princess who floated around after the shows ended, asking if anyone wanted "to get it for real," would float to other places that drew the desperate. None of us had real homes, but Earl and I seemed to be the only dopes with no place else to go.

As it neared twelve thirty, I hoped that Earl might be straight with me for just long enough to offer some direction. "Earl?"

"What?"

"What are you going to do after we close?"

"Drive down to Zad's on 2nd Street and get drunker than shit."

"I mean after the theater closes for good." He took the kind of sharp breath that usually presaged a smart-assed comment. "And don't say, *The same thing.*"

He gave the blade on the splicer a few practice swipes and looked up. "I've always wanted to retire as an elevator operator. I want to die in an elevator in some old downtown office building. Just slump forward on the throttle and send it crashing into the ground floor. Take a few suits with me." He offered a wicked and worn-out grin.

"You gonna miss this place when it's gone?"

"Kid, there's nothing to miss here." Earl checked his watch and stood. "It's just a job."

"Yeah, but it's been more than ten years. Doesn't that mean something?"

"Not a fuckin' thing." Earl took his keys from his vest pocket and headed for the door. "It's like these movies. They don't mean anything; it's just some silly shit meant to get some witless bastard's dick hard. We're all whores here, kid." He put his head down and left for the booth.

I tossed the bank book into the safe and locked it, before heading down to the lobby. Behind the candy counter, a pair of thirtysomething women in red vests and matching skirts turned magazine pages in bored synchronization. To each side, tall arches framed in elaborately molded trimming led to a dim anteroom with a broken marble fountain at its center. From there, four doorways led to the lower part of the auditorium. I pushed through the door at the far right, its ornamental glass inlays long ago busted out and replaced with plywood. I stood at the back of the room, watching the light wash over eight hundred empty seats and two dozen lonely heads.

Every month, a 3rd Street hustler named Buck gave me an ounce of grass in exchange for looking the other way when he cruised the auditorium. Third Street had an unofficial policy of not allowing unaccompanied women into theaters—mostly for fear that the vice squad was watching and would shut a house down on the grounds of being a place of prostitution. It was a mile easier for men to work the 3rd Street movie houses, and they had been, according to what Buck once told me, almost as far back as the silent era. It bothered some to high hell, the cops especially, but I didn't care. The vice squad, revolted by the idea, assumed that no one would willingly permit it. If they busted a woman tricking in your establishment, they'd try to shut you down. If they busted a man, all you had to do was shake your head indignantly, and they'd do no more than scold you like a disappointed parent.

But it also meant that each month I could sell that bag of grass to Janet. Janet was a waitress at a diner across the river on Michigan Street. She came to the Princess on the third Friday of each month, just after the coffee shop closed. I'd let her in the side door, and we'd sit together on the balcony while she smoked a joint and I sipped whiskey from a paper cup. After a decade-plus of fifty-five-hour workweeks and a steadily increasing drinking habit, she was—aside from a handful of South Side barflies who could hardly remember my first name—my only real social contact outside of 3rd Street.

The Princess had ten days left when she visited for her April bag. We'd been sitting together, wordlessly, for a half hour before I told her.

"What, like, forever?" she said through a cloud of smoke. She was, as usual, still in her work clothes. Her hair was a knotty mess, and she rested her clunky nurse's shoes on the rail in front of us.

"Yep. Final curtain."

"So, no more dope?"

I shrugged. "I guess not. I mean . . ."

"*Fuck.*"

The silence resumed. We'd had the setup for about two years now. I'd asked her on a date near the start of it all. She said no. I wasn't terribly attracted to her, but she had a way about her that intrigued me. She was normal, which to me was different.

"I'm not sure what I'm gonna do after we close," I said after a few minutes.

Following a long pause, Janet blew another cloud of smoke. "What, for work?"

"For work. And, just . . ." I stared off at the screen through the haze. A Hollywood wannabe-turned-gigolo was balling some desperate nymphomaniac in a scene that was all back skin and butt crack. "I've been doing this so long, I don't know where else I fit."

Janet rolled her head toward me. "Seriously?"

"Yeah. I'd be kind of lost without this place."

She laughed. "How old are you?"

"I just turned forty-one."

"And without *this*, you'd be lost?" She pulled herself up in her chair as bare breasts shook from side to side on the screen. "Don't you have any dreams? Didn't you ever want to do something with your life?"

I had to think about the question.

"Maybe use this as an opportunity. It's a chance to totally change who you are." Her eyes were slits, and she spoke with a wispy voice. She was nicer to me when she was high. "I mean, is this . . ." She waved her fingers in front of her at all the empty seats, the sad heads, and the comically exaggerated face of the Hollywood wannabe getting rubbed off. "Is this you?"

"I don't know. I really don't know."

She shrugged and slumped back down. "Or get a job at another dirty theater. If that's what you want. You should do what you want."

I sat back too. I took another long sip of whiskey and let it linger in my mouth, angry and cheap. In my mind, I asked her to come home with me. I wanted to smell the fry grease on her clothes and hear those ugly shoes drop to the floor of my tiny apartment: CLOMP, CLOMP. I wanted her belly pressed against mine and to watch her apathetic face as we humped to no conclusion. I wanted the squeeze of someone I hadn't paid or found in a misery sweat at the far end of a long, sorry bartop. In my mind, I asked her to come home with me. Even in my mind, she said no.

"Janet?" I asked aloud.

"What?"

"My guy owes me one last bag. Come by on the twenty-ninth, it's a Sunday . . . and I'll have it for you." It was our last day of operation. A crew would clean the place out on the thirtieth, the final day of the lease.

"Okay," she said.

We went back to staring at the action, wordlessly.

When I was growing up, I never stayed in one place long enough to feel at home. My mother came from some cow town in the middle of the state. She got pregnant young by a man who was already married. There wasn't much forgiveness for a crime like that in Depression-era cow towns, so she left for the big city, where I was born. She worked often, doing what she could and what they'd pay her to do. We moved a lot, hopping from apartment to apartment, school to school. Milwaukee is tribal to its core, and kids banded by school or by neighborhood or by church and always by race. I was the constant new kid, an outsider in my own city.

The one constant space I had was the darkness of the nearest movie house. With a working mother, I was left mostly to raise myself, and the movies became my keeper, and the movie houses became my family. There was the Rainbow on 27th and Lisbon, with its wooden seats and popcorn served in paper cones. There was the Pearl in Muskego Way, with its marquee that lit up the entire corner. There was the Franklin on Center Street, where you could neck with the bad girls from North Division High. There was the Pix on Howell, where sailors courted hookers while their freighters were tied off at the docks. And then the Princess. For twelve years, the Princess.

We had a week left when I met with Dick Bradlee at the Sugar Room, a pasties-and-g-string jazz bar on the corner of 3rd and Wells. It was midafternoon, before the band or dancers went on, and we sat in a corner booth, a pitcher of beer between us on the table. He was giving me instructions for the end. I took dutiful notes on what to remove from the house, who was coming to get what, and so on and so on and so on. He had yet made no mention of what might happen to me or Earl.

The process was cold and smooth. Any equipment of value had been sold to an operator from Chicago. Some salvageable furniture was being taken for a suburban Bradlee Corp. hotel. The concession counter was to be looted by a carnival company from Tennessee. Whatever was left would be abandoned to the real estate company that owned the building. And the building would most likely sit empty until God-only-knows-when. He was planning a burial, but not the funeral.

He finished his orders and refilled his glass. Dick had never been sentimental. He hacked limbs off the dying family business tree without so much as a glance toward the past. When he bricked over the regal grand entryway to the old Hotel Bradlee on Wisconsin Avenue, once the trademark feature of his father's trademark property, people in the city howled that he was disrespecting the past, flushing an important historical structure down the toilet of modernism. Others lauded him, citing it as a shrewd business move, a loss of the thumb to save the hand.

It was neither. Dick was simply doing as he did, strolling

dumbly down the path of least resistance while he waited for his mother to die so he could fully divest himself of the millstone he had inherited. Once, back in the early 1960s, when we were still regular drinking buddies, we were hosting an after-bar in the balcony with a pair of 3rd Street girls and a hot reel on the screen. Dick's girl said something about how great it must be, to be born into money as he had been. Dick sighed and shook his head. "I was born into responsibility," he replied tragically. I had no doubt that Dick really believed that load of horseshit. He was too narrow to see his lot in any other way and too dumb to be any less narrow.

Finally, I asked him about my future with the company.

"Well," Dick said, widening his eyes, "I'm not really sure what we'd have for you."

"There's nothing in management?" I asked.

He exhaled a rough, beery lungful of air. "I don't think that . . ." He shook his head. "We're done with 3rd Street. Damn near out of downtown altogether. So . . ."

"I can travel, you know."

"It's not that," he said, staring at me like I was supposed to know. I knew, but I wanted to make him say it out loud. "I mean, what, we're gonna put you out in Brookfield? We don't have much use for a 3rd Street guy in Brookfield."

I nodded slowly and drained my beer.

"No offense. Hell, I'm gonna miss 3rd Street, but this is the way of the world."

"Severance then?"

He nodded. "Yeah, uh, a month?"

What could I say? I accepted and shook his fat hand.

"I do have an odd job for you, if you are interested."

"Sure."

"Okay, sometime in the week after we vacate, they're

gonna walk through the theater, just to make sure it ain't trashed." He took a slip of paper from his pocket and scribbled something on it. "The week after, on this date and at this time, I got a crew ready to . . ." he leaned forward, slid me the paper, and whispered, "get the copper wire and fixtures. It's not my gig, but I'm getting a cut, and I told them I'd have an insider who could show them around. Could be good money—cash—if it all works out."

I picked up the paper. The beer had gotten to me; something had gotten to me, and I felt dizzy. "You're gonna wreck the place for copper wire?"

Dick shook his head. "Not me. But . . . yeah."

I sank back in the booth, and Dick motioned to the waitress for another pitcher. "*Your kingdom come, thy will be done,*" I muttered.

Dick turned back to me and nodded, grinning.

Earl called them his *fuck books*. They were scrapbooks he kept of film clips snipped from skin pictures. It was a longtime tradition among projectionists in blue houses to snip a few frames from each nude scene in a given film before shipping it off to its next destination. It was so well practiced by the early sixties that the telltale crinkle of a splice running through the feed sprocket would instinctively draw a projectionist's eyes to the screen in anticipation of seeing some flesh. Earl had started snipping in the late fifties when the censor board was ordering boobs and buns eliminated from nudist colony pics. His ledgers contained most of what the city had never been allowed to see and a little something from every hot reel that ever ran illicitly. Most had given up on collecting after distributors began to raise holy hell and threatened to blacklist theaters that didn't crack down. It seemed that by the time a print had been in circulation for a year or two, and after fifty or more projectionists had taken their cut, it could be trimmed of nearly all its nudity.

I was loading up some boxes in the office when I noticed the stack of books on a bottom shelf. "Earl?"

He was on break between shows, reading a newspaper. "What?"

"Are you taking your fuck books with you?"

He had kept them up meticulously over the past decade and a half. Each film labeled, each snip carefully affixed in photo mounts so it could be removed and ogled through a slide viewer. It was practically a life's work. But while it was an obsessive project while it was active, it was now a mere sentimental relic.

"Nah," he said. "Thought I'd try to sell them, maybe. That one-legged guy who runs the bookstore out on Lisbon buys weird shit like that."

In an instant, it all came to me: the show that would drop the curtain on the dirty Princess. "How much do you want for them?"

The last day was sunny and warm. It was a Sunday, typically a lousy day at the box. And the weather would probably make things even slower. It was a day for grilling hamburgers or drinking cold beer on porch steps. It was the kind of day that peeled off the most marginally respectable denizens of 3rd Street, leaving only those too crippled to walk away. We were still featuring the same tired double feature, still billed as *Come One, Come Al* on the marquee. I'd gone up and down 3rd Street in the preceding days, breaking the news of our demise and inviting people to come pay their respects. On the last day, there would be a single 10 p.m. show that would be free to all and open to men and women. I invited the barmen, the whores, the dancers, and the drunks. I told them that liquor would flow, and a grand time would be had. I wanted a full house. I wanted a festive atmosphere. I wanted this old trash house to dim her lights in a proper fashion.

By the time the sun set on Milwaukee that Sunday, I was bleary and half drunk, frantic in trying to execute my farewell. I stepped outside for a smoke and, at five minutes to showtime, saw Janet round the corner of Wisconsin and 3rd, dressed in her usual work clothes and wearing those awful black shoes. I stood under the glowing marquee, a warm evening breeze stinging my face. I grinned a bit and waved and walked up to meet her. We said hello to each other in front of the next-door massage parlor. Behind me, the old "hot print" floodlight lit the theater's façade, bringing to marvelous life its battered and cracked grandeur.

"I don't want to hang here too long," Janet said. "I just got done with a double shift."

"No problem," I told her. "It's a short program tonight."

"I mean, if you could just—"

"Take a seat downstairs, in the front. I gotta make sure we're ready in the booth," I said, backtracking to the glass doors of the theater. "I'll be down in a few minutes." I opened a door, and she walked inside.

I rushed up to the booth, where Earl was checking everything over. "How are we doing?"

"This is all fucking stupid, kid. Why not just run the movies like normal?"

"I told you a thousand times, Earl, I need to do this."

I had been at the theater since four a.m. First, splicing together the snips from Earl's fuck books. It was, all told, only about two minutes of material, a machine-gun spray of filth that fluttered across the screen so frenetically the brain hardly had time to recognize what was happening. So, I set to building. Every spare sprocket or wheel that I could find, mounting them all over the booth to create a long, messy path through which a single loop of the dirty film could flow. By early morning, I had it all set up: an endless reel of every bit of sex to ever put its foul light on the Princess. In the B projector, the second part of the two-projector setup we used, I loaded a long-forgotten instructional reel that I'd found while cleaning up. They would be played over each other, mashing together wicked and wholesome, sex and love, smut and art. I had finished it just in time. The Princess would close as an art house—of sorts.

"Are you sure this is even gonna work? I don't think this is gonna work."

"Earl, goddamn it. Just go with this!"

He shook his head. "Whatever you say, boss."

"So, we're set."

"If we're not, we never will be."

"Perfect." I buttoned my vest. "Watch for my cue."

I dashed back downstairs and took the back way to the old stage door. I walked out onto the stage, and the house lights briefly overwhelmed me. When my eyes adjusted, I saw that I was standing before a nearly empty house. Mostly it was just the same old bums and drunks who made up our Sunday crowds. My shoulders sank. I had envisioned a rogue's ball. What I got was a dozen people with nowhere else to go. Thirteen if I counted myself.

"I want to welcome you all to the last show at the Princess Theater," I announced to the room. "The Princess opened in 1909 . . ." I sighed. "Ah, fuck it." I waved my wand toward the booth, and the lights sank. As I walked down from the stage, the show began. Some rumpled trumpet music started up and a title screen reading *The Waltz for Beginners* lit the screen, a jumble of nudist-camp breasts flashing on top of it.

I dropped down next to Janet; her face bent with perplexity. "What . . ."

"I just wanted to do something worthwhile, after all my time here. I guess nobody gives a shit, though."

"Why would anybody?" she asked.

I had almost expected sympathy. A billowy waltz started to play as the instructional went into its first demonstration. A tidy couple, dressed in ages-old formal wear, pressed close and began their steps. A smattering of pale-tinted breasts and half-covered ass cracks flashed across them.

"This is just weird," Janet said. "Let me buy my bag and get out of here."

The bag—I'd forgotten about it. It was a lie, one that I'd hoped she'd forgive when she absorbed the weird joy of the Princess's last romp. I stood and reached down to her. "Would you dance with me first?"

"What?" she said sharply.

"One last waltz for this old dump. It would mean a lot to me."

"Just give me the—"

"There is no bag," I said. This was the scene in the movie where the heel comes clean. I'd seen it a thousand times growing up. The girl is impressed with the fellow's honesty, and they embrace while the score rises and the picture fades. This wasn't romance or love—I knew that. But maybe, in that theater and on that lonely last day, it might have been just enough for a shared moment. "I made that up to get you to come tonight. This night was supposed to be special, but it's a total bust. I thought maybe if we—"

"What is wrong with you?" she spat. "I've told you before I'm not interested. And then you lie to me and expect me to do some weird sex ritual with you in front of all these losers?"

I didn't say a thing. There was, really, no more to say. She stood and shoved me aside, knocking me backward over the stage stairs. I lay there on the dirty floor as she marched up the aisle. Somewhere in the darkness, a lone drunk laughed. And there I lay, while one dance ended and another began, a hundred bare tits a minute covering it all. I pulled the flask from my pocket and took a long drink. This was how the Princess would end. There would be no salvation. There would be no farewell.

From the glow of the house door thrown open by Janet, a shadow started down the aisle. As it drew nearer, I took another long drink. A slow and sad waltz echoed through the auditorium. In the morning, crews would begin to arrive to haul off equipment and furniture. The morning after that, I would be unemployed. I had followed Dick's instructions nearly to the letter in cleaning out the theater. But I had left one item out of place. It was a large envelope addressed to the inspection agent of the real estate company that owned the property. There was a note inside. It detailed the time and date that a break-in had been scheduled with the intention of burglarizing the vacant building. And it asked a favor: that the enclosed book be returned personally to Beverly Bradlee, the former tenant. It was the theater's logbook, with detailed notes on every picture the house had run since last year. *Thy will be done.*

The figure stood over me. "This is fucking stupid," Earl said. "*You* are fucking stupid for thinking it up."

"I know."

He put out a hand. I reached for it. He recoiled. "No,

the flask." I passed it over, and he drank. "You know, kid, you either gotta live in your world or theirs."

I furrowed my brow, head buzzing from the rotgut whiskey. "I don't know what that means."

"It means I lead." He pulled me up and led me onto the stage. "You know how?" he asked, putting his palm to mine.

"It's been a long time," I managed as he put his other hand on the back of my shoulder.

"Wait for it . . ." he said. And so we stood, as far apart as our arms would allow, until the music came around. "And one, two, three. One, two, three . . ."

As the battered old soundtrack tooted out a slow and sorrowful song, the old man and I danced clumsily, casting a pair of misshapen shadows on the screen behind us.

SUMMERFEST '76

BY REED FARREL COLEMAN

Murray Hill

I knew I was fucked the second I opened my eyes. The blacktop was covered in a thin, nearly invisible layer of ice that beckoned people to drive a little faster, to brake a little harder, to die a little sooner. My vision still bleary from sleep, I noticed that if the streetlamp hit the ice just right, it sparkled, though it was a sparkle not of delight, but more the twinkle in a killer's eye at the moment of ecstasy. The sight of Locust Street that night in November 1976 made me wish I had driven the last few hours instead of sleeping it away. *If I'd been driving, I thought, I would have seen it coming. I would have known. I would have dropped her off and turned right around for home.* I like to think that's what I would have done, but it's horseshit.

"We're here," she said, road exhaustion thick in her voice. There was something else in it too. I didn't know what it was then, but forty years on, I know. Then, the only thing I knew was what it wasn't—enthusiasm.

I was fucked, all right. Royally . . . with a cherry on top.

This wasn't the Milwaukee I remembered from the summer when the sun brushed its warm fingertips across my cheeks, and the sky was so blue it hurt me all the way back to Brooklyn. It had been the best summer of my life because love—real love, not lust, not that stuff I mistook it for when I was seventeen—had found me. Love had light cat-green eyes, and its name was Lisa. She began to consume me the first second we accidentally brushed up against one another in line at the Pabst Pavilion at Summerfest. She was an actress, a dancer, an artist, studying at UWM. She supported herself by slinging beer at Century Hall, a cavernous old bowling alley that had been converted into a bar, restaurant, gallery, and performance space. And it was at Century Hall that the destruction of the person I used to be began in earnest.

At Summerfest, in line, waiting for the Pabst, we'd chatted a little.

Sorry.

Sorry.

Beer always this cheap in Milwaukee? I might have to consider relocating.

Where are you and that accent from?

Brooklyn . . . Coney Island.

Oh my God, I love New York. Broadway, Times Square . . .

You've been?

Twice. I'm going to live there when I'm done with school.

Come visit.

She smiled at the offer, but it wasn't a smile to send me on my way. *Get outta here, son. You're botherin' me.* On the contrary, it was a smile with interest in it. A smile with potential. After she'd gotten the three beers she'd ordered, Lisa turned to me.

I've got to go now. Friends. You know how it is. She actually looked disappointed. Then, as she walked past me, she stopped. *I work at Century Hall. I'm on tonight. Ask for Lisa.*

Where?

Century Hall. Just ask anyone.

And that was that. She disappeared into the swarm of people along the shore of the small ocean known as Lake Michigan.

I think I would have found Century Hall that night had it been on the dark side of the moon. It was considerably easier to find than that. Everybody in Milwaukee seemed to know Century Hall. She fairly shook when she came to the table and noticed it was me sitting there.

"You showed up." She flashed that smile again.

"Did you doubt it?"

She crooked her neck, shrugged. "There's always a little doubt."

"Not with us."

I couldn't believe those words came out of my mouth. *Us! What us?* But her reaction was answer enough to that question. She leaned over and kissed me on the mouth. *Yes, Virginia, there is an Us.* It was a first kiss I will never forget. Forty years later, in spite of how we eventually ground ourselves into dust, I think about it and can almost feel her lips on mine.

"I get off at eleven."

I sat in that seat until eleven, afraid to move for fear that it would all disappear.

The next morning, I woke up with Lisa's body pressed against mine, and the taste of her was full in my mouth and on my face. Becoming conscious of it, and sore as I was, I got hard. Then Lisa noticed and took me in her mouth.

We parted later that morning with tears and promises. Tears and promises I don't think either of us were willing to forget. But that night in late November of '76, when she stopped the car outside her apartment, I think we both wished we had been more willing to consider forgetfulness.

Now here's the funny thing. *Funny?* Okay, not funny. Ironic. What I'm telling you about isn't really about Lisa or about how we set about beating each other into submission and smashing ourselves into small pieces, pieces so tiny and ragged that reconstruction wasn't an option. We were fated to be Humpty Dumptys, never to be put back together again. I wish that's what I was telling you about. It probably wouldn't even be worth the telling, actually. I mean, that's what people do to each other sometimes, right? They meet, fall in love, and eat each other alive. And the thing is, I'm not blaming Lisa. I was just as guilty—guiltier, maybe—for what happened to us. She asked me to move there, probably thinking I wouldn't come. But I said yes, though in my head I knew it was likely a mistake. So, there was love between us, but not honesty.

After a week of lying around her apartment, feeling sorry for myself, I ventured out into the prewinter wonderland that was Milwaukee. Here's something you may not know: New York City is a pretty sunny place even in late fall and winter. I hadn't realized how sunny, nor how much I missed the sun, until I noticed that all I ever saw out of Lisa's window was grayness. Oh, that's not totally fair. It was grayness interrupted every other day by lake-effect snow.

Bottom line was, I had to get a job. Lisa had asked me to live with her. She hadn't offered to support me. And there was the fact that things had already begun going sideways between us. Our sex, while still intense, had taken on an uneasy and angry tone. Her scratches along my back a little deeper. My thrusting a little harder. I guess we were determined to express ourselves one way or the other.

My job hunt lasted all of seven minutes. I walked up the block, crossed the street, and went into a medium-sized grocery store called Eastside Emporium. A neon sign in the window boasted that it was the only store on the East Side open twenty-four hours a day, 365 days a year. All I'd wanted was a cup of coffee to cut against the windchill and regret. I left the store with my coffee and a job.

Both sides of my family had been in the grocery business,

and when I saw the *Help Wanted* sign by the deli counter, it was practically a done deal. And when the owner, Myron Katz, a transplanted Chicagoan, heard my Brooklyn accent, my use of the Yiddish word *meshugge* instead of crazy, and my willingness to work the graveyard shift, I was officially an Eastside Emporium cashier.

"And Robby," Mr. Katz said, placing his age-spotted hand on my shoulder, "the people in Milwaukee are good people. Sweet people, really, for the most part, and there's a nice Jewish community here . . ." His voice trailed off.

"But . . ."

He smiled a sad smile. "You might want to watch the Yiddish, *boychik*. This isn't Brooklyn. *Ton ir farshteyn?*"

I nodded. "*Ikh farshteyn.* I understand."

My days took on an awful sameness. I would be so wound up after working until six in the morning that I couldn't go right to bed. So, I'd go out for breakfast with my coworkers. After breakfast we usually wound up at one of their apartments, getting stoned, drunk, or both. Around noon, I'd head back to the apartment. First, though, I'd go check out the new records at 1812 Overture or Ludwig Van Ear. Then I'd stop in at Axel's or Kalt's for lunch and a beer. As things got progressively worse between Lisa and me, I forsook beer for stronger spirits. It got so bad that I used to say my two best friends in Milwaukee were named Jack—Yukon Jack and Jack Daniel's.

I'd get home around one or one thirty, and Lisa would be off at school. Half in the bag and exhausted, I'd collapse into bed and sleep until five thirty. I'd shower, brush my teeth, and head over to the store. Lisa and I hardly saw each other except on weekends. And weekends inevitably included dinner with her parents and her sister Karen in Wauwatosa, during which Lisa's mom and dad would stare at me, shaking their heads in disgust and disbelief. I wasn't fond of them either. Karen was cool.

Within two months, our destruction was nearly a fait accompli. Our love seemed to have drained away with the last snowmelt. But it was more than that, worse. It did more than simply vanish. When it was gone, I think both of us were utterly perplexed that it had existed at all. The encounter at the Pabst Pavilion at Summerfest felt like a billion years ago in two other people's lifetimes. Those intense, hours-long, late-night phone calls full of love and yearning had evaporated. Our sex had devolved into a pro forma exercise in a consensual need for release, and it was performed with all the passion of a computer screen cursor. By mid-February, I was out of Lisa's apartment. By March, I was out of her life. I should have gone back home. There were a hundred points during my time in Milwaukee when I should have left, but I was twenty and stupid and full of pride.

After I moved out of Lisa's place, I moved in with John Woolridge. John and I worked the graveyard together at the Emporium, and we got along pretty well. His parents had moved to Florida and left their old shitbox house across the highway from County Stadium to him. It was during those two weeks, the ones between my getting my walking papers from Lisa's apartment and my permanent pink slip from her life, that it happened.

It was four in the morning in the third week of February 1977 when he walked in. He didn't look more ornery than most of the other shitfaced assholes who stumbled into Eastside Emporium early in the morning, looking for munchies or someone to grouse to. He was about six feet tall and two hundred pounds of nasty. He wore a weathered, torn Harley motorcycle jacket and reeked of nickel-bag pot. His eyes were shot with blood, and his mouth tilted lazily down to one side.

His brown eyes were misaligned so that the right one seemed to be staring off into the distance.

He threw a bag of potato chips, a bag of pretzels, and a package of Usinger's brats on the belt at my register.

"That all, man?" I asked, and started ringing him up.

He didn't answer immediately. He seemed focused on something over my shoulder.

"Those flowers at the end of the register, how much are they?"

I smiled at that because he didn't strike me as a flower kind of guy. But hey, you never know, right? I'd almost forgotten the little bouquets were there. I hardly ever sold any, but Myron liked the flowers. *The world can be an ugly place,* he once confided in me. *Flowers bring a little beauty to it.*

"Six bucks," I told the customer.

"For those crappy flowers? Fucking cheap kike Jew motherfucker who owns this place," he said without a hint of self-consciousness. "I should fucking burn it down with him in it."

He saw the look in my eyes, but instead of apologizing or explaining—as if there was an alternative explanation besides anti-Semitism—he smiled. It was a cold, cruel smile, the droop going right out of his mouth.

I didn't say a word. I didn't do anything except ring him up, bag his stuff, and take his money. After the guy left, I went into the back storeroom and punched the walk-in freezer door. I spent the rest of the shift in the ER at Columbia Hospital. The hand wasn't broken, but it was banged up pretty bad. The pain and the bruising would eventually go away. The self-recrimination would not. My inaction ate at me. I blamed it on being tired. On being in a strange place. On my trauma over Lisa. It was all of those and none of those and a million other things. In the end, it didn't matter. I hadn't done anything. I'd stood there and taken it. I felt something people in the twenty-first century don't understand—shame.

With my hand the way it was, I couldn't work. But I could drink and drink and drink. Mixing the booze with the stuff the doctor at the ER had given me for the pain, with the self-loathing, changed me. John noticed and made it a point to stay away from me. Lisa noticed too. No, we weren't living together anymore, but we were still seeing each other. I guess it was sort of like when doctors do all those tests to make sure someone's dead before they make it official. Lisa and I were just doing our due diligence. We knew in our hearts that whatever we'd had or thought we'd had was gone. We just needed to make sure.

"Robby, are you all right?" she asked, placing her hand around my wrist. It was the next-to-last time I would ever see her and the last time we touched. "You know I still care about you."

"I'm fine," I lied.

It was only fair since she had lied first. All she really cared about was when I was going to leave for Brooklyn. I didn't blame her. In her shoes, I would have wanted me gone as well.

That night, after I dropped Lisa off for the last time at Century Hall, I went to Kalt's on Oakland Avenue, across the street from the Emporium. Frankie, a waiter who'd taken care of me and a lot of the crew at the Emporium, lit up at the sight of me. Frankie was gay, pretty openly too. In 1977, in Milwaukee, Wisconsin, that was a pretty brave thing to be. His bravery increased the intensity of my shame, but I was almost as happy to see him as he was to see me.

"Hey, Robby, I heard you were hurt," he said, patting my bandaged hand. "Want me to kiss it and make it better?"

"I'm not your type, Frankie."

"I don't have a type."

"I'm straight."

"That's what they all say."

We both had a laugh at that.

"Yukon Jack on the rocks with a Blatz chaser?" he asked, knowing the answer. "I'll be right back with that."

Then I heard it, a voice I'd heard only once before. It came out of the shadows at a corner table across the restaurant. It was a loud, boozy voice full of nastiness and preening discontent.

"Come over here, Frankie. I got something long and hard waiting for you."

"Cut it out, Karl," another voice said, coming out of those same shadows.

"Fuck you, Tim," Karl said. "Frankie and I go way back. After all, he's the queer that made Milwaukee famous. Ain't that right, faggot?"

Karl, so that's your name. It was Karl, the anti-Semitic fuckface who'd wanted to buy the flowers at the end of my register. Apparently, he was liberal with his hate and cast a wide net with it that included not only Jews but gays as well. And in that moment, I decided Karl and I would get well-acquainted. At least, I would get well-acquainted with him. I hurriedly drank my Yukon Jack, skipped the beer, and left too much money as a tip for Frankie.

I parked my beat-up '69 Tempest a few spots down from Kalt's doorway and waited. Fifteen minutes later, Karl came staggering out of Kalt's with someone I assumed was Tim. Tim tried to help Karl stay upright, but Karl wasn't having it. He kept slapping Tim's arms away. I rolled down my window so I could hear their conversation.

"Leave me the fuck alone, you donkey motherfucker."

Tim had had enough. "Fine, asshole. Suit yourself." He walked off, leaving Karl to lean against a stucco wall.

I watched as Karl collected what was left of himself. Five minutes later, he took a few deep breaths and managed to cross Oakland without getting run down. The only thing open on that side of the street was Axel's. Of course, Eastside Emporium was across Oakland as well, but it was still relatively early, and he would have had to cross Locust too, to get there. I didn't think old Karl had it in him to make it across two streets without collapsing. I was pretty sure he had his sights set on more drinks. And Axel's was the kind of place where the beer was cheap and the scrutiny was nearly nonexistent. My guess was right. Axel's it was.

I didn't follow Karl in. I waited on him. He closed the place and sat down on the sidewalk as the lights went dark inside the bar. Eventually, a cab came and took Karl away. I tailed the vehicle, keeping my distance. I wasn't sure why I bothered. Karl was too drunk to notice, and the cabbie certainly wouldn't have cared. The cab came to a stop on South 5th Street in front of a beige brick building that housed a machine shop. Karl rolled out of the backseat like a human blob. He lay there in the gutter for several minutes until it began snowing. That got him stirring, and I watched him go through a big metal door that, I guessed, led to an apartment above the machine shop. My guess proved correct when I saw a light pop on a minute later in a clouded glass window on the second floor above the shop.

I showed up at the machine shop at five thirty the following morning and waited for Karl. At seven, he appeared. He went across the street to a parking lot, emerging a few minutes later behind the wheel of an old Chevy pickup. He drove the pickup a little less than a mile to a salvage yard in the Menomonee Valley just by the freeway. There, sitting outside the fence, I watched him work the forklift, moving the hulks of squashed cars from the crusher to an area where he stacked them like cordwood. He left work at seven p.m.

What I realized after following Karl for a week was that there was an awful, unremitting sameness to his days. We were twins in that way. He would end his days with a cheap meal and a cab ride to Kalt's and/or Axel's. Then a cab ride home. In the meantime, I let my beard grow in, and I quit my job. I had a new job, and his name was Karl. Myron said he was sad to see me go, but wasn't blind. He stuffed a hundred-dollar bill in my pocket and patted me on my now-furry cheek.

"Go home, *tatellah*. This place isn't for you."

"You're right about that, boss. It was a pleasure." We shook hands.

Later that week, I stopped following Karl and began insinuating myself into his life, such as it was. I avoided Kalt's because I couldn't risk Frankie blowing my cover, nor did I want to risk Frankie's disapproval. But I was all about Axel's, and that extra hundred bucks Myron had given me went a long way to helping my mission. I didn't figure Karl would've recognized me from our one previous encounter, but the beard made it a certainty. And Karl was easy enough to befriend. I told him my name was Tommy. He wouldn't have cared if my name was Tinker Bell. All you had to do was buy him a few beers, a shot or two, and bitch about how the world was shit. You commiserated with him about how the niggers, spics, Jews, and A-rab fucks were taking over, and you were a friend for life. Nor did it hurt that I drove him home and saved him cab fare.

Here's the thing, though. I didn't really have a plan. Oh, believe me when I tell you I had any number of murderous fantasies about him. I thought about going back to the Emporium to visit one of the guys and stealing a deli knife with which to cut Karl open. I dreamed about feeding his guts to him as he bled to death. I thought about running him down as he drunkenly crossed Oakland Avenue in the dark. The cops would be unlikely to charge me. I thought of a hundred ways to end his worthless life, but in the end I decided I wasn't going to risk my entire future on him. That was until the night Lisa and two of her friends from work came into Axel's. Karl and I were at the far end of the bar as Lisa, Mary, and Toni settled in at the opposite end.

"Lookee here," Karl said, spotting Lisa and her friends. "Three pieces of meat for the taking."

Karl, as I'd learned, was a big talker, but not much of a doer. So I was willing to dismiss his grossness and chauvinism as just more bullshit. Then he sealed his fate.

"See that one?" He pointed down the bar. "Name's Lisa. I've had my eye on her for a while. Bitch works at Century Hall and lives around the corner on Locust. She's gonna be mine . . . one way or the other." He smiled that same smile he'd shown me that night at the Emporium. "Truth be told, I hope she turns me down, because I'll enjoy it that much more when I shove it down her throat. I'm tellin' you, Tommy, my man, I'm gonna enjoy hurtin' her. She's gonna bleed and then beg for more."

I kept Karl there until closing, an hour after Lisa and her friends had gone. I'd had to hide my head a few times as first Mary, then Toni, and finally Lisa, passed me on the way to the bathroom, but they never spotted me. That was the last time I would ever see Lisa. Later, I found out that she married soon after I left town and that she was pregnant within the year. Then, a few years ago out of the blue, I got an e-mail from her sister Karen. The e-mail consisted of a phone number and a request for me to call.

"Lisa's dead, Robby," Karen said. "Cervical cancer."

"I'm sorry to hear that." And I was. Hearing it felt like getting whacked across the ribs by a two-by-four. "But why—"

"She wanted me to call and say she was sorry for how things worked out between you guys. That she really did love you intensely and that she never wanted to feel that kind of love again. She said it just hurt too damned much."

Truer words had never been spoken. It just hurt too damned much.

Anyway, I drove Karl back to South 5th Street that night as I had every night for seven days running. Only this time I helped him into the shop instead of up to his apartment. He didn't put up a fight, because I had slipped a few of my ground-up pain pills into his last two beers. His dead weight was tough to handle, but it was worth it. He didn't protest when I placed his head under the hydraulic metal press machine, the kind they used to stamp wide steel sheets into various shapes. I would have liked to have killed him slowly so that I could have savored the sound of his skull cracking. So that I could have watched the blood and brains squeezing out of his eyeholes. But it was over in a flash, his limp body dangling from the stamp plate.

I stayed in Milwaukee for a few more weeks, half expecting the cops to knock on the door of John's old shitbox. The knock never came. The papers said they thought it was suicide or maybe an industrial accident. What it was was a mercy killing. Mercy for Frankie, and me, and for Lisa, the pretty girl with the cat-green eyes who should have been more careful in the line buying beer at Summerfest.

COUSINS

BY JENNIFER MORALES

Silver City

C arlisa came back from the army changed. A hitch in Afghanistan would change anyone, but it was maybe more extreme for my cousin. Carlisa came back and asked us all to start calling her Carlos. Call *him* Carlos. He chose my niece's fourth birthday party to deliver that request to the extended family, a month after he returned.

The news didn't land easy on my tía. "Better they should've killed her there, the Taliban or whoever," she said to the guests assembled at Candela's banquet hall, "since she's dead to me anyway." Tía Consuelo kissed the birthday girl on the head, grabbed her purse, and made for the door.

Tío Enrique took it about the same, it seemed. No comments about the Taliban, just a disbelieving grunt and a slow suck on his beer before he plunked it down on the pink tablecloth. The party fell apart after that.

I followed my cousin out. "Lisa—sorry, Carlos," I called after her—him. "Carlos, wait up."

Carlos had always been handsome, and the edges laid on by military service in the rugged mountains of the Hindu Kush didn't hurt. His sharp jaw and high forehead gave him the fierce, alert look of a panther. An emerging black mane just growing out of the GI crew cut added to the catlike appearance. Tía Consuelo's kids got the looks. My siblings and I got the—well, I don't know that we got anything special. Stubbornness, maybe. Or a lack of caution.

"I don't need any more hassle, Marta." The streetlight caught the tears in his dark eyes.

"I'm not following you to hassle you." I put a hand on his forearm. Under his thin cotton shirt, I felt the muscles tense.

"Lisa!" Our cousin Pamela leaned out the door of the party hall. "Tía says get your stuff outta her house. You can't stay there no more."

I turned back toward the open door. "Fuck you, Pamela."

"Watch your mouth, Marta. I'm just the messenger."

"If delivering messages was all you were doing, you'd deliver them to the right person." I reached an arm around Carlos's neck. "This here is our primo Carlos. ¿No lo conozcas?"

Pamela scowled and slammed the heavy door shut behind her.

I loved pissing off self-righteous Pamela, and if I could do it while defending my favorite cousin, so much the better. Perfect fucking Pamela.

"Thanks," Carlos said, wiping the tears from his eyes. "Come back with me to the house?"

Packing up his things took less than fifteen minutes. Most of his clothes and personal items were already—or still—in his army bag. He tossed in a couple of photos from the shelf above his bed and grabbed his watch from his desk drawer, zipped up the bag, and said, "Let's go."

He stayed with me in the upper flat I shared with my ex, Brenda, for a couple of days, then cleared out one afternoon while I was at work. I found a note on the kitchen table, a bottle of Tapatío holding it down against the June breeze pouring in through the window over the sink.

Getting a room at the Wayfarer. I'll see you around.

The Wayfarer was one of several rooming houses in Silver City, the neighborhood where we grew up and still lived, on the near South Side. This one catered to new hires at the mining equipment factory, ones whose first checks hadn't come in yet or who spent them on the bottle instead of building up a security deposit for a more permanent residence. Still, among its run-down, miserable peers, the Wayfarer was the least run-down. No less miserable, though.

I went to see Carlos a few days after he settled in. His room was on the third floor, up a narrow set of stairs drenched in a dubious mélange of smells. The thin walls leaked the noise of a dozen televisions and radios.

"What are you doing here, Li—Carlos?"

He was sitting cross-legged and wedged into a corner on the twin bed that took up most of the room. A book, face-down, a yellow legal pad with his gawky handwriting, and an open laptop fanned out around his knees.

"Just living." He shrugged.

I sat on the edge of the bed. Carlisa and I had been close once—sleepover cousins, keep-a-secret-from-our-parents cousins. Sitting on his bed had been something I did reflexively, but I felt my cousin stiffen at my invasion of the narrow space.

"What's got into you?"

"I don't know." He closed the laptop and then the book, covering them both with the notepad. He drew his knees up to his chest and crossed his arms over them. "I just feel weird in my body right now. I'm not sure I want anybody to touch me."

The screenless window was cracked open to the summer air. The sound of a car crash rattled the glass, though Carlos didn't get up to look. I did. A navy-blue sedan was in the intersection, its bumper snapped off and the driver's door open. A woman emerged from a green SUV with its front lights smashed. The other driver, a bulky man in a Bucks cap, was yelling at her. I kept my eye on the situation as we talked. I didn't have much of a plan in mind if the man went after her, but I'd go down there in a second if something went foul. I didn't appreciate people giving our neighborhood a bad reputation.

"It's like, I don't even want to *have* a body right now—not this body, anyway." He shoved his fingers into his hair, a frustrated move I remembered from our eighth grade algebra study sessions.

"You talk to your mom?"

Carlos peeked around his tented hands and sneered. "What do you think?"

Word along the family grapevine was that Tía Consuelo had banned Carlos's name from being spoken in her house and that Consuelo, Enrique, and our abuela had gone in for a consultation with the priest at St. Vincent's. Something was brewing, though I didn't know what.

The cousins were divided—some saying live and let live, others keeping their opinions to themselves for now, maybe hoping the whole thing would just blow over. And then there was Pamela and her husband Ronnie Junior, Pentecostal converts who took this family crisis on as their personal mission for Christ. Pamela gave me a few messages that I would never pass on to Carlos, stuff about submission to God.

"Yeah, it's probably best to just lay low for a while." Three floors below, the sedan driver stopped yelling and hunched over his car hood to write something down. The woman stood far away from him, talking on her cell phone, her shoulders shuddering like she was crying. "It's maybe too much to ask, you know? For people to come around overnight?"

"I didn't ask them to come around overnight, Marta. I just wanted to let them know what's going on with me." He unfolded his legs, scooted against the wall, and patted the edge of the bed. "You can sit down."

The situation outside seemed calm enough, so I sat. "Thanks."

"They didn't get *you* overnight."

"That's true." My coming out gay was a shock to my nice Mexican Catholic family. I never dated boys in high school, making me seem like an even nicer Catholic girl. When I told my mom at nineteen, she was devastated. My dad stopped speaking to me. After a couple months of silent dinners, I took the hint and moved out. It was two years before Mami could look at me without tears in her eyes, but eventually she and Papi softened up, and I was allowed back into the fold.

"They'll come around, Carlos."

"I doubt it. You heard what my mother said to me, wishing I was dead."

"It's family. They'll get over it. Nothing more important than family, right, primo?" I put a hand on his knee, squeezed it, trying to lighten the mood.

He jerked his knee away. "I said don't touch me."

"Sorry." I stood and stepped back to lean against the opposite wall.

"You don't have to stand—it's just . . ." He waved a hand at me. A shadow passed over his wrinkled brow.

"Something else going on, Carlos?"

He stared down at his hands, then rubbed them together and cracked his knuckles, the routine he went through just before he spilled something big. He went through the motions a few more times until there was nothing left to crack, then set his black eyes on mine. "You can't tell nobody."

I shook my head. "Course not."

Carlos chewed on his lower lip as he worked the first few words out. I couldn't help but think that he looked like the girl he no longer wanted to be, pretty and scared.

"In the army . . ." his voice was high and shaky, "I was part of this ad hoc crew they had stationed way out in the boondocks. Doing guard duty for some new operation, small-scale mining. Well, they were digging anyway, but very carefully, like they were looking for something precious. I don't know why we were there—they kept us in the dark—but our job was to guard the site and provide cover when helicopters or trucks came or went. That's it. Our crew was so small that they had us all housed together, men and women. No separate facilities at all."

I swallowed hard.

"There were only three of us—I mean, women." He flinched at the word. "And, you know, it's the army. We all take a lot of abuse, a lot of . . ." He cleared his throat, and when he spoke again, he was holding back tears. "I mean, we were under a lot of pressure, out in the Kush, not knowing what or who we were protecting. It just got ugly."

I sat on the edge of the bed and leaned back against the wall, so we were facing the same direction. I didn't want to watch his face.

"Ugly how?"

He drew his knees back up to his chest, his voice a whisper. "This one guy, Barclay, he was hitting on me, nonstop, but I kept telling him no. Then one night, a bunch of us were hanging out after our shift, drinking beer. I went out to the priv, and he followed me there, told me he didn't take no for an answer." Carlos's breath was tight and uneven. "I couldn't fight him off. He just left me there, lying next to the latrine."

He was sobbing now, but I didn't want to risk touching him. The shadowy gap between us grew cold.

"Did you report it?"

Out of the corner of my eye, I saw Carlos shake his head.

The sun was getting low, a golden beam pressing through the window and painting the dirty wall across from us a sickly peach.

"I'm sorry that happened."

Somebody cranked up some reggaetón in one of the houses across the way. It was going to be another hot, loud night on Pierce Street.

"Did he do anything else after that?"

"No. I asked to be moved to the opposite shift—I didn't say why. Barclay left me alone after that, and I just tried to do my job and go on with my life, you know? I only had two more months left in my hitch. But his buddies were always looking at me a certain way. He must have bragged to them." Carlos nodded as if answering his own question. "Of course he did. What a big guy. What a triumph."

His bitterness swept across me, and I shivered. "Is that when you decided to become a man?"

Beside me on the bed, Carlos stiffened. "Don't be an idiot," he hissed. "That's not how it works."

"I didn't mean—"

He let out a derisive laugh. "I thought you were the woke one, Martita. So sensitive! Defender of the downtrodden!" His mocking stabbed me to the core.

"I'm sorry."

"I can't fucking trust anybody."

"I said I'm sorry."

It was getting dark, but neither of us moved to turn on a light. Instead, in my embarrassment, I got up and went out the door. I shouldn't have. I should've stayed. Or at least taken a good last look at his face.

Pamela's kid Paulina told me what happened next.

I had let a week go by since that talk in Carlos's room. I didn't know if he wanted me around, and it seemed like everything I did or said was the wrong thing anyway. But once I resurfaced from my swamp of irritation and shame, I couldn't find him. I called or texted a dozen times, but he never answered. Things were busy at the computer store where I worked, and I couldn't go by his place at the Wayfarer until late Friday night. The guy across the hall said he hadn't seen or heard anybody in that room for a couple days.

I called my mom from the street outside. "Have you seen Carlos?"

She made the humming noise she always did before she lied or held something back. "Today? No, mi amor. Not since yesterday."

"Yesterday? Where did you see him yesterday?"

More humming. "Ah, well, she went to talk to her mom and—"

"You should say *he*, Mami."

"Well, they had a little talk, and then I don't know where she went."

"That's it? You have no idea where he is now?" An icy feeling rushed down my spine. My mom could be evasive for a lot of reasons—politeness, shyness with strangers, fear—she did it all the time. But this felt different.

"You could ask your tía."

"I'll do that."

First thing the next morning, a sticky July Saturday, I walked to Consuelo's house. People were out washing their cars, the foamy water swirling with the crushed soda bottles and half-empty takeout containers in the gutters. Kids tore through yards on my aunt's block, chasing each other with squirt guns. I stopped Paulina, my cousin Pamela's daughter, as she whooshed by me on the sidewalk.

"Hey!" She pulled away from me laughing. "If I stand still they're going to get me." She took off again, her long skirt tangling around her legs as she dodged an ambush by Nestor, her brother.

On her next pass, I caught her again. "Hold up. I need to ask you something."

Paulina bent over, hands on her knees, huffing from the run. "What?"

A paletero's jangling bells caught the attention of the other kids, and they ran off toward National Avenue and ice cream. Paulina's eyes followed them.

"I'll buy you a paleta in a minute, Lina."

Paulina held up her fingers in a V.

"Okay, two paletas, but first you have to tell me: have you seen Carlos?"

"We're not supposed to call her that. Her name's Carlisa." At age nine, she was not ready to buck the lessons her Pentecostal parents were laying down about the strict line between the sexes.

"But you saw her?"

She nodded. "A few days ago, I guess. She went to Tía Consuelo's and Tío Enrique's house. My mom and dad brought her."

"What do you mean, *brought her*? She didn't go on her own?" Then an even more uncomfortable question came to mind. "And why were you there?"

She shrugged. "We were all there. Well, not you." She pressed her lips together, her brown eyes dimming as it dawned on her that this might hurt my feelings. "I mean, everybody who has a problem with Carlisa, they all wanted to talk to her and . . . Can I go now?"

"No, tell me what you were going to say." I gripped her shoulder, and she strained under my hand. "And *what?*"

"Mom and Dad made her dress as a girl. They brought her to our apartment first, and Mom and I helped put her makeup on. And we curled her hair in front."

I imagined that black swoop of hair twisted on a curling iron and the image turned my stomach.

The paletero was jingling his way down 33rd Street toward us. I dug into my back pocket for my wallet and gave Paulina a few dollars.

"Thanks!" she said, running off toward the bells.

The chemical fruit smell of detergent wafted across Consuelo and Enrique's porch, announcing laundry day. Consuelo answered the door.

"Hi, tía," I said, but she just lifted a plucked eyebrow and motioned me to follow her.

She led me to the bedroom, where she resumed putting away my uncle's shirts. "You here to apologize?"

"Apologize? Me? For what?" Out of habit, I reached into the laundry basket on the bed to start matching socks.

"You're the one who opened the door to this. This tontería with my daughter."

"How?" I cuffed a pair of her gray socks and threw them back into the basket.

"You two were always close. Too close, I thought. All those sleepovers. All the whispering. But your abuela was always like, *Don't worry, they're just primas. Girl cousins are always that way.*" Consuelo turned and pointed the crook of a clothes hanger at me. "But now look. I told your mother your gay experiment would come to no good."

I tossed the mountain of unmatched socks back into the basket and shoved my hands into my pockets to keep them from my aunt's face. "It's not an experiment. I'm twenty-seven years old, and I've been this way my whole life. And I didn't make my cousin gay."

"No, you didn't. Even worse. You gave my daughter the crazy idea of rejecting her whole identity. Of telling God that He made her wrong." The fire in her eyes made them glow white. "You telling God He got Carlisa wrong, Marta?"

"He didn't get anything wrong. Carlos is perfect just the way he is."

Consuelo brought the corner of the hanger right up to my nose. "Don't you ever say that name in my house again."

I set my hand on the wire and let the weight lower it. She allowed it to happen. Some of the anger drained from her face, leaving her looking pale and tired. She fished in the basket for another shirt.

"Did Ronnie and Pamela bring my cousin over here the other night?"

"Yes."

"What did you talk about?"

"I asked them to bring her so I could tell her that if she wanted to be part of this family, she was going to have to dress like a woman and act like a woman. And if she wasn't willing to do that, I didn't want to see her anymore. God didn't give me a son. He gave me a daughter."

"You got Pamela and Ronnie to dress her up like some kind of doll to tell her that?"

Consuelo smoothed her black hair with an awkward hand. "I thought she looked great."

"Yeah? How did his face look?" I stepped up to my aunt. "Happy to be made up like the daughter of your dreams?" I grabbed her by the shoulders and pushed her into the closet doors. Her eyes filled with fear. "Happy? Did she look happy, tía?" I gave Consuelo another little shove then stormed out, sweeping the laundry basket onto the floor as I went.

The house had been dark and cool. Outside on the sidewalk, the noon sun blinded me. I stumbled up the block, not realizing where my feet were taking me until I was halfway there.

Ronnie sold cars at Arellano Motors on 37th Street, and he worked most Saturdays. I burst into the small sales room, where sweat I had earned walking the six hot blocks turned to ice in the air-conditioned space.

"Where's Ronnie?" I asked the secretary. She was in her seventies and matched the fading utilitarian decor perfectly, as if she were a fixture included when the place was built back in 1950.

"He's making a sale, dear."

I hadn't noticed him in the lot out front, but Arellano's spread their inventory onto all the side streets too, taking up valuable neighborhood parking spaces. It pissed people off. "Will he be back soon?"

She squinted at her watch. "Oh, sure. He's been out there for a while. Back in a few minutes, I'd guess."

I stood staring out at the rows of cars parked in the narrow lot. If I had seen Ronnie when I first came in, I would've punched him first then asked questions. The wait gave me time to settle down.

This rage wasn't new. I had felt it all along—every time

some relative asked me when I was going to stop dating women and marry a man. Every time someone told me how pretty I'd look in a dress. Every time someone referred to my girlfriend as my *roommate*. The rage had simmered all that time, but I managed to keep a lid on it. Until today, shoving my aunt like that. I was sure everyone had heard about it already, Consuelo on the phone to my mother, to her other sisters, to Pamela.

I had almost decided to step out and head home when Ronnie appeared. He was in full-on car-salesman mode, a fat pasted-on smile giving the impression that he was glad to see me. He even threw out his hand to shake before it clicked who I was. When he recognized me, he gave me a quick hug and kissed both my cheeks.

"Marta, what brings you in? You buying a car today? What're you driving these days, still that Toyota?"

"I'm not here to talk cars, Ronnie. Where's Carlos?"

He put his thumbs in his belt loops and looked down at his shoes, chuckling like I just cracked a joke. Then he looked at me, his blue marble eyes glinting playfully. "I don't think I know any Carloses. But I did see your cousin Carlisa on Thursday. She looked good."

I got right up into his face and whispered, "Don't you call him that."

Over Ronnie's shoulder, I noticed the secretary's eyes widen. She dropped the paper she was holding and clenched the edge of the desk with her white fingers.

"I heard she decided to re-up," Ronnie said.

"She's going back to the army?"

"Sounds like it."

That was news. But maybe he could reenlist as Carlos? Regardless, I could see how my cousin would choose living in a war zone in Afghanistan over the battle here in Silver City. At least the government would pay him to fight that war.

"Good," I said. "Anything to get away from you."

"Hey now, Marta, I didn't have anything to do with her decision."

"Yes you did. And you know it too. Making her dress up for Consuelo's little dog-and-pony show. Probably shoving your stupid Bible pamphlets in her face the whole time." I felt a churn of bile in my throat.

"Ronnie?" The secretary put her hand on the desk phone. "You've got a call waiting for you on line two."

The phone hadn't rung since I'd been in there. I mad-eyed the secretary, and she looked down at her desk.

"Well, I guess I've got to get back to it." Ronnie patted my elbow. "I'll take it in back, Betty." At the door to the office, he paused. "Marta, it's better this way. The army straightens out a lot of crooked lives, by God's grace. Maybe it'll stick this time."

I thought of what Consuelo had said at my niece's birthday. I bet not so deep down inside Ronnie thought Carlos would be better off dead too.

"If Carlos gets killed over there, Ronnie, I blame you!" I was shouting, but the door to the office had already closed.

On my way back to my apartment, I texted Carlos: *why did u go along with Ronnie n Pamela dressing u up like that?*

I didn't get an answer.

The plan emerged over the next several days, a conflagration stoked by my guilt over insulting Carlos and my fury at Ronnie and Pamela and the rest.

The only hard part was going to be having to pretend I liked Ronnie for a few minutes.

I drove to Arellano's on Friday, almost a week after I'd confronted him there. I had a duffel bag in the backseat and my gun, a little Smith & Wesson 442 I kept for nighttime walks in the neighborhood, in my coat pocket. I didn't like storing it there, so close to my heart, but the holster would've been too obvious.

I pulled up behind Ronnie's truck in the lot, parking him in just after seven, closing time. The summer sun was getting low, flashing through my windshield as I turned off the engine and got out.

The bells hanging on the glass door announced my arrival, but nobody was there to notice. Betty's desk chair was vacant, a cardigan sweater draped over the back. Through the frosted windows set in the wall dividing the waiting room from the offices, I watched Ronnie's shadow moving from room to room turning off lights. Then the door swung open, and he saw me. It took a minute before his shaken face settled into the salesman's mask.

"Marta, what a surprise."

I shrugged, feeling the weight of the gun sliding against my ribs, and put my hands in the front pockets of my jeans. "Yeah, I just wanted to apologize. For the way I talked to you the other day." I felt the twitch of a sneer at the corners of my mouth, so I looked down.

Apparently, the move made me look genuinely ashamed because Ronnie moved to my side, wrapped his arm around my shoulders, and squeezed. "Hey, don't feel bad. No real harm done."

I looked into his face. The deep blue eyes—the kind that show up in my Mexican family only by way of marriage—held that unctuous variety of Christian concern, Jesus forgiving me my sins by His indulgent proxy.

"Yeah?" I faked relief with a smile and a shake of the head. "Sure."

As if the thought had just occurred to me, I said, "Hey, let's hit Mamie's. It's blues night."

"Oh, I don't know, Marta." Ronnie stepped to the wall behind Betty's desk to key in the alarm code, then gestured to the door. "We've got thirty-five seconds."

Once outside, he locked the door and peered at his truck. "Pamela's not really happy if I'm out after work."

"Oh, come on. Let me make it up to you by taking you out. You've worked hard all day. One drink—a soft drink, okay? And we'll listen to a little music, and I'll bring you right back here to pick up your truck."

My lies were stacking up, but the guilt about them evaporated the second I brought to mind images of Carlos standing in front of his mother in makeup and a dress.

Ronnie's resistance dissolved into something like sympathy. I smiled. He was going to say yes out of sheer pity for my wicked, queer soul.

"Sure," he said. "A soda and, let's say, a half hour of blues." He reached a comradely hand out to my shoulder and turned me toward my car. "I guess we're taking the Toyota. I seem to be parked in."

Mamie's was only four blocks away, and it was a beautiful evening. There really wasn't any reason to drive, except that Ronnie was a car salesman—he didn't walk anywhere—and I needed somewhere semiprivate to punch him in the face.

I did just that. I'm left-handed so even from the driver's seat I had enough clearance to take a good swing. He fell back against the passenger door, stunned. I clicked the driver-controlled locks.

"Marta?" He put a hand up to his cheek.

"That's for Carlos." I pulled out the 442. "This is for Carlos too." I reached over the seat and grabbed the duffel bag and threw it at him. "Open it."

He unzipped the bag mechanically, keeping his eye on the gun.

"Put it on."

Ronnie pulled out the dress I had picked for him—a frilly low-cut party dress in lavender.

"Oh, come on, Marta. You can't be serious."

I moved the gun closer to his nose. "I'm pretty fucking serious right now, Ronnie. Put it on." When he hesitated, I tapped the gun to his temple and said, "The color will bring out your eyes."

He started to pull the dress on over his work clothes.

"No," I said, "the man outfit comes off first."

"Marta . . ."

"Do it."

He did, and it took everything I had to keep my gun sighted on him as he flailed his way out of his shirt and pants and into the dress.

"There's shoes in there too." Matching lavender satin pumps, women's size twelve. I'd found them at a bridal shop near Southridge.

As he bent to put the shoes on, I pressed the mouth of the gun to the back of his sweaty neck. A surge of murder ran through me, but I let him straighten up. I needed to complete the job as planned.

"Happy now?" he asked, gesturing at the getup.

"Nope. There's more in there."

He dug into the bag again, bringing out a tube of lipstick and one of mascara, and a case containing a selection of eye shadows and blushes. "What am I supposed to do with this?"

I raised an eyebrow and heard his breath snag.

"This is . . ." he began.

"This is Friday night, Ronnie. And you're just getting beautiful."

He fumbled with the lipstick first, tingeing the blond whiskers around his mouth a ruby red.

"¡Wátchale, primo!" I flicked down the passenger-side visor and opened the mirror. "Have a little self-respect."

His hands shook as he drew the wand from the mascara tube. He looked at me as if I might help him, but I just sat there, taking in his nervousness, the black cross-hatched mess he made of his eyelids.

"Good thing you can cover that with shadow."

The car filled up with the smell of his sweat. I enjoyed it, the scent of his fear. The pits of his sleeveless dress were stained deep purple.

He chose a pale shade of blue for his lids then moved on to the cheeks, rouging them like a doll. When he was done, he tossed the lot back into the bag and looked at me. He bit his lower lip.

"Don't do that. You'll ruin your lipstick." I gestured with the gun. "Put your hands up on the dashboard."

He followed my instructions, and I started the car. The drive to Mamie's took less than two minutes, though it felt like years. The small gun was heavy in my hand. In the parking lot I told him, "We're going to slide out of the car on my side. Then we're walking into Mamie's, and you're going to act natural."

"What's natural about this, Marta? Please?" His voice had melted down to a damp whimper, a luscious sound as good as the whiskey I was looking forward to ordering.

"Just be yourself, Ronnie." I spat the words into his face and opened my door. I pulled him out of the car. The shame seemed to lighten him. Although he had fifty pounds on me, at least, he slid out like a baby.

I pressed the gun into his side, burying it in the frills of his dress, and led him inside.

The bar was packed. The band hadn't started yet, but the crowd was doing its best to warm the place up. Drunks spilled aside as we moved into the center of the room and the people around us noticed Ronnie and grew quiet.

An asthmatic dude in a Brewers T-shirt elbowed his way through to a spot four feet from us. "Ronnie?" he asked, half laughing, his brown eyes pinched in curiosity. "It's Matt. From church? Why are you—"

I cut him off: "It's a church fundraiser. Didn't you hear about it, Matt?" I pressed the gun farther into Ronnie's ribs as he squirmed. "Ronnie's dressed up like this to share in the humiliation that Jesus felt at the hands of His persecutors."

Matt gave a skeptical nod.

I felt hot with the ridiculousness of the situation, of this story I was spinning, yet I went all in. "We're going to pass the hat around the bar, for donations for the church missions. You should take a picture for the newsletter, okay?"

Matt looked doubtful, but he reached into his pocket for his phone. Obediently, he took several pictures.

"I'm going to throw up," Ronnie muttered.

"Good," I whispered in his ear.

He wasn't lying. He puked right then, all over his fancy dress.

I pocketed the gun and drew out my phone. I snapped a few photos of Ronnie as he wiped the vomit from the corners of his mouth, his eyes cursing me.

"Well, my job is done here," I said cheerfully, and patted Ronnie on the back as I left.

I was going to have to leave town for a few days. I had a suitcase in the trunk.

I stopped by the liquor store for a bottle of whiskey, since I didn't get that drink at Mamie's after all. In the parking lot, I scrolled through the photos. Ronnie looked miserable, slump-shouldered and stained. I don't think Matt entirely bought the church-mission-fundraiser story, but at least he saw Ronnie and took pictures. Ronnie would suffer, knowing that the pictures existed at all, whether they got submitted to the church's newsletter or not. And God, I was sure, saw Ronnie's suffering and saw that it was good.

Or I did, anyway. Ronnie's suffering was good.

Before I texted the photo to Carlos, I opened the bottle and took a nice swig. I doubted he would respond, but a minute later I got a reply.

Ur going 2 need 2 explain that

1st explain this: why did u go along with Ronnie n Pamela dressing u up like that?

A long pause, ten minutes during which I slugged back a couple more shots. Then:

I thought if I did it she wd see

See what?

how ridiculous I looked

I thought about Consuelo's pale, worn face.

She saw it. I don't know if that was exactly true, but it was the best I could do.

why did u do that? Carlos texted.

2 Ronnie? 2 make him feel the same way they made u feel

He will NEVER EVER feel the way I do

My head spun. I had failed Carlos again. The whiskey and the lingering smell of Ronnie's sweat in the cramped space made me sick to my stomach. I opened the car door and puked onto the asphalt.

I thought it would make u happy, I texted when I recovered.

u don't understand anything, do u?

I ignored that. I just wanted the whole episode to be over. My hands twitched on the steering wheel, giving me the urge to drive and just keep driving.

u on yr way back to the Stan?

yep, next 2sday. Got the weekend off tho

Ima come see u—send me the address and I'll b there.

No, don't do that.

I wanted to ask why not, but I knew there were a hundred legitimate reasons he didn't want to see me right then. Me, being the most likely reason.

I let it go. I washed out my mouth with whiskey, and I drove.

ALL DRESSED IN RED

BY VIDA CROSS

Franklin Heights

While sitting on her porch with her sister, Ms. Lora knew she smelled death when she caught a whiff of the scent from her sweater. It was a raspberry color with smooth wool sleeves and a cowl neck. She admired the wool cowl neck, but when she fiddled with the woven ridges, she got a whiff of dust and dime-store eau de toilette. Walgreens parfum. Lavender.

This sweater once belonged to an older white woman with white-yellow hair. The hint of a mothball smell suggested the woman had stopped dressing in regular clothes, so maybe the sweater had sat in a drawer or a see-through plastic bag made for comforters.

Ms. Lora had bought the sweater secondhand from the Immaculate Heart of Mary's basement store. The store was under the Immaculate Heart of Mary's community room. The community room was on the first floor, and the second to tenth floors were senior citizen apartments. Ms. Lora shopped at the secondhand store. It was called the Immaculate Heart of Mary's Clothing Boutique. Most of the items that lined the store's movable metal clothing rods came from Immaculate Heart of Mary's senior residents. Ms. Lora knew that some of the clothes were delivered to the boutique upon someone's death.

She shopped at the boutique with her sister, Ms. Abby.

They arrived every Monday, because Monday was half-price day, and the store clerk greeted them with a fake smile: very bright, very cheerful. The store clerk always said, "Hellooo, Ms. Lora. Good morning, Ms. Abby."

The two women would mumble a "Hello" or "Hey." Sometimes, the store clerk thought she heard "Bitch" or even "Tart."

Ms. Lora and Ms. Abby were always first at the door. The store opened at nine a.m. They arrived at eight thirty a.m. or eight fifteen a.m. and sat on the two brick walls that lined the pathway to the entrance of the basement's double doors.

To get to the doors from their car, they would wheel their walkers down the pathway. The driveway was on a decline or an incline depending on which way you were going. The sisters walked and rolled slowly down the driveway to the boutique.

Ms. Abby was stooped over. She had a bad back and big hips: a big round rear end that may have once pleased the boys. Now, she could barely pull her hiney along with her.

Ms. Lora was thin and wiry. She could walk without a walker but preferred one for the driveway's hill.

Once inside the store, the two ladies would crowd the aisles. One sister would take one aisle, and the other sister would take another. They would rest their shopping carts in front of their walkers, and behind those two items they would stand (in Ms. Abby's case, she was always bent forward). The ladies would move back and forth and up and down the aisle, and by the time another customer came their way, a sister would move to the end of the aisle to block the person's entrance.

They came from Franklin Heights, Milwaukee, Burleigh, the 53206 zip code. They lived in and owned a duplex. They had inherited the space, and each could have had her own apartment, but they decided to share the lower unit. The upper unit sat empty. They were retired postal workers, and the ladies had a routine. They woke at seven a.m. every day. Ms. Lora washed and began coffee by seven thirty a.m. Every day she said, "Abby, you want coffee?"

Every day Abby said, "Yeah," as she shuffled to the bathroom. The ladies didn't talk much. They had all day, all week, all year to say more.

The bedrooms in the apartment were almost Jack and Jill. Two rooms were joined by a short hallway and a bath. The hallway led to each room and the kitchen. By eight a.m. the ladies were either sitting on their porch or off to the boutique or holding their own clothing sale in their yard.

They watched television together for lunch and dinner. Most days, they observed things and said, "See that?"

"Umm-humm."

They were in bed by eight p.m. By nine p.m. they heard gunshots. Every night. The shots ended by nine p.m., and Ms. Lora would call to Ms. Abby, "Abby? You ah-ight?"

"Yeah."

They beautified their home with flowers. Their front lawn was covered in annuals during the summer. Their home was a deep mossy green on the second floor's exterior and a mustard yellow on the bottom. They liked their lives, although things could be better.

Their parents had been the first blacks to move to the block in 1976. Quickly, it had become all black. By 1985, the neighborhood had become drug infested. But they liked their home. Liked their neighbors. Nodded hello to some. Said "See that" about others. They watched the cops drive quickly down the block. One police officer was driving so fast one day he ran over a child. That was 1996. Ms. Lora and Ms. Abby sat on their porch and yelled, "See that?" to each other.

They traveled to the boutique because there were no secondhand stores in their area. There were no supermarkets.
No furniture stores. No coffee shops. No clothing stores. No
auto supply stores. No malls. No McDonald's. No pharma-
cies. No sit-down restaurants. No nothin'. Although there were
plenty of churches all around, the ladies were not dedicated
to a church. They listened to Sunday worship on the radio
every Sunday. On Sundays after two p.m., during the summer
months, they sold clothes in their backyard.

So, they traveled to the southern suburbs of St. Francis,
Wisconsin, to Immaculate Heart of Mary's Catholic Church
once a week to shop, and they traveled there once a month
to eat.

When they shopped at the boutique, they often picked
things up for their yard sale. Ms. Abby would hold a shirt up
and say, "Jimmy?"

"Yep. He'll love that."

Their carts were always piled high. When they moved to
check out, the clerk would pick up an item, check the price
tag, find a beige square with the price of three dollars crossed
out and *50 cents* written beneath the original number.

The clerk could never stop herself from laying an item
down with a heavy hand. Her rings and bracelets and palms
would hit the counter whenever she had to punch in fifty
cents for a three-dollar shirt.

The clerk would never forget the time she called her manager over to look at the tags. He bustled past the three of
them and, waving his hands, said, "Ring it up, Sheryl. Hello,
Ms. Lora and Ms. Abby. Will you be joining us for pancake
breakfast?" He was afraid of them: shaking.

Immaculate Heart of Mary's pancake breakfast was an

all-you-can-eat affair. Immaculate Heart hosted one on the first Saturday of every month. For three dollars a person, from seven a.m. to one p.m., Ms. Abby and Ms. Lora ate pancakes for breakfast and lunch.

Ms. Abby and Ms. Lora knew the room well. A big rectangle. The elder men and women who could walk well sat in the back and allowed the people who walked with some difficulty to sit closer to the door and closer to the serving tables. Ms. Lora and Ms. Abby sat in the middle. They didn't belong. They lived in Franklin Heights, Milwaukee: a city neighborhood that no Immaculate Heart residents cared to visit. Most Immaculate Heart residents were white, a few were Asian, and a few were Latino. None were black. Ms. Lora and Ms. Abby wore red, square-shaped dresses every time they came for the pancake breakfast. They stood out.

Immaculate Heart residents found it awkward. They had held a meeting to inquire about Ms. Abby and Ms. Lora. Many residents attended. One resident, who seemed to be the most vocal, Jeb Turnwall, spoke over the chatter to say, "We just want to know if they are safe."

Who could answer that question? Not management. No one had really spoken to them.

The chatter would continue, and then Jeb would speak up again and say, in an exasperated tone, "Are they dangerous?"

Again, no one knew.

Jeb Turnwall knew Franklin Heights. He had frequented the area for prostitutes. When he was younger, he loved going up there and driving down a dark street until a black shadow popped out. For ten or twenty dollars, he could be satisfied. But he was too old now. Couldn't drive well. Plus, there was that time with the one girl who had pulled a gun on him for all his money. He had paid her ten dollars. He had five twenties left. So he knocked the gun out of her hand, slapped her, picked up the gun, and shot her in the head. It took all of five minutes. He shot her two more times in her face and, sitting the unregistered gun on top of her, he walked out of the alley to his car and never returned. But that was way back. When? 1990? 1993? He didn't remember. Jeb had owned a small convenience store with his wife (who'd passed away). He shot deer during deer season and told himself it was all the same.

Now, at the Immaculate Heart of Mary's meeting, management said, "We'll just let them come to the pancake breakfast, but keep an eye on them."

And that would have been it but for Mrs. Billy Green: a devout Christian who had seen her alcoholic husband die of a seizure. She said, "I think they are possessed."

And that's where the rumor began.

And it would have remained a rumor, but Pauline Fortis told Ms. Lora and Ms. Abby about the meeting. Pauline thought it would get them to stop coming to the pancake breakfast. It didn't. In fact, Ms. Abby told Pauline Fortis that she and her sister *did* have special powers. Ms. Abby would not say what kind of powers.

So, on Saturdays during the pancake breakfasts, the residents would watch the two sisters. They had even come up with some notion of what Ms. Abby and Ms. Lora's powers were. Jeb said that he figured that when Ms. Abby got up to walk, she moved slowly around the room as if she were playing Duck, Duck, Goose. Jeb noticed she just walked bent over to the rhythm of Duck, Duck, Goose. Jeb said, "If she stops in front of you, you're it." He reminded everyone of Josephina Kennell. One day, Josephina sat wearing her purple cowl-neck sweater, then Ms. Abby walked and stood in front of her. Some months later, Josephina was gone.

"What does that mean?" Pauline wanted to know.

"It means," he said, "one of us is the next to go."

"Well," Pauline laughed, trying to lighten the mood, "that's obvious. This is a senior citizens' home."

On one particular Saturday, Ms. Abby did walk around the room. She was looking at the paintings. Some were pretty nice and would sell, she thought. Ms. Abby pushed herself forward and continued to walk with her walker.

It was an interesting spectacle that filled the residents with fear. The power that this woman had in her boxy red dress. The power that they had given her. It was horrific.

She called quietly to her sister, "You like that one?"

Ms. Lora said, "Yeah."

Ms. Abby then stopped in front of a painting's green-matted frame of flowers. The painting rested just above Jeb Turnwall's head. Ms. Abby didn't even notice him. She didn't notice his face turning pink and his exhalation of air and his hand moving quickly, quickly for him, as he fumbled to reach the handgun he wore under his sport coat in a holster. He pulled it out and pointed it at Ms. Abby. He could hear people saying something (hushed mumbles, startled burst of sound), and he saw Ms. Abby look down at him as if for the first time. He shot her in her fat stomach. And she stumbled back with brown blood flowing out of her wound. He shot her again in her cheek, and her hips hit the floor, and then her back slammed to meet the linoleum. He shot her one more time while she lay on the floor, and the bullet landed in the side of her chest.

Jeb sat in his chair, shaking. He wasn't the same deer hunter. He willed his hands to be still and thought briefly about his youth and how he used to be able to hold the gun with one hand and not two. He rested the gun in his lap and looked around like he'd wet himself. At that moment, he had the eyes of a little boy who had been caught sneaking ice cream or stealing quarters.

"Jeb!" Pauline called out.

Ms. Lora screamed. People ran to her. To hold her still.

People moved to Jeb. To take the gun from him.

Ms. Lora was in shock, crying. Of course, she was trying to figure out what had just happened. A little bit later, she even said to the police officer who was talking to her, "What just happened? She was my sister? Why did this happen? What's wrong with that man? Why did he shoot her?" Mostly, she cried. She cried on an officer's shoulder and into the palms of her hands. She cried and looked around to see where she was. She was outside in the parking lot. The residents had walked her out just before the cops came.

An officer offered to drive her home.

"No," she said.

An officer told her where they were taking her sister. "Would you like us to take you there too, ma'am?"

She watched as Jeb Turnwall was driven away in cuffs. It became clear she had to go somewhere. She couldn't just stand there in shock. But she could no longer move. This tall, wiry woman could not move her legs. One of her hands rested on the officer's shoulder, and she began to sense his discomfort.

When Ms. Lora saw her sister's body being wheeled out, she forced herself to lift her foot and point it in the direction of her sister. "Yes," she said, "I will go to where my sister is going."

"Okay, ma'am."

She held the officer's arm as she walked up the incline to the street where his squad car sat. It was near her car. "I'll take my own car. Can you follow me?"

"Yes ma'am."

"You see," she said, "you see, I don't want to get lost. I am not from around here." And she began to cry again. A slow weeping that ended in her gasping for breath. "No, I will follow you," she said to the officer.

"Okay, ma'am."

"I will follow you." She began to breathe regularly.

"Okay." He helped her into her car.

"I'm ready," she said. "I will follow you out. I will follow you out."

PART II

Sweet Misery Blues

FRIENDSHIP

BY JANE HAMILTON
Ogden Avenue

We had reached the point in our lives when we were most interested in bicycles. Not make and material, and repair was beyond us—please God, let us never have to patch a tire or monkey with a chain. We were all about the riding. That's how we explained ourselves. Every morning we woke wishing we could mount that simplest of machines—we did admire the elegance of our Treks and our Schwinns. At home and at work and in spin class, too, we wanted nothing more than to vanish, sunshine or light rain, into the great wide open.

It's a developmental phase, we thought. First comes love, then comes marriage, the baby in the carriage, including getting out the door to earn a living, and when much of that is done, you'll want a double or triple crankset, twenty-seven gears, padded shorts, some crotch butter. You're riding; the cool air is on your bare arms. It is so simple to be happy.

There were four of us with this affliction, middle-aged ladies on bikes, bringing to mind, of course, Margaret Hamilton. *I'll get you, my pretty, and your little dog, too.* We claimed that joke as our own before anyone else could say it. In light of this phase, we weren't taken by complete surprise when Sally John—her first name, a Southern thing—suggested we sign up for a bike trip, seven days in the Pyrenees.

"Mountains," one of us noted.

Sixty miles a day, a Sisyphean change of elevation, no sweetly rolling hills made by the last what-have-you glacier but jagged mountains that in an instant had been thrust into the world. Proof you don't want to venture too far beneath the surface.

It's hard to say if the going up the mountain or sailing down frightened us more. We knew we'd have to train, that the trip would challenge us at every level, test our limits, etc. In our consideration, though, we certainly didn't think, *This is the perfect crime.* We thought, *Jesus Christ, will we be strong enough, fast enough, and mentally prepared?* We marveled at our friend, laughing, saying, "Sally John suggested this!"

"Seriously?" one of us would chime in.

Sally John was—there is no other way to say this—the fat friend among us. Thirty to fifty pounds overweight on any given day. A lot of extra baggage to haul up the mountain. A big-boned beauty. That's what her husband was said to call her in the privacy of their bedroom. Sally John letting us in on their pillow talk. "My big-boned beauty," he would say out loud in his satisfaction. Edwin was his name. He himself was a man you'd term scrawny if you saw him in his everyday clothing.

Despite her weight, she was not unfit, Sally John. She was the least cycle-crazed of us, but she enjoyed riding her bike, a commuter, a hybrid with upright handlebars, a basket, a bell. Her primary exercise, her religion, which she shared with her trainer, was bench pressing. We feigned interest but did not listen as closely as good friends should. Sally John could get very technical about body mechanics.

At the time of our trip, Edwin and Sally John, the Abbots, had been living in Milwaukee for about a year. We later came to blame Milwaukee, or, rather, we held the Cream City responsible for what happened. Milwaukee, a place that frankly held no fascination for us. Edwin—never Ed—and Sally John had been New Yorkers for thirty years, their move from the Upper East Side a shock. He'd been a social worker at the VA campus down on 23rd Street, and Sally John had risen up the ranks from a lowly nurse to chief nursing officer at Lennox Hill Hospital. We figured she made at least half a million bucks. Not that it mattered to them. In the nineteenth century, both of their families had produced captains of industry, the lucky Abbots, stupendous stacks of dough still fluttering down upon them, glorious cash from railroads, printing presses, paint, and varnish. Their trust funds had made possible a five-bedroom apartment not far from Central Park and the Metropolitan Museum. We never got over it, we in our rent-controlled quarters in various parts of the city. Even when the couple had two small daughters, they'd kept a routine of work and pleasure, walking to the museum on Friday nights, for instance, sitting in the Great Hall Balcony drinking champagne and listening to the offering, usually a string quartet or a pianist. They did so for romance, to keep the flame flickering. The fluted glasses, a soft cheese, a small crusty loaf, a stroll hand-in-hand to look at one great master, and home to bed.

What made them leave that romance behind for Milwaukee? A row house, that's what. Edwin's father died, leaving them a newly refurbished town house on Ogden Avenue, one of the Abbot Row houses. Without telling us, they sold their apartment on 82nd Street. Edwin, a man seemingly without dramatic passions, had persuaded Sally John, telling her the move would invigorate their lives. We said, "Who moves to Milwaukee to be invigorated?" He was as insistent as he'd ever been. The row houses, he explained to us, had been built in 1889 for Edwin Hale Abbot, the president of the Northern Pacific Railway. Sally John's Edwin had been named in full for his grandfather, her Edwin Hale, a man who, once they'd moved, would have a model train world down in the basement, a world complete with the usual: cows and haystacks, carrot tops in garden rows, tunnels through mountains, a saloon with parking for horses and motorcycles, and hardworking little people outside the general store.

When we first visited we were on the whole politely amazed, only scoffing at the most obvious evidence of philistinism. The di Suvero sculpture at the end of Wisconsin Avenue, for one. Hideously orange, an industrial hulk that blocks the swanlike Calatrava, blazingly white, hovering at the lake's edge. We took one look at the di Suvero and said, "Are you kidding?" What city would commission Santiago Calatrava to design their art museum, a city with a gorgeous body of water as backdrop, and blot it out in the approach with a third-rate heap of orange-painted steel I-beams?

Edwin claimed to admire di Suvero's *The Calling*, Edwin pleased to defend his new city. He persisted in the conviction that Calatrava admired it too, and indeed had been inspired by it, showing us an interview as proof. It was a form of kindness—we came to believe this—Edwin considering each artist's mind, Edwin's suggesting that the illusion of ease and suspended gravity were features each work shared, Edwin, a person who was never dismissive or glib.

From the start, we had no argument with the row house, my God, we could see the appeal of that real estate. The house had a marble foyer, and although it was narrow, there was the spaciousness of high ceilings and the three floors, plus the basement, each room with comforts designed for delight. The master bath was the size of our living rooms, the long clawfoot tub gleaming on the dais, and the shower had a steam feature you could infuse with eucalyptus. *Only in Milwaukee,* we used to say to Sally John.

Sally John had no trouble securing an impressive job in the health care galaxy there, chief of some part of that Milky Way. She was fantastically smart, and if she'd been born later, in the 1980s rather than the 1960s, and if she hadn't been such a self-doubter, she could have been a brain surgeon. When we were together, the three of us without Sally John, we always spent a substantial portion of our time discussing her. You might say she was our main subject, Mrs. Abbot cut out from the big topic of our friendship. Through the decades we'd often talked about her habit, the glitch where, in spite of her self-doubt, she'd choose difficult new hobbies, or she'd find herself promoted to jobs that seemed to her impossible. Jobs, we agreed, that would push an average woman over the edge. She'd been put in charge of 3,500 health care providers at a major institution when she was thirty-three, for instance. She'd taken up the oboe at age forty. Who does that? At forty-five she gained membership to an exclusive fitness club on Park Avenue, even though she always worried about being socially inferior to just about everyone. It seemed not to have bolstered her confidence, knowing that her great-grandparents had been among Mrs. Astor's chosen Four Hundred in the Gilded Age. Sally John had charmed some doctor-god to death for the fitness club invitation and also smote her trainer, Nolan. There was a period when she spoke of no one but Nolan and the squats he demanded of her, Sally John making us laugh as no one else could.

Although we'd been witness to Sally John's mode of operation starting in college, it was in the Pyrenees that we witnessed her methods at close range. It was in France that our understanding was refreshed—*Ah, yes, this is how she's always exercised her personality, this is how she gets what she wants.* We once again had to stand in awe of our friend. She'd chosen a trip that was well out of her league, she'd required that we accompany her, and then, once we landed in the village of Montjardin, she wasted no time zeroing in on the alpha male, Coach Martin, the leader of our band of eight bike riders. At the first dinner, the meet-and-greet, she grabbed the seat next to him. She soon made herself vulnerable. Hand to her bosom, her large blue eyes tearing up—she confessed to fear. To doubt. Waving away the long story, the remote father, the intractable mother, the beautiful older sister, she wouldn't bore him with the details of her upbringing. A therapy animal, a purse-sized dog, had been helpful to her through her twenties, before anyone had thought of such a thing. But she did want him to know, her failings aside, that she was not a wilting flower. She was committed to the trip, she was serious about the mountains, she wanted to learn, to improve, to grow. As a cyclist and a person. She laughed, she cried, Sally John athletically drinking the red wine of the region.

We reflected that in Sally John's universe the alpha male always came to her aid. There was not a story in which the man refuses her or is unmoved by her appeal. Often, it has to be said, the engagement with the head honcho resulted in sexual intercourse, the affairs sometimes long-term.

How much did Edwin mind? As a therapist, he presumably understood personality types and disorders at a deep level, through the years treating narcissists and maybe a few sociopaths as well as people with regular old unhappiness. Sally John, six feet tall, with high plush breasts, had a most wonderful face and terrific hair. We were always raving about her blond hair, the highlights so natural looking, hair that even into her fifties was silky. She'd wear it in a French twist, or one ropey French braid, or two braids of no nation, wrapping them around her head as if she were going up the path to fetch her sheep. Her gigantic eyes were a lovely soft blue, and her lashes startling black, the tears shining in them, little glistening ornaments. Skin: creamy and smooth. A big juicy mouth that opened with a musical laugh. She couldn't help telling us that her lovers often remarked that she was amazingly wet. It's not that we were prim, generally, but that report embarrassed us. "Wow," one of us said. "Huh," another pronounced. Out of range, we cried, "She thinks vaginal lubrication is an accomplishment!" We said, "Put that on her tombstone: *Here lies Sally John. She was amazingly wet.*"

Did Edwin understand her? A question we couldn't help posing. The answer varying. As opposites attract at first glance, he was quiet, morally upright, and dry. You might even conclude he was a bore. His pale, narrow face, his small brown eyes, the nondescript hair—none of his features drew attention. At their dinner table, he usually said very little, Sally John regaling her guests with hospital and insurance horrors, most always with policy that supported what sounded like malpractice. She'd turn to her husband now and again to say, "Isn't that right, dear?"

"Oh, yes." He always agreed. If he rarely laughed it was because he was serving and clearing the dishes and tasting the sauce in the hopes it was transcendent. He cooked, reason enough, we always thought, to remain madly in love with him. He was not humorless, that is certain. Still, if you could make him light up or even snort, you felt as if you'd cracked into a vault. He enjoyed crisp assessments of politicians and short tales of absurdity that were true. There was nothing more rewarding than Edwin's smile; his face transformed: warmth, appreciation, perhaps even mercy shining upon us. Possibly he'd forgiven us for slandering the di Suvero and calling the people of Milwaukee barbarians. We suspected he knew that we knew everything and that we knew he knew. Not only about the lovers, but also about our being privy to the Abbots' sexual routines and proclivities. Every time Sally John suggested a roll in the hay he was ready at once. We knew that his member was not as aggressively hard and long as one of the lovers'—which further endeared him to us. We knew that he was always grateful. "My big-boned beauty," etc. We did feel that we understood his suffering, and perhaps most important, we were sure that without the rock of Edwin Hale Abbot, Sally John would have imploded, that personality of hers busting apart, the woman shattered.

We grew even fonder of him after he moved to Milwaukee. The old brew town seemed in fact to invigorate him. He had color in his cheeks; his eyes seemed to open wider; there was a lightness not only in his step but in his being. We'd say something mildly amusing, and he'd laugh, one vibrant *ha*. When we came into the library he'd look up from his book, he'd shake off his deep thought and invite us to sit, inquiring about our work, our husbands, the grown children, his interest, after all our years in his company, marvelously genuine. It was almost as if he felt an urgency, now that we were in our fifties, to get to know us more fully.

Every morning, in the perfectly appointed bedroom, he hopped from the bed that seemed like a king and a half, an emperor bed, Sally John, legs splayed, occupying far more than her own side. He'd walk into the dressing room to put on his biker duds, his shiny black shorts, the glossy yellow jersey, in minutes ready to head out to the path along the lake. It was he who was the real biker. Fifty miles even in the rain, eighty to a hundred on Saturday. No slouch, Edwin Hale Abbot. He'd explain away his strength saying, "Yes, but it's flat."

Among ourselves, we admired his tight little glutes, his knotted calves, his waifish but steely thighs, the general buffness of his torso—so much revealed in the biking costume. He had no interest in joining a group, no desire for a band of brothers who'd draft and compare their customized bikes, who'd gather to perform maintenance. He'd strike out, maybe as happy as he'd ever been. Riding through woods, right in the city, coming upon a beer garden tucked away off the path in a forest. Edwin in a fairy tale, the gingerbread house through the thicket, the possibility for the brief companionship of strangers or a magical conversation with a squirrel. Back on the bike, he'd pedal up through Brown Deer toward Port Washington. Maybe he'd find a different way home, Sally John off to work, the mess of her breakfast dishes in the sink. He'd clean up, eat his own cereal, take a shower, put on his civilian clothes, and begin his day receiving patients in the downstairs office. Most typically he saw couples breaking apart, teenagers with depression and anxiety, young men searching for meaning, women hoping to find love.

When he didn't have clients, he walked the two miles to the movie theater. It was hard to believe he walked more than he had in New York, but his Fitbit told the truth. Everything he wanted was close enough, no need for taxi, subway, or bus. He'd pull a granny cart behind him up to the Whole Foods. He'd walk farther on to the bookstore. His barber was a few blocks away, a real artist, he said, a woman named Shaza Palooka. We said, "You made that up!" It was with indignation that he replied, "I did no such thing. That is her given name."

Shaza Palooka was twenty-nine years old, four foot eight, with two black buns at her temples, and who, for some reason, was already stooped. At every appointment, she spent a full hour cutting his short hair with her little tiny scissors. Together they had a Milwaukee love fest, discussing all the advantages of the city, Shaza puttering around his head and face. Shaza, who would step back to examine her progress, coming back to him, pressing the pads of her fingers to his skull, fluffing her work, saying, "Hair, oh hair, Edwin! You just have to cajole it, don't you? Edwin, you have to befriend it."

What, then, was the dark side of such a life? What is the darker side of a Midwestern city, beyond its particular history of oppression, beyond urban blight, crime, and poverty? The worst thing that happened in the Abbots' first year was the theft of a neighbor's kayak, gone from the back shed. We wondered about a cultural vacuum, we wondered about loneliness. It's possible that Shaza Palooka was the only adult, besides Sally John and his clients, to whom Edwin spoke at length, Edwin in a trance while his hair, strand by strand, floated to the floor. We wondered if it was during the haircut that the idea of Sally John's bike trip occurred to him.

Maybe he'd become obsessed with the notion of perfection, something he could not possibly achieve with big messy Sally John fucking her brains out with an anesthesiologist from Whitefish Bay. Would life be better without Sally John hauling her purse the size of a duffel bag into the kitchen after a day's work, Edwin setting out a good supper with a full-bodied wine? She'd collapse on the sofa afterward up in the library, somewhat drunk, pointing the remote at the TV, soon fast asleep. Maybe he considered how it would be, if, when his daughters came to visit, Sally John wasn't grilling them, doing her best to micromanage those young women's lives. Sally John had the habit of finding fault with their boyfriends, the daughters early on learning to keep their lovers away. We all want to murder our spouses, and even if, in the heat of the moment, we mean it, we of course don't actually mean it. Did Edwin, of all people, mean the thing he would never have said as a joke?

We'd always wondered why he hadn't divorced her. How many affairs had she had? We'd lost track. In New York we'd perpetually felt sorry for him, having to accompany her to hospital galas, a great number of people in the room aware of Sally John's infidelities. Edwin, head up, noble chin, talking by the bar with one of the husbands about his bicycle. Did he stick with her because, you know, he loved her deeply? Whatever that means! We no longer knew what love was, or how to think about it, if the word was adequate, if it could mean inertia, affection, hatred, and habit all at once. Maybe he'd listened to enough couples in therapy to know that even if he divorced Sally John, he was stuck with her.

We could understand his wishing she might disappear. The relief of that erasure. The solace of such loneliness, the comfort of missing her. Edwin with an even lighter step walking up Farwell to the Oriental Theater. The pleasure of coming home to a dog; he'd get a small brown mutt, a loyal creature his patients would like to pet. He could sink into the problems of his clients, their misery something he could appreciate even if he no longer shared it. When he finished for the day he'd put the dog in his pannier, its sweet little head meeting the wind as he rode out into the late afternoon. On the weekends, after his bike ride, he'd construct bridges and new towns in the basement, the train country expanding from the table to the floor and into the laundry room. He would glue lakes and streams, fields and forests, to fabric that served as earth. Oh, his dominion! The daughters would visit more frequently, they'd make him dinner, and their boyfriends would show up too, everyone talking, no one silent or shy. Could it be that a vision so simple, a vision of ordinary life, with a specific quality of quietness, was Edwin's guiding principle? A vision that seemed possible in Milwaukee, one that he came to want with a longing that is usually reserved for illicit love.

We didn't learn that the bike trip had been Edwin's idea until the first night in France. The eight campers were seated at the table in the chateau that was our base, the four of us old friends, and four others, strangers from Britain, in addition to Coach Martin and his wife, the cook. Sally John was telling the group that she was now living in Milwaukee, in Wisconsin, a city and state that, in truth, she said, she was having trouble thinking of as home. A tear sparkled in her lash. She got everyone shaking their heads over the alarming homicide rate, the drive-by shootings, the culture of poverty that was hardened in the African American community. As she was speaking about the dire eviction problem, she was so winning, dismissing her knowledge even as she clearly understood the crisis and was offering solutions. When she mentioned that her husband had suggested the Pyrenees trip, it was as if Edwin would have done anything to spare Sally John, if only for a week, the pressures of a city riddled with crime.

"Edwin suggested the trip?" we said.

"I told you that, girls!" We still called each other girls.

We didn't dare look at each other, didn't know what our bewilderment might say. Maybe after a minute we laughed to ourselves, thinking of Edwin at that moment on his morning ride, returning to a kitchen free of Sally John's breakfast dishes.

The next day she was freshly distraught. We had before us a fifty-mile ride, a 3,000-foot change in elevation, some or other terrible grade to climb for our warm-up. She said, "Edwin told me I could do this. He was sure."

We did not have much of an understanding of her training regime—a few excursions down the lake path, as far as we could tell.

"He encouraged me to make this trip but I—I'm scared shitless, girls."

"We are too," we assured her.

She said, "I'm just going to speak to Martin. I'm going to the bike room to have a chat with him."

When she was gone, we said, as if Edwin was right there with us, "What the fuck, Edwin Hale?"

One of us said, "He wants her to die."

"He wants us all to die."

We laughed.

There was a puzzling detail that stuck with us: she did not own a pair of clip-in biking shoes. Edwin had not advised her that on a trip of this difficulty no one would be wearing tennis shoes, every biker equipped with proper shoes and pedals. He didn't say that not having such basic equipment would be like showing up for the steeplechase without a horse. The rest of us had brought our own pedals and knew enough to secure them to the bikes Coach Martin was providing.

We could not understand Edwin's lapse in judgment, his disregard for his wife. On that first morning, he was no doubt asleep alone on the great plains of that row house bed. Maybe for the sheer hell of it, he'd left his model train running downstairs, his own world humming. Coal cars circulating. Lumber passing by towns that did not require wood. He'd sent Sally John abroad without shoes, knowledge, or strength, having enlisted her to our care. He hadn't asked us, hadn't pointed out to us in a private e-mail that this would be the case. He no doubt understood our love for her and took it for granted that with us she would be safe. Maybe, we mused, as soon as he woke up in five or six hours, he'd go directly to the dog pound to get his new true friend.

On our way to the mountaintop that first day, we rode through a forest and up to a plateau where great woolly brown cows strolled, the bells around their necks clanking as they went from tuft to tuft. How strong Coach Martin was, and of what good cheer, riding very close to Sally John, one hand on his own bike, the other on her back, pushing her up the narrow road. We could hear her laughter from down below, Martin apparently telling her stories to pass the time.

While we waited for them at the summit, we wondered with more seriousness if, say, Edwin in fact had a plan, sending Sally John to France with us. We'd begun to wonder if actually, he didn't want her to die. Not one of us laughed at the idea the second time. Or maybe he thought she'd survive, of course she would, but he'd have the satisfaction of her failure; he would secretly, lavishly, enjoy her humiliation. He knew that we, the friends, would be fine because we had trained in spin class and up in Vermont on the weekends.

Or maybe, we thought, he hated us too.

As Coach Martin and Sally John got closer (her laughter louder), we wondered if Edwin didn't know his wife at all, if he'd underestimated her, if he hadn't envisioned the alpha male taking up the great cause of getting Mrs. Abbot to the summit. When the Siamese biker twins finally came into view, at the last hairpin turn, our fellow riders, younger than we were, began to cheer, calling Sally John's name, shouting *Champ!* and *Trooper!* and *Winner!*

We laughed bitterly then. That thing she did, she was doing it! And they were rewarding her, calling her brave for completing an exercise for which she hadn't bothered to prepare. We knew, even if they did not, that Martin was going to have to push her up every climb for the next six days. We wanted to call Edwin, to tell him to take the goddamn dog back to the pound, to inform him we were sending his wife home before she got into bed with Martin. We were thinking to say, *We know you now. We understand how much you loathe her.*

Sally John throwing her arms around Martin and the other fellows did make us feel for Edwin more fervently than we ever had before.

As the days passed, it was funny that although we were in France, and enjoying our rides, savoring our own hard-earned strength, and the remarkable countryside, and the meals at the chateau, we most often were thinking of Edwin. We naturally especially had him in mind after the accident, after Sally John's fall. A crash most logically would have happened on a long descent, but Sally John tumbled coming up to a roundabout in a busy town we had to pass through to get to our home base. The tragedy took place on day five. Martin, that morning, had ridden with Sally John to the bike shop, had put her in clip-in shoes and the requisite pedals. She'd been scared to death of course, but she'd done very well until the late afternoon, when, with the roundabout in view, she got flustered. A car coming on struck her.

For a few days, there seemed little hope that she would live. Such little hope, in fact, that we discouraged Edwin from getting on a plane—what was the point? She'd be dead by the time he arrived. And, in the weeks after, when she was improving, when she had stabilized, the three of us taking turns at the hospital, we reiterated that he would have the care of her for quite some time to come, and that he should spend his energy getting the house ready for a patient who would be confined to her bed, and who, while breathing on her own, and seeming to understand the conversation around her, had lost the power of speech.

Of course, Edwin's life changed. And ours did too. We became far more acquainted with Milwaukee than we'd ever imagined we could, the three of us rotating in and out of duty at Ogden Avenue. We came to appreciate what we thought of not as the philistinism of the city, but rather its gentleness, its humility. The lake's fresh water seemed an innocent cousin to our ocean, and the hip young people looking as they do the world over, those kids on Brady Street drinking their coffee and gazing at their tablets, seemed content, seemed not to care that they weren't in Brooklyn. The city, to our way of thinking, was glad to be under the radar, confident in its beauties, trying in meaningful ways to correct what was brutal. We came to think the di Suvero industrial spareness was just right, the sculpture like a sunburst, announcing the glorious, improbable swan on the lake. It seemed to us, in sum, that Milwaukee was a place of possibility and surprise.

Sally John's money was of real use, funding our travel, and also our retirement. In addition, it paid for the home care angel who arrived in the mornings to bathe our girl in the library-turned-bedroom, to make her just as gorgeous as ever, that great silky hair still expensively streaked, a moisturizing foundation smoothing away her age, her enormous eyes opening and closing as we read magazine articles and the books of her youth out loud to her. And sang, we often sang. Also, on the hour we paraded the ninety-pound chocolate Lab, Moto, in and out of the room. Sally John could squeeze our hands in answer to our questions, and she seemed to enjoy the food we spoon-fed into her lovely big mouth.

You might have thought that our attention to our friend, the coordination of activities required, as well as scheduling the visits, would have strengthened our already strong bonds. We, the three of us, did, as always, work effectively as far as the details went. Furthermore, we really were not competitive in our caretaking capacities. And yet, a curious thing happened. Gradually, without our realizing, we began to be closed to one another. Not that we acknowledged this, not that we weren't, as always, in constant communication. We expressed our love, as always, in our e-mails and texts and in person, signing off with *love*—no name attached, only *love*. And in person always saying, "Love you!"

It was through Shaza Palooka of course, of course it was the hairdresser, all of us becoming her clients—so cheap, those hour-long cuts—the woman so close to our faces, her soft hands moving through our scalps, that we learned—or thought we were learning—the secrets of our circumstances. We knew what we did not wish to know, that one of us, and maybe another, also, had started to share that enormous bed with Edwin Hale Abbot. Shaza didn't say so directly, but when she mentioned that one of us enjoyed the linen sheets made especially in Italy for the custom-made bed, when she remarked that the other wished the shower was slightly larger to accommodate two, when she paused midcut, the scissors stopping, to marvel at Edwin's strength—we knew what she was speaking of, we knew what confessional Edwin had chosen, what priestess was his own.

Edwin Hale, the dark horse, and ourselves too, we supposed; we ourselves were surprising. But on the whole we thought of him, of Edwin, who we came to believe had orchestrated all of the events, the near-death, followed by the friends visiting, one after the next after the next, way out into the future, each of us with our particular charms. *Only in Milwaukee*, we'd say to Sally John, Sally John the person we talked to now, Sally John the friend who knew everything.

TRANSIT COMPLAINT BOX

BY FRANK WHEELER JR.

Midtown

Monday, 1232 hrs: 5621 / 0922 / 151 / N-23

"There's a new definition for the word *racist*," I said. "Stop me if you've heard this one. A racist is now defined as any Republican who wins an argument with a Democrat."

"Ha-ha. Very funny. I'm a Democrat."

"I was too till I started working in Milwaukee," I said. "And you'll think that joke is hilarious by the end of the shift."

My probie and I walked to the bus stop on North 17th, just at the edge of the Transit System property. He was fidgeting with his belt. Wasn't used to wearing the gear yet. Expanding baton, pepper spray, cuffs, radio—they were all still foreign.

"I'm just saying," I told him, "they're gonna call you a racist."

"Who's they?"

"The shitbirds. The troublemakers we see every day on the bus."

"But I'm not one. I'm not a racist."

"That's a non sequitur."

"A what?"

"It means it doesn't follow. Whether or not you are a racist has nothing to do with them calling you a racist. That's where we are with this now. It's just a strategy they use to make you shut up and back off. It can be used for anything, and any word that is used to describe anything by definition has no meaning."

"Sure, I get it. So what am I supposed to do with that?"

"Do your job. Just know they'll try to hurt you with whatever they can no matter what you do."

"Why would they do that?"

"Simple answer is you're white, and they're bored."

"Write this down," I said as the bus pulled up to the shelter. "Four sets of digits, just like dispatch says it. Bus number, operator number, run, route. Leave a blank for the operator. Bus fifty-six twenty-one. Run one fifty one. Northbound twenty-three." The doors opened, and we waited while several people alighted. Then Probie and I got on the bus.

"What's happening, professor?" the driver said, smiling at me. He was a middle-aged black man, fat and bald, wearing the Transit sweater vest.

"Good to see you, Rory," I said. "Got that operator number?"

"Badge nine two two," he said. I nodded to Probie, and he wrote that in his notebook too. It was packed. Every seat taken, people standing in the aisle all the way to the back.

"Okay," I said, "so we both take the front post. Normally, one of us would go to the back, but it's too crowded."

"Ten four," Probie said. We stood on opposite sides of the aisle just behind the yellow line with my back to the driver.

"How was your vacation?" I asked the driver over my shoulder, still looking at Probie.

"Great fishing up there, man. You should go up some time."

"They let me out of this circus long enough, I will."

"You training another newbie?"

"Rory, this is Probationary Officer Miller. He served in the army like you did."

"Glad to have you, kid," the driver said.

Monday, 1414 hrs: 4974 / 0853 / 202 / S-27

Probie and I were at the front of the bus on the southbound route twenty-seven, stopped at a red light.

"Don't look at the map," I said, "and tell me how we got here."

"Um," Probie stammered, "route twenty-three all the way up to route eighty at, where was it, Villard? Then eighty to route twenty-seven."

"You know where you are now?"

"Twenty-seventh and Atkinson."

"This is the Hot Spot," I said. "Know why they call it that?"

"Why?"

"That's the name of that liquor store across the street there. Also, this is where most of the shootings happen. The greatest concentration of it is right here, within a few blocks' radius. And for a couple months this summer, we had the highest per capita murder rate in the country. Even beat out Baltimore and Chicago."

"Damn."

"Don't get off the bus here after dark. Not if you don't have to. Just pass through."

"Ten four."

The light turned green, and the bus went through the intersection and pulled up to the bus shelter directly across the street from the liquor store. The driver opened the doors and let about a dozen people off. Black male, late teens, got on the bus, holding an open beer can.

"Nope," I said, stepping in front of him before he could walk up the aisle. "You know you can't bring that on."

"Man, what I do?" the kid said. "I ain't do shit."

"Can't bring open alcohol on the bus," I said. "Either dump it outside or wait for the next bus."

"Why you gotta be like that, man? This some racist bullshit."

"Those are the rules," I said. "County ordinance."

"Fuck yo shit," the kid said, shaking his head. He curled his free hand into a fist. I watched him and waited. Probie watched us both.

Behind the kid, an older black man came through the door, also carrying an open can of beer. The kid turned and saw him. He moved toward the older man and pointed to go back through the door.

"Come on, Dad," the kid said, "we can't ride."

At the end of the shift, as we rode back to the fleet building, Probie spoke up: "Why'd they call you *professor* earlier? The driver, but also somebody in the roll call room did too."

"'Cause I used to teach history."

"No shit."

"For a few years at a community college. Never finished my PhD."

"Why not?"

"Humanities department turned ugly. I got tired of working for the propaganda wing of the Communist Party."

"Think you're overstating it, maybe?"

"Not really. The sad thing about paying attention to history is you know what's going to happen, and you're powerless to stop it."

Tuesday, 1625 hrs: 5478 / 0683 / 139 / S-57
Black kid in his late teens got on the bus right as we turned onto Water Street. As he walked past Probie in the front, I

saw the kid was talking to himself and shaking his head. With wild, unfocused eyes, he looked around the inside of the bus. He covered his mouth with both of his hands. Moved his hands away and waggled his fingers. He walked past me where I stood by the back door. He paced up and down the aisle, talking to himself.

"Bitch, I told you," he said. "Better listen. I told you. How come I gotta keep saying this shit."

Probie looked at me. I shook my head no.

"Bitch, I ain't talking to you no more," the kid muttered. He turned and stared at me for a second as he paced the aisle. "Ain't gotta be like that. Don't wanna kill nobody."

The kid went into the back area of the bus and kept pacing and talking. Probie moved down to my door.

"What do you want to do about it?" Probie asked.

"Wait," I said. "We provoke him, and it's a whole other world of trouble. Wait and see if he gets off by himself."

"He's scaring people."

"They know we're here. And it's better for everyone if he gets off the bus himself."

The kid kept pacing. He slapped himself once, then twice. "Motherfuckers always watching me."

"Try not to look directly at him," I said to Probie. "Go back to your post in the front."

"Motherfuckers always wanting something."

The kid sat down two rows from where I stood. He rocked back and forth. Slapped himself a few more times. Then the bus came to a stop at Wisconsin Avenue.

"Ain't doing this shit no more," the kid said, standing up. He walked to the back exit where I stood. I moved aside from the exit.

"Y'all motherfuckers can burn in hell," the kid said as he

opened the back door and stepped out onto the sidewalk. "Jesus ain't gonna save none of you."

The door closed and the bus moved forward, crossing Wisconsin Avenue. We waited one more stop and got off the bus too.

"Should we have done something?" Probie asked.

"We could have called the police," I said. "But what do you think he would've done if he'd heard us call the police?"

"Run?"

"That or freak out. Get violent. Then we've got a real problem on our hands."

"But he needed help."

"Sure he did. Like half of Milwaukee. Is this the first EDP you've seen up close?"

"Here, yes."

"Emotionally disturbed persons are a dime a dozen. Plain fact is that a lot of mental illness goes untreated here. People fall through the cracks more often in this city than others."

"Well, that sucks," Probie said.

We walked up to the stop for the westbound route twelve.

Tuesday, 1655 hrs: 5210 / 1055 / 251 / W-12
The Downtown Transit Center was quiet. Our bus idled in the parking area while Probie and I took advantage of the layover to use the bathroom. Probie looked sick when he walked out.

"The smell?" I asked.

"I saw blood on the floor of the stall."

"You didn't use the stall, did you?"

"No, but I could see the blood just from standing at the urinal next to it."

I walked into the bathroom and looked around. Sure enough, there was blood visible under the stall. It was only a small spatter, and brown. I nudged the stall door open with my boot. It was empty.

"Somebody shot up in here," I said to Probie, "then squirted the hypo on the floor. Blood's dried, so he's probably long gone."

"Should we report it?"

"What would that accomplish? They're not gonna clean it more often. I can't think of a public property in Milwaukee that isn't a biohazard. Hence, we carry gloves."

Our radios squawked, *"Northside Transit officers. Passenger harassing an operator. Bus fifty-two twenty, operator four three nine, run one twenty-three, southbound thirty on Sherman at Hampton. Report said the suspect was a very large black male wearing headphones. Driver said you guys knew who it was."*

"Shit. Deshawn's out on the town tonight."

"Who's that?"

"Our favorite person. Mentally unstable, six-foot-five, four hundred pounds, and loves to fight."

"Damn."

"You know it's about 2 percent of the population that's immune to pepper spray, right? Of course Deshawn would fall into that category too."

"So what are you supposed to do?"

"Not get in a fight with him."

"How can he just keep doing this? Don't the charges add up for him?"

"He's in an outpatient mental health treatment program. Keeps him out of jail as long as Milwaukee doesn't press charges that are too serious. And he knows exactly where that line is too. Most of the time he keeps on the safe side of that line."

"So he just wanders around looking to beat people up for fun? And nothing we can do?"

"We can do our job, but we can't expect help," I said. "Oh, hey, that reminds me, how long did the driver say his layover was? Let's do a quick building check."

Ronnie, a white male, about thirty, was asleep in the stairwell. "Wake up, Ronnie," I said. He didn't respond, so I repeated myself a few times. Then nudged his leg with my boot.

"Lemme sleep, man," Ronnie said.

I told Probie, "Take a picture of him like this for our report." I put on my gloves while Probie focused the camera on the company phone. I picked up the bottle on the stair next to him.

"That wine?" Probie asked.

"Cooking wine," I said.

"Naw, man, that's *sherry*," Ronnie said, not moving to get up.

"You know how this goes," I said. "You can get up and walk, or we can get you up and carry you out. If we have to carry you, we call MPD. Think on which way you'd rather it go."

"I'll get up," Ronnie said. "Jesus, you fucks. Can't you just let a guy sleep?"

"There's other places to sleep besides here."

Probie and I waited while Ronnie sat up, pulled himself with the rail to a standing position, and walked down to the stairwell exit.

"We find him in here about once or twice a week," I said.

"Can't he stay in the shelter? There's one just up the street."

"Can't drink in the shelter."

Wednesday, 1251 hrs: 4995 / 0656 / 250 / N-Blue Line
Sondra, a black female in her sixties, got on the bus with her

pull cart full of groceries. Probie and I were in the Transit vehicle, taking calls. Dispatch said it was a passenger harassing another passenger. When we got on the bus, I saw right away what had happened.

"Get away from me!" the passenger, a black woman in her thirties, yelled.

"Get away from me!" Sondra yelled back. "Lord Jesus bless you!"

"Just stay over there!" the passenger said. "Don't touch me!"

"Bless you, bless you, just stay over there!" Sondra said, patting the woman on the shoulder. "Don't touch me, Lord Jesus!"

"Quit it, you crazy bitch!"

"Quit it, you crazy bitch, uh-oh, oh-no, God bless you, Jesus bless you!"

Sondra had some kind of dementia. She liked to say blessings for people. But she often couldn't remember how to say them. So a lot of the time she just repeated what the other person was saying.

"Hey, Sondra," I said. "How've you been?"

"God bless you, boy," she said. "How've you been?"

"Come on over here and sit with me," I said. "Tell me about your church."

Sondra stepped back from the angry woman, looked at me, shook her head, and then followed me to the back of the bus with her pull cart in tow. I sat on the bench facing the door in the back. She sat down next to me.

I stood up and told her I'd be right back.

"We're gonna do a ride-along," I said to Probie. "That means I sit with her and keep her quiet while you follow the bus in the vehicle until she decides to get off. Should be just a few minutes since she lives close by. Go tell the driver what we're doing."

Probie nodded and took the keys from me.

"Ain't you even gonna kick her off?" the angry woman yelled.

"No need, ma'am," I said. "We'll stay back here and keep quiet. Won't be a bother anymore."

"Better not be," the woman said. "Crazy-ass bitch."

I looked back at Sondra, and the bus started moving again.

"So, they have a new garden out behind your church," I said.

"Oh yes, yes, God bless you," she said. "There's a new garden. And peppers and tomatoes and onions and beans and corn."

"That's really nice," I said. "And can anybody pick from it?"

"Jesus bless you, Lord bless you, and anybody can pick the vegetables from the garden. And lettuce and squash and zucchini. The church tends the garden and anybody who needs to can pick from it. Jesus bless you."

"I really like that idea," I said. "I should tell my pastor about it."

"Tell the pastor," she said. "Professor. I know you. Lord Jesus bless you. You the professor. I know you, and Jesus know you."

"I know you too, Sondra," I said.

After a few blocks, Sondra took her pull cart and got off the bus. I thanked the driver and passengers for their patience and got back in the vehicle with Probie.

"Getting her to talk about her church's garden works," I said to Probie.

"Which church?" he asked.

"The one she's thinking of, according to some of our other Transit officers, the pastor was murdered fifteen years ago. Congregation scattered. Building's burnt out now. But she remembers the garden."

Wednesday, 1525 hrs: 5602 / 0925 / 221 / S-57

Bus fifty-six oh two waited for us on the corner of Water

and Wisconsin. We boarded and spoke with the driver.

"Dude in the back wearing camo," the driver said. "Saying weird shit, got people nervous."

I looked in the back of the bus and saw him immediately. Black male, looked tall in his seat, built, shaved head, camo T-shirt stretched tight over a ballistic vest. His eyes were darting around, trying not to make contact.

He stood up in the aisle and sprinted to the back door, tried to shove through, but the door was locked. He began kicking it with his black combat boots, yelling, "Driver, back door! Back door, driver! Back door now, driver! Now, now, now! Back door, back door, back door!"

I nodded to the driver, and he released the back door. The man stepped off the bus and walked quickly down the sidewalk to the intersection. Probie and I went back to the vehicle and waited for the bus to move away.

"Let's watch him for a minute," I said.

"What for?" Probie asked.

"See if he gets on another bus."

We watched him cross Wisconsin and walk south on Water Street. When he was about halfway past the bank, I pulled into traffic.

We followed him to Water and Michigan. He turned and saw the Transit vehicle, crossed Water Street through traffic, and waited for the light. Then he crossed Michigan, looking over his shoulder every few seconds. He kept glancing around until Clybourn, where we lost track of him.

"Where'd he go?" Probie asked.

"Probably one of the bars there. Gonna wait us out."

We watched that side of the street for a minute, then pulled away and stopped at the light on Clybourn.

"There he is," I said. He was half a block east, crossing

through traffic, still heading south. He'd just gone into a bar and cut through an alley.

Probie and I watched as the man pulled a small handgun from his waistband behind his back, tossed it into a storm drain, and kept moving.

"Jesus," Probie said. "You see that?"

We were parallel with the man when he walked into the Milwaukee Public Market. I started driving us back to the Transit fleet building.

As I drove us back to fleet, the radio squawked, "*Northside Transit officers. Black male harassing other passengers. Driver says it's you-know-who.*"

"We're not going to that?" Probie asked.

"Others are closer. And we have a report to write," I said. "Firearm takes precedent."

"We should have guns," Probie said to the supervisor. I sat at the computer on the east wall of the roll call room, typing our report. Probie seemed shaken after seeing the gun.

"We don't decide that," the supervisor said. "The client wants us unarmed."

"But it's not safe. Some of them carry guns."

"I'm not disagreeing with you on that. But we have to do the job the way the client wants."

"So has anybody talked to the client about it?"

"You're more than welcome to write a memo."

"Sure," Probie said, "I could do that."

"I'll deliver it for you when you're done. But you could save time if you just put it in the box."

"Where's the box?" Probie asked.

The supervisor pointed to the trash can by the computer.

Atop it was a paper shredder. The trash can was labeled, *Transit Complaint Box*.

"If I take it to the client, or if you put it in the box," the supervisor said, "the results will be the same."

Thursday, 0941 hrs: 5023 / 0767 / 132 / S-27

"Bitch stole my phone!" the old black man yelled in through the door to the bus. The woman who had just gotten on was thin, smelled bad, scratched at bugs that weren't there, and was eating a breakfast sandwich. Leticia was a regular.

Leticia stood back from the front entrance, chewing, peering at the man outside. He looked at Probie and me and stepped back from the door.

"Bitch stole my phone!" he yelled again, pointing at her. The driver covered his mouth so he wouldn't laugh.

"Shut up, you stupid old motherfucker," Leticia said, still eating her breakfast sandwich. She turned and began asking passengers for money for her bus fare, one after another down the aisle.

"You nasty bitch!" the man yelled. "She's a damn prostitute! She stole my fucking phone!"

"Shut the door," I said to the driver.

"This is too good, man," the driver said.

"We don't want him to board like this, and we can't kick her off with him right there."

"Spoilsport," the driver said, laughing.

"Get her!" the man yelled. "That nasty hooker stole my phone!"

"Sucked your dick, didn't I!" Leticia shouted, spitting bits of the sandwich.

The driver shut the door, and Leticia resumed asking passengers for money.

"Nope," I said. "None of that. Yours is the next stop."

"You couldn't just let me ride?"

"Sorry," I said, "you're getting off up here."

Leticia took the last bite of her sandwich, pointed at me, and said, "Motherfucker rape me! Faggot, dick-sucking motherfucker rape me! He rape me! Go suck your mama's dick!"

The bus stopped two blocks away at the next stop, and the front door opened.

"Time to go, Leticia," I said.

"Ain't one of y'all motherfuckers got enough change for me to ride?" she said to the passengers.

"Let's go," I said.

"I get the money, just gimme a minute. Racist motherfuckers."

"By county ordinance, you can't panhandle on a bus, you can't swear on a bus. So you'll have to catch the next one."

"Fuck yo shit, snowflake cracker bitch."

"You rather talk to MPD?" I asked. "I know they like you less than I do."

Leticia turned and walked off the bus, raising her middle finger to everyone aboard.

"So, you know why we don't carry?" I asked Probie.

"Yeah, 'cause the client doesn't want us to."

"And why doesn't the client want us to carry?"

"I don't know. 'Cause it looks bad, I guess."

"Exactly. Transit answers to the county board. Arming the Transit officers would look like the board members were admitting things were getting out of hand."

"But they are. Things are definitely out of fucking hand."

"But admitting it would cost votes. So there you have it."

"Maybe I ought to carry anyway. Like an ankle holster nobody would see."

"Bad idea. You'd violate the contract. You lose your job and maybe face jail time if you ever have to pull it, even if you're defending your life."

"I'd still feel safer with a gun. I know some of these morons are carrying."

"It's mostly the dealers who carry. And the ones who ride the bus, which isn't most of them, have something to lose. They keep quiet and mind their business. Never cause trouble for us. The ones who do, the shitbirds, they don't typically carry."

"How do you know that?"

"'Cause most of them are addicts. The vast majority of the shitbirds are. Guns cost money. And if they had one, they'd have sold it already. Worry about a knife on them. Or a screwdriver. Guns are unlikely."

"What about dude yesterday? We saw his gun."

"He's a whole other type. Surprised he wasn't wearing a tinfoil hat. I don't even want to think about him. But honestly, I think he was a lot more scared of us."

Thursday, 1913 hrs: 5232 / 1033 / 103 / W-30X
Black male got on the bus drunk and told the driver he didn't have to pay because the driver owed him. Didn't he remember? He owed him.

The driver refused to play along and told him to pay or get off the bus. After half a minute of arguing, the drunk man tried to go over the clear plastic divider and grab the bus driver. He threatened to kill him. Then the driver called security.

"*Downtown Transit officers,*" dispatch said over the radio.

We took the call and headed to the bus in a Transit vehicle. The drunk man had quieted since his outburst. He sat on the side bench in the front of the bus, directly behind the driver. The driver gave us a quick rundown of what happened. I recognized the passenger but couldn't remember his name.

"Tell me what happened," I said.

"Dude got a attitude," the drunk man said.

"He said you grabbed him, told him you were going to kill him."

"Man, I ain't do shit," the man said, rolling his eyes. "He the one with the problem. You can't treat folks this way."

"So here's what I can do," I said. "I'll get you a transfer, and you wait for the next bus."

"Motherfucker, you can't do this. I ain't do shit."

"It's all on video, man," I said. "All of it. Let's get you that transfer, and you can get right back on the next bus."

"Fuck yo shit, white boy."

"Okay," I said, "think it through. This bus doesn't move as long as you're on it. If you take the transfer, you get where you're going faster."

I looked over at Probie, who was still talking to the driver. I motioned him over, and he took a position on my other side.

"Y'all gonna kick me off, huh? Just like fucking Nazis."

"Like I said, sir, we'll put you on the next bus."

The man grabbed my arm and tried to yank me off balance. I pivoted to the side, stepped back to break his grip, and reached for my pepper spray. Probie grabbed the man by his other arm, pulled him out of his seat, and forced him to the ground. I moved in to secure the man's other side.

"Fuck you doing, motherfuckers?" the man yelled.

Probie got his cuffs out and quickly put them on the drunk man.

* * *

We waited at the bus stop. I'd called MPD. Told them we'd detained a subject who'd assaulted a driver and a Transit officer. The drunk man sat on the bench in the bus shelter with his hands cuffed behind his back. Probie stood next to him with one hand on the drunk's arm as a precaution.

"Y'all can't do this," he said.

"We didn't do this," Probie said, "you did this."

"Don't talk to him," I said. "Not unless you can improve the situation."

The stop was on Wisconsin Avenue, just west of Marquette University. Lots of traffic. Lots of curious onlookers. There was a very good chance we were being recorded.

"I ain't going back to no jail," the drunk man said.

The radio squawked. Our supervisor was asking for either Probie or me to call him. Probie took his hand off the drunk man to click the radio mic on his shoulder.

And with that, the drunk man got off the bench and walked out into the intersection.

"Dude, come back over here," I said.

"Fuck you," the man said over his shoulder. "Ain't going back to no jail." He walked toward the oncoming traffic.

Horns blared and tires screeched as cars swerved around the drunk man.

"You're just making a mess!" I yelled.

"Ain't going back to no jail."

"You didn't hit anybody!" I yelled. "You know how this'll go down! The cops will turn you loose two blocks away from here most likely! They don't have time to worry about minor stuff like this!"

He looked back at me.

A car stopped five feet in front of him and honked.

"Fuck you, bitch!" the man shouted. "Run me over or go around!"

"Nobody's gonna run you over," I said. "You're just adding charges right now."

"You don't know shit."

"I know you come back here right now, MPD probably lets you go. What do they care? Like I said, they have other problems. They're chasing down murderers, drug dealers. But you wait out there till they get here, you're definitely going back in. You cause an accident, that's a much bigger deal than disorderly on a bus."

"How the fuck you know that?"

"'Cause that's how it works every time," I said. "Come on back over. You're just wasting time now. My partner and I have been working almost twelve hours today. Give us all a break, huh?"

The drunk man watched two cars pass him. Then he walked back to the sidewalk. "I ain't sitting on no bench. I'll stand."

"That's just fine," I said.

Friday, 1423 hrs: 5002 / 1103 / 122 / W-60
Probie and I stood near the bus shelter on Burleigh and Sherman, but outside the police tape and broken glass scattered on the sidewalk. MPD cars were starting to pull away now. Our supervisor walked over to us.

"You guys can get on the next one," the supervisor said.

"Looks like they're wrapping up," I said.

"Pretty straightforward. Shooting in the shelter. Dude followed the victim off the bus. Robbed him when he got to the shelter. Then shot him."

"Shot him *after* he robbed him? Why?"

"Fuck knows? Only got him in the arm too. They took him away in the ambulance a few minutes before you got here."

"They don't need anything from us?"

"Don't think so. They're picking up the video now."

"Any description yet?" I asked.

"Victim said black male wearing a long coat. We'll get a better one from the video and have that out later today. Should be easy enough. He said they were the only two who got off at this stop."

"Should we be looking for him?" Probie asked.

"When we get the description, yes. And if you spot him, absolutely do not engage. Call MPD first, then call me."

I nodded, and the supervisor went back to talk to the detective.

A little later, we took the Blue Line downtown and got a sandwich from a shop on Wisconsin Avenue. We met another team of Transit officers there, Mack and T-Bird.

"Y'all saw that shooting up on Sherman?" T-Bird asked.

"Yeah, we got there after. All we saw was glass everywhere."

"Sounds like half the bus shelters in Milwaukee," Mack said.

"White boy gonna make it?" T-Bird asked me, nodding toward Probie.

"He'll be fine," I said.

"That's crazy, though," Mack said. "Dude follows a guy off the bus, robs him, then shoots him after he's already got the money."

"Don't try to rationalize it," I said.

"I see you got your vest on today," T-Bird said to me.

"After we saw dude with that gun a couple days ago, I figured I'd start wearing it again," I said.

"Yeah, I got to dig my shit out again," T-Bird said. "Milwaukee's getting *extra* retarded."

Friday, 1650 hrs: 5303 / 0767 / 153 / N-76
The route seventy-six pulled away from the stop and drove down 60th. Probie and I crossed 60th and waited at the stop on Capitol.

"So, tell me what we're doing," I said to Probie.

"Catching the Red Line to Atkinson, then hopping on the nineteen back to downtown."

"Sounds good," I said.

The radio started talking at us: *"Northside Transit officers."* It was our favorite person.

Deshawn was harassing the driver on the westbound route sixty-two. The call came out from Capitol and Fond du Lac.

"Fuck," I said, turning to look east. "They said bus fifty-one eighty-one, right? That's what you heard?"

"Yeah, that was it."

"That's the bus," I said, pointing. On the other side of the street, the route sixty-two was two blocks away, coming right toward us.

"Are we supposed to do something?" Probie asked.

"We don't have time to get to the stop before the bus arrives. It'll be gone before we get across the street. No, nothing we can do now."

The bus stopped at the corner. Let off several passengers. Drove off, beating the light. And Deshawn was standing on the corner, a head taller and twice as wide as everyone else.

"That him?" Probie asked.

"Yup."

"He's crossing Capitol," Probie said.

"I see that."

"So what do we do? Do we detain him?"

"Last time that happened took six officers. If he comes to our stop, we deal with it. If they cancel the call by the time he gets here, he's not our problem. No need to create trouble."

Deshawn waited for half a minute at the corner, then ignored the light and crossed 60th. He had his headphones on and nodded with a beat. As he approached the shelter, we heard the music too. Deshawn looked us over before he sat down on the bench inside the shelter.

"Stupid pig KKK racist motherfuckers," he said. Then he growled twice, mimicking a tiger, and laughed after that. I rested my hand over the top of my holstered baton.

The radio crackled, *"Northside Transit officers, cancel that call for help. Subject alighted from the bus without further incident."*

Probie looked at me and gave up a deep exhale, shaking his head.

Deshawn put his thick, meaty hand up to his earphone and sang out in a high pitch, *"Y'all fucking pigs! Y'all racist motherfuckers! Y'all KKK pigs gonna die like little bitches!"*

"Okay," I said to Probie, "let's go back to the other stop."

Probie walked over to me, nodding.

"Do I know you, man?" Deshawn said to Probie, standing up off the bench.

"Nope, you don't know me," Probie said.

"Fuck you look at me then?"

"Don't talk," I said to Probie, "let's just walk."

Deshawn grabbed Probie by the shoulder and shoved him. Probie fell and knocked his head against the thick shelter glass.

I pulled my baton and clacked it open. Out of the corner of my eye, I saw a young man hold up his cell phone to record what was happening.

"Get back!" I yelled at Deshawn.

He ignored me and stomped on Probie. His head broke through the pane, and shelter glass scattered everywhere.

I stepped in and swung the baton at Deshawn's knee, but he moved, and the blow glanced off his thigh. Before I could step back, Deshawn leaned in, grabbed me by the throat, and squeezed. I felt a couple things pop inside my neck.

"Cracker bitches can't come up here without paying," Deshawn said to me. "You gonna pay me what you fucking owe me."

I swung my baton at the side of his head. He flinched when it connected, snapped his headphones, and drew blood.

"Fucking little bitch gonna die, man."

I swung again. Then a third time.

"Pussy-ass bitch—"

My fourth strike cracked open his temple.

Deshawn stopped talking, fell to the sidewalk, and let go of me.

First, I checked that Probie was still breathing. He was, but it was getting harder for *me* to breathe. I was getting light-headed. Then I tried to call on the radio, but my throat wouldn't allow for words. I took out our Transit cell phone and pressed the emergency button that would summon the sheriff's department.

I could hardly breathe now.

When I looked over at Deshawn on the ground, I saw he wasn't breathing either. I moved in to confirm. Shook him. Still no breath. No surprise given the blood pooling around his head and the brain matter hanging out over his ear.

I crawled on top of him, yanked up his shirt, and began doing chest compressions. Probably it wouldn't matter, but I had to do it if I was able. I felt a couple of his ribs crack on the first compression. Kept going.

And then I couldn't breathe at all.

I tried to keep going, but I just fell forward. I could hear a police siren a couple blocks away. But in Milwaukee, they could be going anywhere.

Before I passed out, I saw the young man still filming all of us with his phone.

If I lived, that might save my job.

THERE'S A RIOT GOIN' ON

BY DERRICK HARRIELL

Sherman Park

There should be two and a half cigarettes left. Terrell knows because he counted. He counted after writing something on Facebook and then smoking half a cigarette. On this morning, the room wasn't spinning, and birds even sang outside the large window beside his bed. He'd forgotten birds sang around here, in this hood, and closed his eyes to momentarily listen. He tried counting how many of them there might be—no more than four, but at least two. He reached for the half cigarette and lit it. Today was Sunday. Terrell figured his mama and her boyfriend had gone to church and remembered he'd told Destiny he'd call as soon as he got up. Destiny was his glorified parole officer. She always said things like "Be safe" and "Call me when you get home." They'd dated in high school sophomore year but were now just friends. He liked it that way. He knew if he could keep her close, he could have her back someday. Terrell exhaled a fog of smoke and thought about all the times his mother repeatedly called him a fool for not committing to Destiny. "Why you wasting your time with these no-good fast ghetto girls when Dessie is right here? I mean, she even does your damn homework, boy," is what she'd say.

It was almost noon. He lay there smoking and slowly started remembering last night's dream of him and Destiny in the backseat of a car. The car was sinking under Lake Michigan, and it wasn't the wet dream Terrell had hoped for. He had no idea how they'd gotten in the car, whose car it was, or who was driving. He only remembered reaching for the door handle and trying to shove her out. He remembered motioning for her to swim toward the surface while his extremities suddenly fell paralyzed. He remembered what drowning felt like.

Terrell grabbed his phone and saw three missed calls and two unread text messages. Mama had messaged, *Don't you go over there today or to that house across the street.* He knew where *over there* was because he'd been over there until late last night. He opened his Facebook page on his phone and saw twelve new alerts. He clicked on the post he'd written before falling asleep:

Finally muhfuckas standing up for something in this city. We tired of muhfuckas hunting us like we ain't shit. I was out in the middle of that shit tonight. We ain't taking this no more.

He looked in the comments section and was shocked to see thirty-seven comments. He put his cigarette out, sat up, and read them all, starting from the very top and then scrolling down. Most of the comments were from the people he'd gone to high school with. He was a shy person in high school and mostly stayed to himself. He understood why his old high school acquaintances might find his speaking out entertaining. The only time he spoke out in high school was when he wanted an extra milk at lunch. But today he felt liberated. He felt assured as if he'd begun to discover some hidden continent within. An unexplored world that could only be found through the violence that occurs when a riot reaches the point of no return.

Terrell raised the window shade and stared outside. It looked like a normal Sunday afternoon. A few dudes walked down the street laughing, each holding a burning cigar, each wearing a white T-shirt. Cars sped down Center Street as if the drivers were hurrying toward something. On the block, the trees looked especially lush, and the house across the street was still lined with cars. One of the cars was a white Impala, which meant Country had ended up spending the night. Country's real name was James, but ever since James went to college down South and came back with a country accent, people started calling him Country, or Fake-ass Country Accent. He remembered Country texting him last night and telling him to stop by once he'd gotten back to the hood. He remembered him saying there was plenty of beer and Hennessy left. He'd seen the line of cars once he'd gotten home and thought of stopping by but was eager to write something on Facebook. He believed somehow the words might leave his stomach if he waited. Or perhaps he'd lose the courage to post something. He wondered if there was still beer and Hennessy left.

Terrell closed out his Facebook app and called Destiny.

"I thought I said call me as soon as you woke up," Destiny accosted in a voice Terrell was all too familiar with.

"What you mean? I am."

"Negro, you just getting up?"

"Yeah, I was tired as shit. What up, though?"

"Nothing. Just making sure you straight and everything from last night."

"Yeah, I'm good. You know ain't nothing gone happen to me."

"Whatever. Look . . ."

"I know, I know. Don't go over there today."

"Yeah. That too. But I was gone say let me know if you trying to get up today. I bet your mama would love to see me."

"Cool, I'll let you know."

"Are y'all doing anything?"

"She said some shit about frying some chicken later. I'll let you know."

"Okay. Don't forget."

"Cool. Oh, and you think you could look over my credit hours and help me sign up for classes this week? I think I only got like three more semesters and I'm out this bitch."

"Yeah. I got you. I got two more. Look at us, Washington High's finest, soon to be U-Dub graduates."

"Exactly. The best to do it."

"Better say that."

"Okay, cool. Well, I'll hit you later or whatever."

"Don't forget."

"I won't. Damn."

"And hey."

"Yeah."

"Don't you take your ass over there today. And don't go over by that trap house across the street either. I'm serious."

"Damn, you and my mom on that shit. I'm chilling today."

"Okay. Just call me later."

"I got you."

He put the phone down and thought about last night. Once he'd heard there was a riot going on, he had to go and see for himself. He remembered being pulled that way. It was hard to explain. The only other time he'd felt that kind of pull was the first time he'd seen Destiny. He had seen her before, but he hadn't really *seen* her. She was closing her locker as he and Rico walked in her direction debating Kobe and Jordan. He remembered stopping while Rico continued walking. He couldn't remember what he'd said to her and couldn't remember how she'd responded. She was the only girl at Washington who wore leggings and didn't look homeless. This was probably because of her toned legs and athletic build. He remembered her perfect complexion that reminded him of his longtime Hollywood crush, Nia Long. When he found out she was on the volleyball team, he never missed a game. Once they became a couple, he never missed school.

Last night, Terrell went to the riots alone. He poured some beer into a water bottle and started walking. The walk seemed quiet, surreal almost. It was that eerie spectator feeling: that almost watching-yourself-from-above feeling. His family had lived in Sherman Park his entire life. Chaos in the neighborhood had become nothing new. But a damn riot was, and it was something he had to see. He had to see a riot. He had to see a riot in his hood.

Terrell remembered approaching the burning gas station and the voices, the chorus of screaming. Agonized black faces shouted through clenched teeth. Red and blue sirens hovered, and the stench of hot gas made his stomach turn. He imagined war smelled like this. For the past few years, police had been making national headlines for murdering young black men. He'd lost count of how many. He had always moved carefully around the police, but lately folks were talking about it on CNN. The law's presence had always made him paranoid. In fact, when he was a child, his father had sued the city of Milwaukee after having his head slammed against the hood of their car one December night. The incident had cost Terrell's father fifteen stitches and a headache that lasted for over a week. Nothing ever became of the case, but for a while the family thought it might make them rich. He remembered clutching a bag of cold fries and watching from the backseat as his father argued with the police officer. Soon after the case was dropped, his father moved to Atlanta. His mother said, "Your father is looking for something and thinks he can find it in Atlanta." Whenever he saw his father after the move, he wanted to ask what was so much better in Atlanta. Terrell figured it was women, because his father had always kept more girlfriends than a man should need. Sometimes, Terrell wanted to curse his father for making him another daddy-less black boy. And although Terrell had never held a gun, sometimes he wanted to point one at his father but not shoot.

Last night as he approached the burning gas station, he wondered what his father would have done. Although he had beefs with his father, he always felt his father knew what to do in any situation. During the entire walk, he'd never considered his next move. He remembered looking for familiar faces or cars but didn't see any. While this was happening less than a mile from home and on a street corner he'd passed almost every day, it felt like another country. It looked like another country. He'd found a group chanting, "Fuck the police!" and stood beside them. Nearby, a group marched and chanted, "Black lives matter!" Cars drove by and either honked or boomed loud music. A group of officers in riot gear about thirty feet away stared in their direction. He remembered looking deep into the face of one of the officers, a white man who stared back at him. Eyes mirroring those of the officer who had slammed his father's face into that cold car hood. He joined the chorus, "Fuck the police!" then took a swig of his beer and shouted it again, "Fuck the police!" Amused at his audacity the night before, Terrell reached for the phone and called Country.

"T, what the fuck, how come you didn't fall through last night?"

"I know, man, I was about to, but I got tired," Terrell responded, rubbing his stomach and remembering that he hadn't had a thing to eat since he'd woken up.

"You got tired, or Destiny had you tied up?"

"Here you go with this shit."

"Fam. What you about to do, though?"

"I don't know, that's why I was hitting you. What you got over there?"

"Shit. Everybody just now getting up. But I go back to New Orleans later this week, so I'm down to throw a few back."

"Bro, I thought you muhfuckas was getting it in last night? And why every time you say *New Orleans* you say that shit like that, like you not from here. All like *Nawlins*. It's *New Or-leens*, Negro."

"Don't hate because I got that Southern flow now. And I told you about counting my drinks. I'm grown and if I want to get it in last night, this afternoon, tonight, tomorrow, that's my business," Country joked, then blew air into the phone.

"Why the fuck you blowing in the phone?"

"I'm having me a little smoke, Mr. Officer. Damn. Oh, I almost forgot, I saw that shit you posted on the book. That shit was real. You was out there, huh?"

"Yeah, that shit was crazy, fam."

"Knowing you, you was out there with no pistol, no plan, no nothing. Just out there."

"How about I don't count your drinks, and you don't worry how I be out here?"

"Whatever, fam. Come over here and sip something with us."

"I'll be through. Is Rico over there? I didn't see his whip."

"Yeah, he here about to cook some shit. Fall through, bro."

Terrell put the phone down and headed for the shower. As much as he wanted to see Country and Rico, he wasn't sure he should be over there. Last month, that house was raided, and a few people went to jail. The house was Theresa's mama's house, but her mama was never home. Theresa had just graduated from Washington High, and although she was kind of young, she could throw a crazy house party. Theresa was also the prettiest girl in the hood. Every guy in the neighborhood had made a move, and he was no exception. Terrell had been telling her for years that he'd take her on a date once she turned eighteen. She'd turned eighteen in June, and he had yet to make good on his promise. Just two weeks ago, she asked if he would take her to one of those "cracking college parties." After the police raid, his mama made him promise to stay away from that house.

Exiting the shower, he also wondered if Rico's wild cousins would be over there. They always had at least one gun and some illegal substance between them. While most of the people around smoked weed, they were the only ones who sold it. They carried weed in bulk. If there was another unexpected raid, that could be a problem. While placing his Packers G hat on his head, he felt his stomach turn. Not the way it turned last night, but the way a hungry stomach does, the way a rioting stomach does. Rico was one of the best cooks he knew, including his own mama. He knew whatever was being prepared across the street would be right on time. Rico had just completed his first year in the culinary arts program at MATC and cooked at the Applebee's down the street. Rico always hooked them up with a free order of off-the-menu wings whenever the restaurant manager wasn't looking. Even when they were kids, Rico could dig into any refrigerator or cupboard and put a gourmet meal together. And these meals weren't gourmet peanut butter and jelly or bologna sandwiches. Rico cooked whole big-mama meals. In fact, by the time they turned twelve, Rico had already perfected lasagna, fried catfish, fried okra, collard greens, baked chicken, and an immaculate poor man's peach cobbler.

Terrell walked out of the house and sat down on the porch, fondled a cigarette, and stared across the street. He'd never noticed how much Theresa's house looked like every other one on the block. All the houses looked the same. But none of the houses had the same things going on inside. He remembered when Theresa and her mama moved there about eight years ago. The elderly couple living there before was one of the last white families in the neighborhood. All their kids had grown up and moved out, but this didn't prevent the bevy of Christmas and Halloween decorations. For years, it was the only house on the block with skeletons hanging from the top balcony, and during winter a large glowing Santa figurine guarded the front porch. Sometimes they'd even turn the inside into a haunted house. His first kiss took place in that dark basement.

Terrell lit the cigarette and started walking across the busy street. An old orange Chevy sped by and beeped its horn just as he made it to the other side. He turned around and stared at the car, unsure of the occupants, or if the horn was even intended for him. Ringing the doorbell, he continued staring down the street. By now, the Chevy was blocks away. Country opened the door holding a bag of chips and a bottle of beer in the same hand.

"Finally, you come to see your people," Country greeted with a huge smile on his face.

"What up, fam. Hey, who we know drive an orange old-school?"

"Orange old-school? Oh, you talking about Wop, Rico's cousin."

"Oh shit. Wop got an old-school now?"

"Yeah. He just got that joint. He brought it over here last night to show everybody. But we know you was too busy being woke and shit."

"Who all here?"

"Why you asking so many questions? Just bring your ass inside."

"Can I bring this cigarette in?"

"Yeah, but go straight downstairs."

They walked down to the basement where a soft musical bass beckoned. The crowd was smaller than he'd expected: Rico was on the phone, Theresa and a girl he'd never seen shot pool on a crooked table, two dudes lay on separate couches staring at their phones, and Country walked behind the small wooden built-in bar.

"What you want to drink? We got Henny and some beers back here," Country said.

"Let me get a shot of Henny and one of those beers."

"Oh, you rolling double-fisted." Theresa smiled while clenching a half-broken pool stick.

"I figure I need to catch up." He sat down on the floor and put the beer to his mouth. Took the final drag of his cigarette and then placed it in a crowded ashtray.

"So, tell us what happened last night, fam," Country said from behind the bar. "I hear muhfuckas was not having it."

"It was crazy, man. Like, I've never seen the hood like that before. It was so many cops and shit. And so many people. And everybody was just mad as fuck. Everybody was just mad and yelling."

"We supposed to be mad. How they gone just shoot that man like that," Theresa's girlfriend said while aligning her broken stick with the cue ball.

"Yeah, for sure we are, but I didn't expect all that. I didn't expect shit to be on fire. That fucking gas station on Sherman and Burleigh was on fire."

"What did you expect?" Rico said, putting down the phone.

"Shouldn't you be upstairs cooking?" Terrell joked.

"I am. Theresa's mama got some ground beef up there. I'm thawing it out right now. I'm about to cook the shit out of these burgers. Let me hold one of them cigarettes, though."

"This my last one, bro."

"I'll go down the street and get you another pack in a minute. Don't be stingy with the squares, bro."

Terrell pulled the box out of his pocket and handed Rico a cigarette, grabbed the shot next to him, and swallowed it down in one motion. He'd drank on an empty stomach before and knew a few shots and beers would distract him from whatever hunger he felt.

"I'm saying I'm glad I went," Terrell said. "I really don't know how to explain it. They've been hunting us forever. It felt good just to tell the police, *Fuck you.* And to feel like they couldn't do shit because we was all together, like united and shit."

"I saw some folks got arrested, though. So apparently they *could* do shit, college boy. And when did you start talking like you a Black Panther or some shit? It was that Africology class you took last semester, wasn't it?" Rico chuckled, smoke wafting from his mouth, as he headed toward the stairs.

"Nobody I was with got arrested, and we was out there. Like, I was with this crowd, and everybody was screaming *Fuck the police* in they faces. And they didn't do shit."

"But they could've, social media tough guy. And like I said earlier, I bet you was out there with no strap or nothing, just screaming *Fuck the police* like you at an NWA concert and shit. Boy, you lucky you didn't get arrested. Your mama would've beat your ass," Country said in a fake country accent.

"So, you going back tonight?" Theresa asked with a hint of concern in her voice. "It's gone be even crazier. Everybody on the book talking about protesting."

"I don't think so. I want to, but I told my mama I'd chill."

"First they killing us and now they trying to get the fucking *Apprentice* dude elected president. This some crazy shit. Bro, I done got pulled over so many times for not doing shit," said one of the guys on the couch without taking his eyes off his phone.

As the shot pulled Terrell's body down, he found himself staring at Theresa, and in that moment realized she was probably the coldest girl he'd ever seen up close. Her red bandanna and red lipstick lit the dim room. Her braids hung low, and the light sneaking through a tiny basement window reflected off her black-rhinestone top. She leaned over the pool table, and with her eyes facing him smashed the cue into the eight ball. She looked at him and asked, "You want next, college boy?" He shook his head but knew that was a lie. He'd wanted next. "Well, let me know if you change your mind," she giggled while sauntering up the stairway.

He wondered how many of the dudes in the basement wanted next. He still had that date promise in his back pocket and considered bringing it up. The beer in his empty stomach sunk him lower and momentarily tethered him to the floor. He knew taking Theresa out meant borrowing his mama's car. It meant waiting until his next paycheck. He remembered Rico one day telling him that Woo claimed Theresa was a freak in the sheets. Rico also claimed skepticism because Woo had a knack for exaggeration and outright lying. Many of the girls in the hood that Woo claimed were freaks had denied knowing him in that way. No one ever asked Theresa if she'd known Woo like that. True or not, he worried about it all. If Woo had been with Theresa, they'd probably went for a ride in one of Woo's nice cars. They'd probably spent some of Woo's money at the mall or out to dinner. And Woo probably showed his experience in the bedroom: an act Terrell had only lied about. Like the time he told Country and Rico he'd lost his virginity in the school's parking lot after junior prom. Or when he bragged about how freaky the white girl in English 101 from up north had been.

"Man, I'm about to go to the crib quick and come right back," Terrell said, feeling the beginnings of a headache.

"But you only been here for like an hour," Country said while pouring two shots from behind the bar.

"I know, but my mama supposed to be coming back in a minute, and I just remembered I said I'd take out the chicken. I'm gone do that quick, handle some other shit, and come right back," Terrell responded, knowing he wasn't coming back. Even though he'd been there for only an hour, it felt long enough. Long enough for him to feel out of place. Last night's riots had stirred something in him. Suddenly, the urge to drink, smoke, and make passes at Theresa had subsided.

"All right, because you know Rico's burgers about to be on hit."

"I already know. I'm coming right back, bro," Terrell lied again.

"Cool. Let's take these shots, fam. And you better not get caught up with Destiny. I bet you still be trying to hit that on the low."

"Don't worry about my business. Wasn't you just saying that when I walked in this bitch?"

"Whatever. When you come back, we have to talk about a trip for everybody to come down to the dirty and see me. You gone love it. And the women down there just different. Bourbon street. You have never seen nothing like it. Not Chicago. Not our downtown when it's cracking. Nothing."

"Okay, cool. Let's talk about it when I come back."

Terrell begrudgingly slammed the shot and headed toward the door without saying bye to anyone upstairs. He didn't want the shot but had become accustomed to consuming things he didn't want. Walking outside, he didn't see his mother's car in the driveway. They were probably at his aunt's. Most Sundays they congregated there after church for brunch and mimosas and more fellowship that would sometimes last into the night. He pulled out his phone and noticed two unread text messages: a reminder from his mama to take out the chicken, and a reminder from Destiny to call.

The normally busy street was empty, and he crossed with ease. Terrell opened the front door and dropped all his weight on the living room couch. That second shot made the room spin a bit. He leaned back, pulled out his phone, and responded to each message. He told his mama he'd take the chicken out and Destiny he'd give her a call. He wondered about last night's riots, what they meant and what kind of change they might bring for black people in Milwaukee. This was history, and it was happening in his backyard. Up to this point, he'd never done a single brave thing. There was the time in third grade when a boy punched him in the stomach, and all he could do was drop to his knees and lick the tears around his mouth. And the time he and Theresa had been in her basement alone, pretending to play pool, but waiting to see who would move first. Terrell froze each time Theresa smiled at him, inviting him to come close to her, to do something brave.

Terrell walked into the kitchen and did what he promised his mother he'd do. When he opened the refrigerator, the smell of old collard greens caused him to gag slightly. Then the doorbell rang, and he cautiously walked toward the front door. He had the slightest idea who it might be but then thought it shouldn't be his mama and her boyfriend already. When he got near the door and peeked through the blinds, he saw it was Destiny. She was standing there in a white tank and fitted blue jean shorts, her head slightly tilted, a phone in her hand. Most often, she only stood that way when she wasn't happy with him. Terrell opened the door.

"So you're not going to invite me in?" she asked, accusatory, as if she knew something.

"Yeah, you can come in, but how come you didn't call first?"

"Because I knew you probably wouldn't answer your phone, Negro."

The two walked into the living room and sat down on the couch. Normally, Terrell would've said or done something flirtatious, but his attention was someplace else. He thought of his friends across the street and became slightly annoyed that none of them protested the night before. He had known them all his life and for the most part felt that they shared a brotherhood. To him, this meant that if one of the brothers protested, then all the brothers protested.

"How come none of them dudes went to the protest?" he asked Destiny.

"None of *who* dudes?"

"Country, Rico, my boys. How come none of them muhfuckas protested?" he responded, his speech becoming a bit slurred.

"Have you been drinking?"

"Oh, here you go with this shit. You always trying to mom me and shit."

"You *have* been drinking, because I can smell it," Destiny replied, now standing up. "And let me guess, you went across the street to that bum-ass trap house, didn't you?"

Terrell stayed seated and silent. He wasn't in the mood to lie but didn't want to argue either.

"Since you don't have anything to say, I guess I'll let myself out." She walked toward the front door. "I hope one day you figure out who the fuck you are and stop moving wherever the wind blows you."

He never motioned to stop her or even looked in her direction. He simply stared at the black television screen. His buzz had started to subside once again, and his midday hangover had returned. He was hungry for a meal, but another hunger swelled within.

Terrell walked down the hallway toward his mama's room. He remembered her boyfriend often saying when he was drunk, "Let a motherfucker bust up in here tonight. I got something in one of them drawers that'll have that motherfucker wishing he picked the house next door." He sometimes added, "And if them pigs ever try pulling me over thinking they about to kill me and get away with it, I got something for them too."

Terrell glanced around, bewildered, knowing he didn't belong in there. Mama's room had been off limits for quite some time, but being in there brought back nostalgic feelings. Momentarily, he felt protected. Like when he was young, and he and Mama would lie in her bed sometimes for a whole weekend. He looked across the room and stared at the dresser. He eased toward it, and without hesitation opened the upper left-hand drawer. There it was—there was the gun. He'd found it on the first try. If he wasn't brave, he figured maybe he was lucky. Like that time sophomore year when they all played spin the bottle, and his first spin landed on Destiny. He reached down and for the first time felt the cold weight of steel. At that moment, he heard Country's voice: *No plan, no nothing.* He didn't know how to check to see if it was loaded but pointed it at the mirror. Then he raised it in the air and then pointed it back at the mirror. He heard Destiny's voice ringing in his head: *Stop moving wherever the wind blows you.*

Terrell remembered leaving the riots last night moments after a shot rang out. People ran in all directions. As he hustled home with a plastic water bottle containing a half-empty beer, he thought of his father's face that night. How blood decorated the frozen snow on the car's hood. It was the first time he'd seen his father bleed. It was the first time he'd seen his father at someone else's mercy. Terrell remembered waiting in a cold seat until another squad car arrived, praying they'd let them go. That night, he rode shotgun in a police car and waited at the station for his mama. Once she arrived, the two of them drove home without saying a word. He thought of all the chances he'd had that night to save his father. If only he could've said something to prevent them from yanking his father out of that car. Maybe he could've told the officers to handle his father with care because the family needed him, that slamming his father's head into a car would change everything.

Terrell lowered the gun into the waistband of his jeans and started to walk toward the front door. He wanted to shoot something, anything. As he walked, he felt the return of third grade tears. He wanted to shoot the boy who punched him in the stomach. He wanted to shoot his father for moving to

Atlanta. He wanted to shoot a police officer, any officer. He wanted to do something brave. With his forearm, he brushed the tears from his face and opened the front door. Riots of sunlight enveloped him as he stepped onto the porch. He looked where the riots had been in the distance and, for the first time since he could remember, he felt free. Terrell inhaled deep and exhaled even deeper. He thought of pointing the gun in the direction of the riots but figured a neighbor might see him. He again heard Country's voice: *No plan, no nothing.* The sun was starting to go down, and Center Street seemed to be on fire. Last night, he had walked east on Center until he got to Sherman Boulevard. A few blocks north on Sherman Boulevard had landed him in the eye of the riots, on Burleigh.

Today, he figured he'd be more inconspicuous. *Isn't that how a person carrying a gun should be*, he thought to himself, *dark, hidden, and inconspicuous?* He decided he would take Center east until he got to 44th Street. Then he would head north on 44th until he got to Burleigh. This would allow him to be within eyeshot of the melee but give the appearance he was just some spectator. Terrell started his trek with a howling stomach. He wanted a cigarette but had no money for another pack. The more he walked, the louder the sirens pierced. He could also hear voices that roared louder and louder with each step. The voices momentarily startled him. While he knew people would be protesting and rioting, he assumed most would wait until later, until night. Terrell walked carefully, so as not to disrupt the shifting metal in his waistband. The thunderous roar of outrage rang throughout his ears and head, and a nervousness rattled about him like it would before he got on a roller coaster as a kid.

Terrell made it to Burleigh and looked in the direction of where the riots had been. The police had placed barricades at the intersection of Burleigh and Sherman, a block away from him. While staring at the crowds in the distance, he started reimagining the incident that started this. He knew it had occurred just blocks from where he stood. He closed his eyes trying to envision the exchange. Two officers pulled over two black men for suspicious activity. The two black men exited the car and fled on foot. Terrell squeezed his eyes tighter. One of the men fleeing was armed with a gun, and as he ran, a cop shot and killed him.

Terrell opened his tear-filled eyes to a blurry scene of sirens and protesters in the near distance. The charred gas station on Sherman provided a threatening reminder of the night before. He hadn't even noticed people had been shuffling past him the entire time he stood there in his apparent daze. "Say his name," Terrell whispered to himself, and uttered the name of the young victim. He then thought of all the young black men who'd recently been murdered by cops and began whispering their names too. "Say his name," Terrell repeated, and whispered his father's name. And suddenly, in an odd moment of clarity, a final shift transpired inside him. Despite what everyone thought about him, he was brave.

Terrell reached into his waistband and grabbed the handle of the gun. It still felt cold. He then pulled the bottom of his white T-shirt over his hand like he'd seen people do who wanted to hide a gun. His feet felt light as he started toward the charred gas station, toward the protesting and squad cars, the loud chants and bullhorns, the fallen buildings and storefronts, the outraged faces, the blue uniforms and holstered guns, the armored police trucks and fire engines, the picket signs and young spectators. Terrell started toward all of these things that beckoned him in the near distance, toward all the riots and riots of immaculate light that would follow.

'MOCKING SEASON

BY CHRISTI CLANCY

Whitefish Bay

B ack when there were still trees in Whitefish Bay, the
boys started sleeping in the hammocks they hung from
them. At first their parents thought that '*mocking,* as
the boys called it, was a great idea. It was as if, at seventeen,
the young men were finally experiencing real boyhoods outdoors, although these modern-day Huck Finns weren't exactly
roughing it in their backyards, not with the accessories their
mothers bought for them, from polyester taffeta tarps to dense
insect screens that, when gazed at from a distance, made their
boys appear to be encased in giant pods of milkweed.

The mothers met early each morning for pep-step walks
through the village, their ponytails bobbing in unison. *Oh,
those boys and their hammocks!* they said with hints of
self-congratulation, even though the idea to give up their
beds was not their own. Of course it was Leif's.

Leif initiated all the youthful trends that swept like brush
fire through Whitefish Bay. He even started the trend of man-
hood back when he was the new kid, when he and his mother
Erin moved to the village from some small town in rural Wisconsin. Marinette? Mukwonago? Merrimac? Leif had been in
eighth grade then, and his early plunge into puberty, along
with his midyear arrival from nowheresville, disrupted the
natural cycles of transition everyone in "The Bay" valued so
dearly. As soon as the first leaf fell, the mothers set plastic

skeletons that appeared to crawl out of their graves in their front yards, and when the snow melted they hung lavender and spring blossom wreaths from their front doors.

Leif already stood over six feet tall back in those days, with lamb-chop sideburns, knees like tree knots, and an Adam's apple as big as a fingerling potato. Soon after his arrival, all the boys started weightlifting, and they took razors to their faces in hopes that their peach fuzz would grow back thicker and more robust, like Leif's.

Erin and Leif's home was one of the oldest in the village, a beer baron's former summer cottage built back in the days before the neat grid system had been imposed on the burgeoning community. Instead of fronting the road like all the other houses, Erin's home was tucked like a secret in a thicket of woods at the end of a short, private drive off Day Avenue, perched on the bluff overlooking Lake Michigan. If the residents didn't make it their business to know about everything village-related, they might not have been aware that the house was even there. It didn't seem right to live where you couldn't be seen. All those trees made it impossible to sneak a peek inside when they walked their labradoodles at night.

The mothers waited almost a year to introduce themselves to Erin. One afternoon, they walked up her long, spooky drive bearing housewarming gifts of wicker baskets stuffed with artisanal cheeses, potter's crackers, wine and jam made from Door County cherries. They were shocked by the hedges, already so overgrown that they threatened to poke their eyes out. They might as well have because it hurt to see what awaited them: gangly juniper bushes and ostrich ferns that were almost tall enough to hide the *Green Party* sign.

Maureen's face was pinched from distaste. "Her yard," she said, "it looks so . . . so *woolly*."

A carpet of ivy choked the stucco walls of the once-grand mansion, and moss grew on the chipped clay roof tiles. Erin emerged from somewhere in the woods like an elf and greeted them. She was tall, blond, and busty. Her hair was feathered, and she wore plastic drugstore flip-flops. She seemed happy to see the women and invited them inside, where the air smelled like eucalyptus. That's when they saw Leif standing in front of an enormous instrument plopped smack dab in the middle of her living room like a casket set out for an old-fashioned wake.

"My, that sure is a big xylophone," Kitty said.

Leif took offense. "It's a marimba."

"What's the difference?" asked Maureen.

Judging from Leif's reaction, she might as well have asked about the difference between the Israelis and Palestinians. "The marimba has a much broader range. It's lush and reso-nant." Leif's voice was low and gravelly. He spoke about the marimba the way the women might have described a bottle of fine wine that doesn't pair well with food. "It has a gentle, per-sonal sound that's best for soloists because it can't cut through the group." He ran his fingertips along the tone plates with a tenderness that made the ladies uncomfortable.

"We moved here so Leif could play with the youth sym-phony," said Erin. "Hey, do you want a beer?" She held up the can of Old Milwaukee she was drinking, and the mothers looked at it as if she were holding a wild animal she'd just caught with her own hands.

That was the first and only time the mothers went in-side Erin and Leif's house, although their sons considered it a second home all through high school. The boys were drawn to Leif's marimba as if to the sound of the Pied Piper's flute. Soon, Whitefish Bay filled up with incessant banging on rosewood keys, a sound that carried across the open water of Lake Michigan and echoed mournfully off the bluff. To the women, it was like the atonal soundtrack to a bad horror flick on permanent loop.

No matter how much they practiced, the boys would never play as well as Leif, and they knew it, which only elevated him in their eyes. They tried to *be* him, although they could never imitate his style, no matter how many trips they took to the Goodwill in Milwaukee. He wore chunky turquoise rings on his fingers and a thick silver chain necklace with an Aztec mask pendant that floated atop his chest hair. His Cuban cigar shirts stunk like mothballs and patchouli. He never took off the Caterpillar work boots that he laced up over thick rag socks; nobody had ever seen him in tennis shoes—not in gym class, and not even in his hammock. His photochromatic eyeglasses didn't change with the light; they were always tinted dark. Leif christened the boys with nicknames that made them sound like 1950s greasers, like The Deuce or Skeech. To get a nickname from Leif was to *be* someone in Whitefish Bay.

Leif's hammock was a remnant from his canceled service trip to Guatemala (where, he told the boys, the marimba is the official instrument). All the parents were crushed to learn that Leif would stay home that summer because Erin of all people was worried about some mosquito virus. Leif's continued presence interfered with their plans to deprogram the boys in his absence. The husbands wanted to get them back into *real* sports like the soccer their boys had grown up with, sports that could earn them college scholarships (Leif played handball and boomerang, and he'd started a curling club that winter). The mothers fantasized about hauling their sons' smelly old vintage crap to the Rescue Mission and dressing them in J.Crew. They fantasized about snipping the hair the boys had started to grow long because they wanted to wear a single fishtail braid down their backs, like Leif's, because Leif said he was part Cree Indian. This was a claim the mothers doubted, even though Leif walked quietly in his big boots, with one foot right in front of the other, which is how they'd heard Native Americans walked.

It would be so nice, they thought, for their boys to be more like the normal kids in neighboring Fox Point and Mequon, who played Grand Theft Auto instead of that creepy instrument, and listened to obscure rap music they found on SoundCloud instead of marimba virtuoso Pius Cheung, who could play Bach's *Goldberg Variations* with four mallets.

But Leif stuck around, as persistent and ubiquitous as the no-see-ums that wiggled through their screens even after they'd set off bug bomb after bug bomb. The minute Jack "Tripster" McCarthy saw Leif lounging in his hammock in his jungle of a backyard, all the boys decided they had to have a hammock too. That was when 'mocking season started.

The mothers eventually learned that the only reason Erin could afford to live in a deteriorating lakefront mansion in the tony suburb of Whitefish Bay, buy a marimba, pay youth symphony fees, and think about sending Leif to Guatemala was because she'd landed a big settlement after her husband was killed in a fireworks accident at a county fair. In her terry cloth short-shorts, Erin could never overcome the two early strikes against her: she was tainted by tragedy and, as Kitty Knapp said, she was "one of those fireworks people."

Widows like Erin didn't belong in the village, a place where picking out the best paint color for the family room was a competitive sport. The women were known around town as "North Shore Nancies." They liked to think of themselves as *optimizers*, intent on elevating anything that was good to great. They made coffee with twice-boiled distilled water and served Ethiopian teff with blueberries in mason jars with gingham ribbons wrapped around them. They knew about all the latest treatments at the aesthetic center: injectables, lasers, ultrasounds. When yoga got old, they started taking classes where they learned how to floss their nerves.

And then there were their husbands, who outdid each other with their cocktails. Jake Kemp introduced a new kind of ice he'd seen on a business trip to LA, cut into perfectly spherical cubes with slow dilution rates. They moved from muddled to shattered herbs and sprayed their concoctions with elderflower from an atomizer without fear of compromising their masculinity.

Everyone took meticulous care of their homes and double-seeded, underground-sprinkled yards. As Kitty said, "Think of it this way: it's as if your house is a face and the lawn is the hair. You wouldn't ever want to be caught with bags under your eyes or your roots showing, would you?" The mothers happily trimmed their topiaries while the husbands mowed the Kentucky bluegrass in neat diamond patterns with freshly sharpened mowing blades and beveled the edges with scissors. Their yards looked *clean.* Before company, the ladies might even feel inclined to wipe down the leaves of their hostas with a damp cloth. The lawns were so lush and uniform that they could be mistaken for slabs of green concrete, with their boys' hammocks swinging gently atop the little white EverGreen warning flags.

Well, all but Erin's. The ladies walked past her driveway and wondered what went on back there. There were rumors of killer wasp nests, marijuana plants, ticks, and garlic mustard gone wild. Janet Marks said she'd heard that Erin even kept a miniature donkey in the garden shed.

Meanwhile, Erin drove around in a rusty black Saab that looked like a boll weevil, complete with bumper stickers that said: *Sleep, Creep, Leap!* and *Lawns Are for Losers.* Everyone felt that one was unnecessarily aggressive.

It didn't take long for the mothers to become less enthusiastic about their boys' new habit of sleeping in hammocks. Their sons refused to come back inside at night. They said they liked the air, the stars, the freedom, and the ergonomic zero pressure points Leif told them about.

The mothers began to sense how strange their houses felt without their children sealed in the drywall and UV windows, breathing in the HEPA-filtered air. They seemed so exposed out there with just a whisper of nylon separating them from the rest of the mean world, although they took some comfort knowing that outside was more like inside with the new waterproof upholstered sectionals and patio rugs, furniture the salesperson at Laacke and Joys called "outdoor solutions."

At night, the mothers stood in front of the windows that looked out onto their pristine backyards, so perfect yet sadly invisible in the dark, and listened for the sounds of coyotes and the giggles of girlfriends, or the footsteps of burglars and child molesters who they worried would snake through the village in their rusty old pervert vans. But all they heard was an occasional cough or wheeze and the hum of the outdoor refrigerator.

They would pause at the doors of their sons' listless bedrooms that smelled less and less like athletic socks and retainer breath and gaze wistfully at the plaid Pottery Barn coverlets gathering dust, the discarded birch mallets, the trophies and ribbons, the calculus textbooks and the Bibles their grandparents gave them that they never read, and they'd think about how they'd molded their lives around their children. They couldn't wait for summer to be over so their boys would come back inside. It seemed like yesterday they were watching them climb the rock walls on their elaborate cedar play systems— and then? Leif. Now, because of him, their boys were out there all alone, strung up, as Kitty said, "like ground meat in sausage casing." Soon they'd be off to college, and this new air of abandonment in their bedrooms would calcify into something more permanent and terrifying.

Apparently, Erin didn't feel the same pangs of loss that they did. They heard that Erin had bought herself her own hammock. On the nights when Erin's weird boyfriend Cody didn't stay over, she'd "toss her 'mock" between the white pines she'd planted when she moved in, as if she needed more trees back there. Erin once told Kitty that she loved white pines because they grew so tall and straight and true, like her Leif.

"What do you think they do out there?" asked Maureen.

"Who knows," said Marci. "Smoke cloves and recite Walt Whitman or *whatever.*"

The women imagined the mother and son drifting off to sleep under the stars, dreaming of Leif's mysterious dad before he got blown to smithereens.

Apparently Cody, Erin's horticulturist boyfriend, was to blame for Erin's jungle of a yard. She'd met him after she hired his company, Middle Earth, to save her trees during the bad drought several years earlier. He drenched her magnolia roots and fertilized her sugar maple with Vigor Trigger after it exhibited iron chlorosis. Erin suggested to the boys that they tell their parents to hire Cody too, but the fathers took the simpler route: they began to cut their ailing trees down. By that summer, so many trees had been cut down that many of the boys had to hang their hammocks from metal hammock stands.

That summer Kitty felt particularly generous—or perhaps *curious* was a better word—and invited Erin and her "special friend" to her annual costume party. She figured that Erin might be a safer guest if she dressed as someone other than herself. That was a mistake. Erin and Cody, pleased, after all these years, to finally get an invitation to a social event in the Bay, happily rose to the occasion. Cody offered a bag of hand-picked chanterelle mushrooms as a housewarming gift. He had twigs and leaves glued into his hair, and he was dressed in a shaggy brown-suede tunic, furry vest, and pointy-toed slippers. "Let me guess," said Marcus. "You're a turd, right?" He gave Cody such a hard pat on the back that he knocked him into Kitty's jockey statue.

Cody corrected him and said he was Noldo, which meant nothing to anyone. He had to explain he was the Tolkien elf of the second clan, which still meant nothing. As for Erin, well, she wore a halo headpiece made with fragrant irises she said she'd picked from her yard, and she was practically naked in a wispy dress Janet had seen on clearance at Oh My Gauze!, the store on Silver Spring Drive. Her breasts were incredibly firm and ripe, and her glitter-covered skin was luminescent under the adorable string of twinkling martini-shaped lights Kitty had strung up around the patio. The husbands, who had all decided to dress as Boy Scouts, had to hold their craft cocktails over the crotches of their brown shorts to hide their erections.

"What *are* you?" Kitty asked Erin.

Erin said she was the wood nymph, Daphne, as if she was surprised Kitty couldn't guess this.

The women didn't know how to talk to Erin, but they certainly didn't want her to talk to their husbands, so they took turns holding her hostage in the corner near the decorative sundial that Erin said wasn't set right. They bragged about their sons' ACT scores and made small talk that got depressing. "Marcus has developed this horrible wheeze," said Janie Aberg. "I think it might be asthma."

"You should see Elliott's hands shake," said Marci, who was dressed up like a cowgirl. "It's like he has Parkinson's, like my dad."

Annie was Jackie O. in her pillbox hat, pearls, and a smear of ketchup on the shoulder of her jacket. "Owen can't concentrate anymore," she said. "He just stares into space, and I'm like, *Are you there? Earth to Owen!*" Annie clapped her hands hard, right in front of Erin's face, making her jump.

"It's all the chemicals they're exposed to," Erin said.

"What chemicals?"

"That stuff you put on your lawns."

"Our lawns are *fine*," they said.

"They're perfect."

"Beautiful."

"It's just allergies."

"Gluten sensitivity."

"Dairy intolerance."

"Well," said Erin, "you might want to give it some thought. They started getting sick about the same time they started 'mocking."

"Whatever."

"You know there's nothing wrong with dandelions," Erin said. "We eat the leaves at our house. We fry them up with—"

"You *eat* them?" asked Kitty, as though Erin had just told her she ate her own shit.

"Sure, they're a rich source of beta-carotene. Not to mention Vitamin C, potassium, fiber, calcium."

"Oh gross," said Fiona. "I'll tell you, it's the dandelions that are dangerous. Remember that ratty overgrown soccer field at Cahill Park? The boys used to trip all over them. I'm so glad they replaced it with Astroturf."

Erin said, "Have you tried corn gluten? Aeration? Those chemicals you use, they're dangerous. You do know that, don't you?"

"Don't be a downer," Kitty said. "Let me get you another drink, hon."

"Cody says that stuff is like nerve gas."

"What does Cody know?"

"He's a certified botanist."

"Look," said Marci, "we've used EverGreen for years, and we've always been fine."

Erin looked over to where Cody stood. He was losing traction with the husbands, who laughed when he referred to the trees in Erin's yard as his "community," and were unsympathetic when Cody told them about the aggressive invasives that kept him up at night, like the mile-a-minute vine, pale swallow wort, and the Alabama jumping worms that were making the soil look like coffee grounds.

"Mow that shit down, you've got nothing to worry about," said Bruce.

"Cheers to that," said Marcus, who was on his fifth of Bruce's signature cocktail—a drink made with potato vodka, blood orange bitters, and shattered tarragon. He called it the FUBAR (Fucked Up Beyond All Reason).

The heat and rain that summer created the perfect condition for buckthorn, goldenrod, and Bishop's gout, leaving no choice but for the husbands to double down on their lawns. When the steam weeders and the EverGreen spray stopped working, the husbands went to the hardware store and marinated their grass in new combinations of chemicals. It was fun for them to compete against the so-called experts at EverGreen, mixing up their own more powerful concoctions. For their wives, it was exciting to watch them try each new application; it was a little bit like getting their hair highlighted when they waited to have the foils pulled out to see if the color would take.

A few weeks later, their grass was as colorless as dead flesh, but at least the weeds had been baked out of them. "With some fertilizer and rain they'll grow back good as new," the husbands said. Everyone held their breath in anticipation of rain, and in dread for the next windy day, when the seeds from Erin's yard would inevitably drift over like all those refugees they read about in the news, looking in vain for hospitable soil.

It was a bad summer. The Fords, the new young couple on Upper Berkeley Boulevard, walked past Kitty's brown lawn with slumped shoulders. Ashley's poor baby had a rare condition and was born without eyeballs. Then Annie, like everyone else, had a suspicious mammogram. "Probably nothing," her doctor said, but still he seeded her breast with metal beads so he could keep an eye on it. Same thing happened to Gloria. The women had done so many self-checks that their breasts were bruised and tender. "Mitts off, ladies!" said Marci, when she saw that they were all checking themselves for lumps while they drank margaritas on her patio. She'd invited them over earlier that day with an e-mail: *Dress code? Village Casual.*

The mothers used to talk about the latest home collection from Serena and Lily. Now Tracy Pearson said that her husband Greg pulled off his athletic socks after an afternoon of yard work, and bits of his skin got stuck in the cotton. Jane's track-star daughter had to quit the team because she'd developed sports-induced asthma. And then there were the poor dogs who'd turned lumpy and practically died all at once. Lymphoma, the vet said. Traci replaced hers with a shepadoodle she named Mutt. Soon, everyone had a shepadoodle.

The boys became so lethargic and sick that the neighborhood, usually a whirl of activity in the summer, was locked in an unsettling stillness under the blinding light of the sun, light that was no longer dappled through the tree branches. Well, except for Leif, who banged away at his depressing marimba at all hours. He was about to participate in a statewide youth competition for a big scholarship. The boys said that Leif was working on an incredibly difficult, conceptual piece called "Fantasy on Japanese Woodprints." Everyone could hear it for miles. It wasn't like any music they'd ever heard before; it made everything seem off, like when they test the tornado sirens at noon on Wednesdays.

During his practice breaks, Leif made a shuffleboard court on Day Avenue with duct tape. He fashioned cue sticks out of upside-down brooms, and he cut up the Frisbees he'd bought at Winkie's Variety Store for discs. When the boys showed up, drawn to Leif as if by secret signals (Leif didn't even have a cell phone), they could hardly muster the energy to even focus on the rules. Daniel "Lunk" Morello had boils on his neck, and he complained of dizzy spells, and Joey "Fizz" Robinson had Bell's palsy. Lunk and Fizz sat on the curb and stared at the pavement.

"What's wrong with you, my brothers?" asked Leif.

"Probably Lyme disease," said Lunk, although Leif couldn't hear him, because the truck spraying for gypsy moths was passing by, even though almost all the oak trees were gone now. The vapor hung in the still air.

"My mom says it's just the heat," said Fizz.

Daz tried to make a shot, but his right arm was rocked with a sudden spasm. The disc hit Leif so hard in the head that he was knocked onto the pavement. His tinted glasses flew off his face and shattered when they hit the street. The boys were beside themselves. They'd never seen Leif without his glasses, or on his ass.

Klode Park was one of the few Erin-free zones in Whitefish Bay, a relic of life before she and Leif had moved in. But suddenly there she was, spread out on a lounge chair like a porn star in her crochet-knit bikini, giant bubble sunglasses, and chunky Dr. Scholl's sandals hanging perilously off her unpainted toes. She was reading a *Smithsonian* magazine. On the cover was a photo of a leopard about to pounce and the headline "Return of the Big Cats."

"Oh, hi, Erin," Annie said. "We don't see you here often."

"It's a nice day," she said.

There was no arguing that Erin had a great body. The women weren't too bad, but they had the occasional varicose vein, and you could see the cottage cheese under their thighs when they sat down, which is why their tankini bottoms had little skirts sewn into them. Watching Erin, they instinctively sucked in their bellies and adjusted the bras to cover stretch marks, cursing themselves for letting their CrossFit memberships lapse. Kitty stood behind Erin's chair and pointed at her boobs. *Fake*, she mouthed.

"I like your suit," said Maureen. "Did you make it?"

Erin set her magazine on her lap and sat upright. Her breasts didn't even jiggle. Her glasses slid down the sheen of grease on her tiny nose. "I bought it at Kmart."

The women almost died.

"We hear Leif's big competition is coming up," said Marci.

"Next week," Erin said. "He's been busy practicing."

Katie said, "You don't need to tell us. We hear him banging on his marimba day and night. The sound really carries."

"Isn't it beautiful?" Erin said. "It's like the music moves through him, like he *is* the music. I never get tired of listening to him play."

"Well, good luck," Kitty said. "We hope he wins."

"Thanks. The piece is so difficult, so delicate. I hope you'll all come to the competition. I put tickets in your mailboxes."

"Yeah, sure," they said, although they had no intention of going.

"It would mean so much to Leif. He's been through a lot. Your boys, they're like a family to him. That's why we moved here, so he could be part of a neighborhood."

This sentiment made the women feel good: a neighborhood, yes. An actual village.

"How's Skeech?" Erin asked Kitty.

"Don't call him that. His name is Connor."

"He was pretty sick the other day. I've been worried. He threw up in my birdbath."

"He's fine. Just a few bad oysters."

"You know I like Connor. I like all your boys. I care about them," Erin said. "But they're all getting so sick, I thought we could talk about it."

Maureen said, "They're just a little under the weather."

"Daz only had one seizure last week," said Katy.

"Nerves," said Annie. "I think it's just the stress of thinking about college. That'll be a big change."

Erin said, "I'm sure it's the pesticides. We talked about this before. Cody says—"

"Cody isn't a doctor. Give us a break."

"Are you accusing us of knowingly putting our kids in danger? Look, we love nature. And we love our boys. Why do you think we let them sleep outdoors? What could be healthier?"

"But they got sick as soon as they started 'mocking. Maybe you could lay off the spray, see if it makes a difference. Just try."

"No way," said Janie. "It's such hard work to get our yards to where they are."

Erin said, "But don't you see a connection? It's as clear to me as the nose on my face."

"I'll tell you what connection I see," said Kitty. "Everyone is sick but Leif. Don't you think it's strange that he's the only boy in Whitefish Bay who hasn't had a single seizure this summer?"

The women nodded. It *was* strange.

"That's because I don't use that stuff," Erin said.

"He's poisoning our boys," said Kitty.

This wasn't something they'd discussed before, although now that Kitty said it, the mothers had to agree: it made perfect sense.

"We're on to him," said Maureen.

Erin tossed her magazine into a used Sendik's plastic red grocery bag, and the women all thought the same thing at once: *She doesn't even have a decent beach bag!*

"That son of yours is up to no good," said Annie.

Kitty said, "I've put it together. Your boyfriend Cory—"

"Cody."

"He just wanted to get some business from us. He got Leif to poison our boys and have you blame it on our lawns so we'd have to 'go natural.' This is part of your gig."

"My what?"

"The gig is up!" said Annie.

"I would never. Cody would never. *Leif* would never!"

"You're all just trying to make a profit off of us."

"God, you're sick, you're all fucking sick." Erin stood up and folded her chair under her arm. "Each and every one of you."

Marci said, "*We're* sick? Your husband didn't die from a fireworks accident, that's what I heard."

"Cody poisoned him too," said Maureen.

Annie pointed right in Erin's face. "You're a black widow."

"You're a *weed*, that's what you are!" spat Kitty. "And you don't belong here."

"Go to hell." Erin marched away, the wooden soles of her Dr. Scholl's clomping on the concrete path that led up the bluff, a sound like Leif's mallets against the keys.

The next week was Leif's big performance. Nobody from the village would dare go see him play, and they forbade their boys from going too. Still, the boys gathered together in Kitty's basement and watched it on the local cable access channel. The mothers, who were upstairs, gathered around Kitty's granite peninsula countertop, plotting their next move. When the boys started cheering for Leif, they decided to wander into the basement to see what all the fuss was about.

There Leif was, in the center of the stage, in front of all the other musicians. He didn't look like the Leif they knew. It was the first time they'd ever seen him in a dress shirt and tie, with a shiny red vest and a nice pair of slacks. There were no rings on his fingers, and his Caterpillar boots were replaced with black dress shoes. He must have been wearing contacts; the eyes he'd hidden behind his tinted glasses were revealed as penetrating, as green as their lawns used to be. The women felt chills run through them; it was like he was looking right at them, like he saw everything.

The boys came to life when the music began, although Channing drooled out of one side of his mouth and Connor had a constant twitch. They were mesmerized as Leif moved through the piece. They knew it well and commented like sports announcers on the series of cadenzas, accompanied first by the violins and violas. When the flutes and oboes made everything "weird," as Maureen said, the boys explained the Japanese and Armenian influences on the piece and how the musicians are expected to improvise on a series of notes.

The mothers wanted to dislike the music, and they did at first, but they couldn't help but get caught up in a sort of spell. The song was strange and haunting, soulful, even beautiful. It grew and grew, building on itself, and Leif seemed somehow to expand beyond what they knew of him, and what they thought they knew of boys and life.

Now they saw what Erin meant when she said that the music went *through* Leif; he was just a vessel. The song was like a story; it transformed from the light, tinkling sound into a march, then a crescendo. They were transported. The family room, recently painted in brassica, an eggplant color Kitty had told her husband wasn't actually purple, disappeared. There was just the music, just the moment.

Leif made them aware of a certain kind of frightening beauty, a transcendence—something they could tell was really, really important and meaningful. Maybe if that moment lasted even a few seconds longer everything would have been different, and the song would have been enough to change them somehow. But then, his arms raised high over his head, he froze like a zombie, his face contorted into a horrible grimace. His mallets slipped out of his hands and tumbled onto the keys. His whole body began to jerk and convulse. Of course, everyone knew what a seizure looked like after watching the boys succumb to seizures all summer, but for just a moment they thought perhaps this was what the music was supposed to do. Maybe, they thought, Leif was caught up in rapture. But then he collapsed.

While Leif was at his rehearsals, the mothers had snuck over to Erin's house and entered a backyard that Kitty called Jurassic Park. "I couldn't live like this," said Annie. "It's so . . . disorganized."

"This is a project," said Maureen.

Under the thick canopy of Kentucky coffee trees and sugar maples, they pushed away the damp stalks and branches that gently grazed their legs. They discovered mayapples and umbrella plants and sprawling butterbur with kidney-shaped leaves as big as their boys' backpacks. Sunny yellow black-eyed Susans seemed to watch as the women squirted the colorless, odorless chemical potions their husbands had made. The flowers on the squash plants wilted, and the cigar-sized hornworms lost their grip, falling off the tomato plants into the yarrow. The chemicals had burned several small holes into Leif's and Erin's hammocks.

"We were just trying to show Erin how wrong she was," said Kate.

"It's not like we tried to poison Leif," said Kitty.

"This stuff is perfectly legal," said Janie.

"And perfectly safe," said Maureen. "If it were that bad they'd ban it, but you can slap down your credit card and buy it at the Ace."

"It's not like he died," said Annie. "He'll be able to play again someday. Once the tremor lets up, he'll get his rhythm back."

"Epilepsy," said Maureen. "I'll bet that's what it was. All those lights on him probably brought it on."

"A shame," said Kitty. "He had such a rare talent."

Erin had taken one look at her yard and knew what had happened, but she couldn't prove anything, and the village police didn't get worked up about Erin's crazy pesticide theories. They had better things to do, like give speeding tickets to African Americans who drove through the village.

The new zoning ordinances the women had fought for went into effect, and Erin's house was deemed a nuisance and condemned. Erin had to sell Leif's marimba to pay his medical bills. She and Leif packed up the Saab and moved to a random town in some random part of the state.

"Whatever," said Kitty.

Still, it felt like Erin and Leif haunted Whitefish Bay with every weed that sprouted in their yards after they left, each one more aggressive and noxious than the weeds they'd seen before: first, the wild parsnip that caused streaky red rashes, then the hogweed with leaves that were three feet wide, and poison sap that could burn and blind.

"Don't worry, we've got this," said the husbands, who donned hazmat suits that made them feel like police in antiriot gear. They power-sprayed stronger chemicals through wider hoses and special nozzles.

The boys were gone, no longer boys. Their hammocks hung limp in the lingering mist.

TWO CENTS

BY Shauna Singh Baldwin

East Town

A man of 6'4" needs a sturdier railing to climb the seven stairs from John Hawks's pub by the river. Even with the cane Ev makes him carry.

Used to be 6'4", that is.

At the top now.

Helmut straightens. *Crick-crick*, say his vertebrae.

Those vertebrae oughta be more relaxed after two Christmas toddies, but by golly that Hawk and his buddies . . . young, ignorant. They aren't thinking about what they're asking for, come January. So it will be a long four years. Maybe eight, 'cause people won't want to switch horses midstream.

Ach, wasn't he like them once? Wasn't Chamberlain? But like he told them, this time there's no superpower that's going to land troops on a D-day, nor bomb them to smithereens to save them.

The clouds are white ovals forecasting snow, and dusk is dissolving the radiant blue over the high-rises. That Irish coffee'll keep him toasty in his parka. His car's in that lot near the arcade that used to be a Gimbels Brothers department store.

What year was it that he parked cars in that lot? Who cares now when those cars got parked. Or who complained about it (and man, did those downtown bankers complain). All he knows is: it was several years before he met Ev.

Ev says never to act like he did the first day they met. Like it wasn't her fault. If she hadn't come sashaying past that Gimbels window he was decorating, he wouldn't have vaulted over a brass bar, the better to see her apple-shaped butt. To this day, he can hear the crash of plate glass and the tinkles as every mannequin rocked on its pedestal. And Ev's high coo, "Are you all right?" (Her voice is more practical now, but warmer than the froggy voices of young gals.) Helmut said he was fine, though his heart was boinging all around. Then he nearly passed out from the touch of her gloved fingers at his temples—kind gals like Ev, they wore gloves. Titanium white, with just a tinge of cadmium yellow—he thought of that shade whenever she served anything topped with good old Cool Whip.

Light in dark. Streetlights shining up to the bridge, then continuing on the west bank. And every light source casts a shadow. Like there's some darkness hidden within light—those restaurant windows stretching away along the River-Walk. *Yin-yang.* The bridge: one filbert brushstroke to suggest its metallic green.

Ev says that wasn't the first time they met. She says they met at a train station when they were only nine or ten. She says she was with her mom, he with his, and he reached over and took her hand. He doesn't remember that, but one of his teenage paintings does show those children. He won a prize for it; it still hangs in Bayview High School. Ev thinks it really happened.

Mother called that painting sappy; got so afraid her youngest might be gay she made him join Golden Gloves after that prize. Renewed his membership every time he won another art prize. Helmut never took to boxing, but after that morning at Gimbels he would have fought anyone and everyone for Ev if he'd had to. Even August Jr.

Oh yeah, he finally hurt his brother real bad soon after he met Ev. Popped him with his one-knuckle. The shoken zuki, hard as John L. Sullivan, like his dojo master taught. So hard, he had to catch August Jr. quick before his head hit concrete. Which could have killed him, just like if Helmut fell today on the sidewalk here.

When Helmut caught him, the coat came away in his hand, and there was Emperor August with his fancy suit split right up the middle, and his white shirt showing up pink skin. Helmut sure hit him good that day. The taxi horns in *An American in Paris* kept blaring as August Jr. sailed off the porch for saying Ev was a dumb Polack. Said it right in front of Ev's dad, who *was* a dumb Polack but always thought Helmut was a dumb Kraut.

So it was Uechi-Ryū, not boxing, that took care of August Jr. That's how August Jr. finally quit beating him up.

The river runs Prussian blue between ice floes all along its banks—Ev would remind him to hold the railing when he gets to the Plankinton Street bridge. He'll stay to the right, on the side of the cigar store and the Riverside Theater, to say hello to Gertie. Kids these days only remember Gertie the statue. Helmut remembers the brown-feathered duck with the liquid eyes who sheltered her babies under this bridge during the war. He and August Jr. took a streetcar downtown just to see her.

August Jr. was already full grown back then. About six feet, same as the guy in the hoodie coming toward him on the bridge. Tougher than Helmut, but Helmut was catching up. He had to. He and August were the only two German kids in a Polish school.

Oh man, when Hitler invaded Poland. August fought the crap out of three crazy kids armed with crowbars to break his legs, and Helmut fought the crap out of six kids who jumped him that day. Helmut got home with a smashed nose, and there was his Uncle Margraff hunched over German radio. Uncle told August Jr. and Helmut to clean up. He said everything would be fine as soon as Hitler invaded America to save the Germans. August got so mad he was German, he pulled the whole sink from the wall. And Helmut remembers himself standing there, blood soaking his only school shirt, wondering, *Save us? Who can save us?*

Jesus was supposed to be the answer. Jesus was the answer to everything for Mother. Jesus had a helluva lot on his hands back then, trying to save all the German and Polish guys who quit fighting one another to sign up right when Helmut did and go fight the same son of a bitch.

Jesus still has. Only now, Jesus, how about looking after this old gumba? Because there's a dark guy in a hoodie, almost as tall as the carved and painted Indian standing outside Uhle Cigars. Which means almost as tall as Helmut. The dark guy's footfall clangs softly on the metal bridge.

The guy in the hoodie doesn't know Helmut used to do the shomen geri, a kick high as his own ear, or a spear-hand nukite so hard he could bring down August Jr. Well, at least Ev is at home and can't feel his arm trembling, his grip tightening on his cane. He's facing forward, feeling the rush of the river below. The carved Indian facing the street looks like he knows but won't tell Helmut what hue of white the snow dust stippling the air is. Good thing none of the guys at the ad agency can see him now. Good thing Ev can't see Helmut now. She'd see he is feeling lightheaded. Should he continue?

A knowledge bubble rising within says kicking or punching is out.

The railing feels solid beneath his fingertips. If the guy

comes at him sideways, maybe he can back up against it, real sudden, real quick. Theoretically, the guy would fly past.

If he comes at him straight, you can bet there'll be two guys in the drink, 'cause Helmut isn't the kind to let go.

The dark guy trades places. It takes Helmut a second to realize the man is now behind him, walking.

Is he looking back? Turning? What if he's coming up behind Helmut, about to take him in a choke hold from behind? Helmut will flip him over his shoulder and shout, "Harrrgh!" and slam him to the ground. And a look of surprise will wash over his face like it did for August Jr. the day Helmut said, "No, no more money, go find another patsy."

The black guy could be coming up behind him, stealthy and quiet as a thief. Tiptoe, like August Jr. must have when he stole the money Ev gave his kid for cutting grass—she called it mowing the lawn. And the black guy could be thinking as August used to, that he could just get away with anything because he always did.

Move forward.

He tries to catch up with the clanging of his cane.

Had there been a flash of white in the hoodie? August Jr. used to smile whenever he was caught. A smile that said, *What, you were expecting something different?* or, *You have to forgive me—it's my nature.* No, there had been no smile.

Doesn't anyone teach kids to smile at their elders these days?

Maybe he didn't smile because, unlike August Jr., he probably knew he'd never get away with whatever he might be planning to do to Helmut.

Are those footsteps? No sound. The black guy must be wearing fancy sneakers. The Michael Jordan kind: dark cadmium red, lamp black, and white.

He listens for breath. Like he had when August was lying there, out cold. Remembering how he worried if he'd killed his brother this time and how he would explain it to Mother.

There's none, only stiffness in his neck from holding himself tall as he did in the Air Force. Which he joined because he could not shoot to save his life or anyone else's, so it wouldn't do him any good at this moment to have—or not have—a gun.

Helmut stops, draws his collar up. The rush of the river seems to have stilled. Snow swirls lazily on the road; the wooden Indian looks like he has better things to think about than notice. The roll of the marquee on the Riverside Theater is still. Now he can barely read the name of some rapper who, like Helmut, probably never finished school. (Artists never finish school, he told Ev. She believed him—or at least she never said he should have.)

All the kids should be out on the street at this hour. People gotta work tomorrow. C'mon, isn't closing time only a few hours away?

The black guy could be following him, getting closer. He might need someone to take him back to Ev. She'll know what to do.

Ev always knew what to do. Would call up and schmooze people Helmut completely forgot right after he delivered on time—he never missed an ad deadline. If she were here, she'd turn and say something nice that would just stop that guy.

Helmut could too, if he could get the words out. Because he knows exactly where that young man is right about now, in his life. Nothing working out, no one making any more jobs. Computers taking over the ones you could have had with no college. He might tell him how he'd had to retire from ad agency work because his hand was too large to ride the back of a mouse, his eyes couldn't focus on a screen. He wants to tell the kid, *I get you. I was like you at your age. I'm like you now.*

But the black guy is probably just like the Polish kids in school. Probably only sees a white guy, a Kraut.

They say only your mom cares a rat's ass who you are.

Not Mother. Nicknamed him Two Cents, 'cause she said that's all he would ever be worth. That black kid probably had some teacher say the same. But his mom would never call him Two Cents—no way. His mom probably worked her ass off for him. But that black kid is probably living without his dad like Helmut did at his age, 'cause who would want to live with August Sr.? Not Helmut or August Jr. A guy who'd leave his wife and go off with her sister. Ev says Helmut should trash the newspaper clipping now. But that's all he has of August Sr.

Never did find out where he vanished, though Helmut once took Ev to Berlin in a vacation sort of way, hoping to bump into him on Unter den Linden or near the Bundestag, places August Sr. had mentioned. If he'd found the man, he would have asked, *Did you not fear us?* And then killed him, probably. Though not in front of Ev.

August Jr. never cared about finding his father. Soon as Mother died, he left for Las Vegas. Kept calling, telling Ev some mobster was going to break his legs, so she'd send him a check. Helmut never believed him till it happened.

The black kid could break Helmut's legs. He strikes backward into the dark with the cane.

Nothing. No one.

No breathing.

"Hey!" he shouts. It's a squeak of bravado. "I see you!"

But he doesn't. Above him, the clouds have blended into indigo.

All he has to do is make it to his car. If the black guy wants to come after him . . . well then, it's time.

August Jr.'s time came after they broke his legs. He called and said it was because Helmut had refused to send him money. But that was just August Jr. making more excuses. Helmut told Ev to tell him so—it was easier than talking to him. Ev wasn't talking to August anyway. She was talking to August's latest lady friend. The one in his Christmas photo. With the red leather skirt. The one with the zinc-white teeth and a horse laugh you could hear clear across the whole United States whenever Ev asked how things were going.

He's moving past the Riverside Theater now, crossing the street. And another crossing at a right angle to that one. Crossing over.

The lines on the black asphalt look like a referee's shirt. There should be referees on every corner blowing their whistles on grown-up kids getting their kicks out of destroying.

Dirty rotten kid, August Jr. called him in that last call. Helmut couldn't remember what August Sr. sounded like by then, but he imagined his voice like August's. No joking, though they were brothers. Said his brother was a *dirty rotten kid* like he meant it. No joking, though Helmut had loaned him money several times by then.

Maybe he was right, he thinks, folding himself into his silver-gray Chevy.

No, he was not. One of the two dirty rotten kids could paint his teacher nude when he was ten. And only one dirty rotten kid painted a picture of Ev reaching for his hand at the train station as if that really happened. That award-winning painting that still hangs outside the teacher's office at Bayview High School.

That painting must be how the hell Ev ever fell in love

with a dirty rotten kid. It helped her imagine his big mitt enclosing her hand, then her enclosing him. *Yin-yang.*

If he ever sees the dark guy again, he'll tell him: *Don't ever let anyone call you a dirty rotten kid. Because there is something in you that someone like Ev will see one day.* Something that let this old artist go, put his cane into his car, and drive past the ferry, down Superior Street.

He should have stopped and talked to the kid. Maybe learned him a thing or two. Too late now, as he's pulling into his garage, hauling himself out of the car a leg at a time. Whole legs, even if they don't work so good.

A private eye called from Vegas after August died and asked if Helmut wanted him to investigate his brother's death, because those broken legs sure weren't natural. And Helmut told him nothing about August was natural, and he wasn't going to spend another dime on that son of a bitch, not even two cents.

Was August Jr. ever afraid of crossing over? Did he ever wonder what's on the other side? Was he in hell before, or after, or—what? There's no way he can be peaceful.

Helmut enters through the side door, calling for Ev. She's usually standing in the bay window, watching for him.

Silence. Unmoving, hollow.

He calls out again, hanging up his cane.

He switches on the tree lights. They begin winking, colorful as memories.

Helmut's heart falls ten stories, banging below his ribs till he can barely breathe.

In the bedroom, her side of the bed is unused. In the bathroom, her toilet articles are neatly arranged. Her sparkly scarves scratch his cheeks as he opens one closet. Her sixty-shoe rack bulges from the other. Her cream gloves are still in their satin-lined box. Her collection of music boxes is dusty.

Ev wouldn't leave him. No matter how bad the dirty rotten kid is, Ev would never leave him.

He stands in the living room till her tree lights begin doubling and blurring. He gazes out of the bay window. Snow is settling on the *Noel* sign, the one he painted for Ev.

The weight of the coming year presses down with the snow.

Maybe he should be glad she's no longer here. Together they'd outlive their savings and the little that comes in via Social Security—which he wouldn't have but for Ev talking him up, sending samples of his work to ad agencies, and invoicing his clients. Ev won't have to deal with the new guy acting like August Jr.: Loud on loving America, proud of never learning anything but how to cut people down. Destroying the hard work of all the folks Helmut fought for.

Helmut stands there a long time.

Please, Ev, tell me you're okay.

He turns the lights on at the top of the stairs and holds onto the railing. He descends, a step at a time, into the smell of linseed oil and Gamsol.

Yup, he still has a few primed canvases in his studio. He sets one on his easel, stares into its blankness.

He will dress her in viridian-green velvet. This time Ev's hand, freckled and wrinkled as he remembers it, will be reaching for his.

PART III

WHAT MADE MILWAUKEE FAMOUS

NIGHT CLERK

BY LARRY WATSON

Yankee Hill

Every goddamn night. Two or three o'clock the elevator doors open, and there he is. And for the next three or four hours, he sits in the lobby like it's his fucking job. Only it's not his job. It's mine. I'm the night clerk at the Whitcomb.

You've wondered about that? Yeah, the Whitcomb is a hotel, but it's nothing like the Hilton and sure as hell nothing like one of those get-your-ashes-hauled-here motels out on the edge of the city or a here-today-gone-in-an-hour drug dorm in the inner city where gunshots might interfere with your sleep. The Whitcomb is a residential hotel. People *live* here. Oh, we get a few guests who stay a night or two, go to the conference, get drunk or laid or both, and then go home. But mostly our people are here long term, like for months, as they try to get the books straightened out at United Widget or get the website up and running for Acme Industrial. And some people here are permanent, like year round. Oldsters whose kids don't want Mom or Dad in a nursing home but want someone to keep an eye on them. Or single working-women who come home after dark and want to walk into a well-lit lobby with someone at the desk to see that they're safe and sound. And if it's after midnight and before seven a.m., that someone is me.

I don't even do much checking in or checking out. Hell,

by the time I come on duty most of our residents are tucked in for the night. And nobody just walks in off the street. We're in a quiet neighborhood on Milwaukee's East Side, where there are more churches than bars. The Whitcomb. Like I say, where people live.

Except for the guy who comes down in the elevator every night. He's temporary. He came here to die.

But not at first. Initially, he came to live. To undergo a series of cancer treatments at our world-fucking-famous cancer hospital. But about a quarter of the way in, the doctors told him, *Sorry, no go. Not working. Might as well go home. Get your affairs in order.*

But he didn't go home, wherever home is or was. He stayed put. At the Whitcomb.

Where, from the wee small hours of the morning to the first blush of light in the east, he sits in the lobby in one of those creaky old green leather wing chairs. He doesn't read. He doesn't listen to podcasts. He doesn't play Angry Birds. He doesn't try to chat up the desk clerk like a couple of our resident insomniacs. He just fucking *sits*. Oh, and he smokes. Every half hour or so he goes out the front door, paces back and forth under the Whitcomb's awning, and puffs his way through one heater after another. Yeah. Cancer. And he smokes. What the fuck. Maybe if you got a death sentence, you'd light up too.

It goes on like this for weeks. He and I are practically the only ones up and moving in the Whitcomb at this time, but we don't say a word to each other.

How do I know so much of his story? Luther, the head of maintenance, fills me in. He was fixing the dude's radiator one day, and he sees a bottle of pills on the coffee table. And Luther, who's never afraid to enter where angels fear to tread, says, "Hey, my grandpa takes those. How are they working for you?"

The guy gives Luther the story. The special hospital, the special doctor, the special treatment. The failure. The future. Which he has practically none of.

"He's an interesting guy," Luther tells me. "You ought to talk to him. Bet you'd get along. Both of you got that same fucking look of doom."

"But I'm not dying anytime soon."

"Whatever you say, man."

Thank you, Luther. Remind me to feature you in my next novel. Except there won't be a next one.

Summer turns to fall, but this guy's wardrobe doesn't change. Cargo shorts, T-shirt, fleece vest, and flip-flops. And as the calendar pages fall, I can't help wondering, *How much longer for this guy?* Yet there he is, every night.

And that finally gets to me.

So, one night I come out from behind my counter and walk over to him. I'm standing there for a good minute before he glances up. Does he look like a dying man? Not really. He looks like maybe he was a linebacker thirty or forty years ago in high school or college. But still pretty damn fit. Big cask of a chest. Legs like tree trunks. A weightlifter's arms. A head so damn big and round you think it ought to bear Jerry West's silhouette. A week's worth of stubble, but what the hell does he need to shave for? His gray hair is cut close and sticks out from his skull like iron filings stuck to a magnet. But his skin looks as gray as a cloudy day. Or like a man who only comes out at night. And his eyes are sunk so deep you wonder if anyone's in there.

"Hey," I say. "You know what? You make me nervous sitting here."

"Yeah?" He gets up and moves six feet over to the other wing chair. "Better?"

"Not really. See, I'm wondering when you're going to finally fucking die."

If this pisses him off, he doesn't show it. He gives this sort of understanding nod and asks, "Why? What date do you have in the lottery?"

"No, man. Just my own curiosity. You're down here every night. I'm wondering if I need to be ready to do CPR or some shit. Like I say, I'm nervous."

"I'll tell you what. I'm giving you my own personal DNR. There. You're under no obligation. Better?"

"Yeah. Much." I turn and walk back to the desk, and when I sit down again, he's gone. Time for a smoke.

But then, two nights later, when he gets up from his chair he doesn't go outside. He walks up to the desk. He leans on the counter. I know he's there, but I keep staring at the computer monitor like I have work that needs my immediate attention.

He just waits. For a man who's on the clock, he's patient.

When I finally look up, I give him the standard front-desk greeting: "May I help you?"

"Who do you want to see dead?"

"Good question." Actually, *great* question. Right away, I decide I'm going to use it in the very near future. Maybe my new pickup line. "I want to say my stepfather, but he's so full of shit he'll probably keel over just from the weight of it any day now. So not him."

"It's not like three wishes," he says, his voice low and growly. Is that the cigarettes or the cancer? Or both? "Just give me a name."

"All right. How about Jenny Landry?"

"How about her?"

"Dumped me for a guy I introduced her to. So, yeah, Jenny Landry. I'd like to see Jenny dead."

He braces his hairy arms on the counter, stands up a little straighter, and says, "Jenny Landry. Okay. Let's make it happen."

I think I understand what he just said, but in this matter, you want to be sure. "What are you saying?"

He points a finger at me. "It's what *you're* saying, man. Jenny Landry, right?" He turns his head for a coughing fit that finally ends with him spitting a little American Spirit chunk of lung into his hand. But the coughing brings a little color to his cheeks. "What have I got to lose? I might as well try to do someone a favor before I check out. So, give me Jenny Landry's itinerary, and I'll see what I can do."

"Jesus fucking Christ," I say, "you're serious."

"As a heart attack," he says. He's got this wide mouth, so his smile makes me think of a wolf. He points to the Whitcomb notepad on the desk. "Write down what I need to know. Where do I find her? When is she there? That kind of shit. And what she looks like. Unless you want to come along on the expedition. You can point her out."

"Fuck, man. You're crazy."

He shrugs. "Just trying to find something to fill the hours." He pulls a pack of smokes out of his vest pocket and backs away. "Let me know when you're ready. But don't take too long." He flashes that wolfish smile again. "Jenny Landry, right?"

As soon as he's out the front door, I whip out my phone and bring up my photos of Jenny. Especially the one she sent me for my birthday. Sweet Jesus, I've never had a better present.

When she was moving out, I said to her, "Walk out that

door, and your body will be all over the Internet inside of five minutes. Within an hour about ten thousand men will be whacking off to that picture."

Jenny didn't miss a beat. "Go ahead," she said. "Get it out there. I'll never look better. Might as well preserve the historical record."

I couldn't do it. Not to Jenny. Not to that body.

By this time, Dying Man is back in his chair. I approach him, and before I can utter a word, he says, "Let me guess. You changed your mind."

I nod. "It's a big step," I say.

"The biggest." He shuts his eyes, and they're closed for so long I wonder if he's fallen asleep. Then he grimaces, and I can see pain must be scraping its way through him.

He opens his eyes, and for some fucked-up reason I don't understand, I say, "Sorry." Like he'll be hurt because he won't get to murder Jenny Landry.

"No worries," he says. "But maybe you've got a second choice? Give it some thought. But like I say, don't wait too long."

"Am I supposed to pay you for this? Because not only am I mostly broke, but I owe a fucking bundle in student loans. What do you want?"

He laughs. At least I think it's a laugh. It ends in another one of those wheezing, coughing jags. "What do I want? What do I *want*? Fuck, man. Figure it out. Nothing you can give me."

I don't need this dude mocking me, so I head back to the desk. I've only taken a couple steps, however, before it comes to me. I turn around and say, "J.G. Burch. Burch with a *u*. Professor J.G. Burch."

"Write it down," he says, and makes that writing gesture

in the air that assholes make when they're calling for the check. "Give me everything I need to know."

I'm tempted just to write the word *prick* and let him take it from there.

That wouldn't be enough, of course. But Jesus Christ, I could fill a couple of these pads with all the reasons someone should take out J.G. Burch.

First of all, he's the reason I'm here, behind the desk of the Whitcomb, so fucking far off the path I was on that I can't even see the way back.

I was going to be a writer of books, a novelist who turned out work that would make Stephen King's oeuvre look like fucking kiddie lit. Novels that would be a kind of thriller-horror-porno-literary hybrid, books that would need a warning on the jacket: *Beware, All Ye Who Enter Here.* The prose would dazzle the shit out of readers while it was turning their stomachs and turning them on. Cross genres? Fuck yes, it would cross genres. Bookstores would need to invent a new section to shelve these bastards.

And I was moving right along toward that goal. Toward that life. I was in an MFA program, not a top one, but what the hell. I just needed a few initials to put behind my name. It was the work that'd matter.

In the first couple workshops, my fiction got the reaction I could have predicted. Most of the dudes ate it up with a spoon. A few of the chicks didn't get it, but most of them put my work through their feminist filters and acted all offended. Not Jenny, though. Jenny said, "It's disgusting. I love it." Then after the first time we fucked, she said, "Well, that was vanilla. I thought from your fiction it would be, you know, filthier. Weirder."

Then the second year the shit hit the fan. J.G. Burch taught the workshop, and I was a fucking goner.

Burch wasn't someone they just pulled in off the street. He was the director of the MFA program, and its star, all because of this dainty little novel he published about a million years ago. It's a love story between a sailor and an old Chinese woman, all rendered in this poetic prose that's dense as a brick and understandable by about four critics. But apparently it was the right four because it's been right up there on the masterpiece shelf since it was published. (By the way, the sailor and the old woman? They never even fuck, as far as I can tell.)

Right from the get-go, Burch didn't like me. He called me *the rough-hewn* Mr. *Veller*, and the first time I had a story before the workshop he gave me the full treatment, complete with props and a reenactment.

In the story, sort of a *Blade Runner* homage but with more human-replicant sex and a desert chase on flying motorcycles, one of the humans gets his throat cut, and as he's dying he *blood-gargles his farewell to Fie*. (Fie's the replicant he's in love with, though in the story they're not replicants but cryptos.)

Before the discussion got going, Burch stood up and called for attention.

Burch is tall and super skinny, and he's like fifty or sixty with long, white stringy hair and crooked teeth that you see all the time because he never stops with his shit-eating grin. But for all that, women still dig him. I heard one of them say he's a David Bowie look-alike. Maybe in an alternate universe.

Anyway, after he stopped the discussion, he reached into the woven wool bag that he always carried instead of a back-pack or briefcase. He pulled out a water bottle that he'd filled with some kind of red liquid.

"I realize," he said, "this isn't the consistency of blood, but for the purposes of our demonstration . . ."

He proceeded to take a big swig, and then he tilted his

head back and, like he was gargling with mouthwash, he said, "Farewell to Fie! Farewell to Fie!" Only he didn't say it; he fucking gargled it!

The red liquid sprayed all over, and of course the class cracked up. And let me tell you, in a workshop, once they laugh at your fiction, you're fucking done for.

Naturally, after Burch's demonstration, there wasn't much in the way of discussion. A couple comments on whether the female crypto's behavior was *sufficiently motivated*. Noah Duggins wondered why the cycles had wheels if they could fly. Noah. Yeah. Who Jenny left me for. I should have seen all that coming with the fucking wheels remark.

Burch wasn't done, though. After the discussion gasped to a close, he looked around the table. He wasn't smiling. And sure as hell wasn't gargling. "The sensibility behind this piece is appalling." All around the room people nodded, like, *Yeah, just what I was going to say.* Right.

But there was still more to come. Burch gave me a C- in the course. A fucking C-! In a course where everyone was sure they'd get an A or, at the very worst, an A-. That pretty much finished me off in the program. Especially since I wasn't exactly tearing up the track in my other classes. And the classes I was teaching I'd canceled a bunch of times. The way I saw it, I was in the program to write, so that was what I was fucking doing—I was writing! I lost my teaching fellowship and the tuition waiver that went with it.

So, adios MFA program, hello to the Whitcomb.

But I swore I'd get back at that fucker. And I knew exactly how I'd do it. I'd keep writing, and I'd push my fiction even further. Darker, bloodier, sexier. I didn't need his goddamn class. I didn't need any class. When my first novel came out, all the articles would say, *Veller wrote most of his best-selling novel during the night, when he worked the midnight-to-eight shift at a hotel.* I'd leave out the part about the Whitcomb being a residential hotel. Let readers think I work in a bulletproof cage.

Except I couldn't. I couldn't fucking write! Every time I tried, I kept hearing Burch. *Appalling sensibility.* I had no idea what the fuck that meant. I mean, I knew what the words meant. Okay, okay, I had to look up *sensibility*. But I didn't know what they meant together. Or how to write another way. So I didn't do it. It's been almost three years since I put a word on a page. Who did I want to see dead? What took me so long to come up with Burch's name?

A couple nights later, when the elevator doors sigh open, and Dying Man strolls out, he comes right over to the desk. He holds out his palm and asks, "You got the information I need?"

I reach into my backpack and bring out the list I've written on the Whitcomb notepad. A pretty fucking long list, all under the heading, *Professor J.G. Burch.*

He takes a long time reading it. Then he nods, folds the paper in half, and puts it in the pocket of his fleece vest. "Where do I find him?"

"Where? Shit, he was my teacher! You can take him out in the fucking classroom, for all I care."

He gives me this long, baleful look. "Maybe you'd rather do this yourself?"

"Okay, okay. You know where the Black Star is? A bar on Brady Street? Burch always invites students to join him there after class. He buys pitchers for anyone who shows up."

Dying Man shakes his head. "Never heard of it."

"Brady Street?"

"Nope."

"Come on, man."

"What night does he usually have class?"

"I'll look it up for you."

"I got a better idea," he says. "Scouting expedition. We go to this bar together, and you point him out to me."

This is too much involvement for me, and I ask, "And then what? You take him out on the spot?"

I got to hand it to Dying Man, he sees right through me. "Don't worry," he says with a grin. "All you have to do is point. You can keep your hands clean."

A week later, Dying Man and I are at the Black Star on a school night.

It's a decent bar, one of a shit-ton on Brady, the street where the 1970s refuse to die, a few funky blocks of coffee houses, bars, cafés, and twenty-first-century versions of head shops—used clothing, posters, bongs, glass pipes, incense, tobacco, and vape. And the Black Star fits right in. It's got about a hundred beers on tap (but the college kids and the hipsters drink PBR), and the TVs are more likely to have soccer on than baseball or football. Like I say, a decent bar. Dark and lots of good-looking women.

But here's the thing. Burch thinks the Black Star's some down-and-dirty dive bar and he's living on the edge by going there. When he meets the class there, he all but tells the students to hold hands and stick close to him. Shit, there's a bar over in the Riverwest neighborhood I'd like to see him walk into. The first time he asked for a drink in that fake accent of his they'd pick his bones clean.

While we're waiting to see if Burch and his little ducklings show, Dying Man and I sit at the bar and nurse a couple of taps.

"Let me ask you a question," I say. "Have you ever done something like this before?"

"What?" he says, holding up his tulip glass. "Belgian beer?"

"Come on, man. You know."

"No. Never."

"What did you do before . . . you know."

"Before I took a room at the Whitcomb? I was on the legal staff for an airline."

"Legal staff? Like a fucking lawyer?"

"Just like."

"So if anything goes wrong, you could handle your own case?"

"I could," he says. "But I won't."

"No shit." I turn back to my beer. "A lawyer. A lawyer and a fucking assassin."

"Not anymore. I haven't paid my bar association dues."

"I suppose you can just say fuck it to just about everything, can't you?"

He sips his beer. "That's right. Dying doesn't have a hell of a lot to recommend it, but it's good for that."

I'd told him that Burch and his fiction seminar would probably show between nine thirty and ten, and Dying Man keeps looking at his watch—gold number about the size of a hockey puck. Keeping track of the time. Yeah, I bet dying's good for that too.

Just when I'd started to worry that maybe Professor Burch had changed his ways and no longer took his students out for drinks, he walks into the Black Star, a posse of four adoring students trailing close behind. They make their way to a table in the back like they have a reservation.

"Okay," I say to Dying Man, "that's him."

Dying Man swivels slowly on his stool and, like an old

gunfighter, watches Burch. Then he turns back to his Belgian beer, satisfied, I bet, that he could take that skinny son of a bitch without a problem. Shit, I felt it myself every time I sat in his fucking classroom.

He says, "All right. I know his type."

"And what type is that?"

"Victim." He drains his beer. "I've seen enough." He pulls out a money clip, peels off a twenty, and drops it on the bar. When he heads for the door, everyone steps aside.

Then he stops on the sidewalk right outside the Black Star. The poet might have thought the fog came in on little cat feet, but here on Milwaukee's East Side it rolls in like smoke from the fucking artillery. In a few minutes, you can't see anything above a building's third floor. Dying Man lights up a cigarette and exhales his own little cloud.

For the first time he offers me one from his pack, but I wave it away. "Let me ask you something," I say. "Why're you doing this? If you want to go out in a blaze of glory, why don't you get yourself an AK-47 and start blasting away?"

"How do you know I won't? And then your professor would just be collateral damage."

I don't say anything. We've started walking now, on our way to the Whitcomb and our nightly ritual. He smokes. I watch.

He finishes his cigarette and flips the butt into the street. "If you think this is about the killing," he says, "you obviously don't understand a goddamn thing. I'm doing you a favor. You still don't get that? You want something done, you can't do it yourself, so I'm doing it for you."

"You plan to do anyone else a favor?"

"That remains to be seen."

* * *

That night, he doesn't come down to the lobby. Damned if I don't miss the bastard.

He doesn't show the next night either. Or the next. Or the next.

Naturally, I start to worry. Nobody told me anything about the guy in 322 checking out—or, you know, checking *out*—but what the hell.

On the fifth night, I ring his room. No answer. Now I'm thinking, *Shit, he's lying dead up there*. Unless his body starts to stink, nobody's going to notice anything unusual. That's the thing about the Whitcomb. You live this close to your neighbor, you respect his privacy. Nobody goes knocking on doors without an invitation.

That's when I resolve to do something that'll cost me my fucking job if I get caught.

I take one of the pass keys and go up to his room.

Now, if you're thinking this is all about Professor Burch and my lust to see him dead, you're wrong. It's not about him at all, not anymore. In fact, I've decided that if Dying Man is there, I'll tell him, *Fuck it, the deal's off, it's not worth it. You don't want to spend the rest of what time you got left worrying about being busted for murder.*

Before I put the key in the lock, I look up and down the hall. Plenty of the busybody old farts at the Whitcomb have nothing better to do than watch for someone breaking one of the ten thousand rules here.

I turn the key and push the door open. The first thing that hits me is the smell. No, no, not a body in decomp. Cigarette smoke. The son of a bitch hasn't always been stepping outside for a smoke. He's been smoking in here. I'm surprised someone hasn't complained. The Whitcomb is damn near a hundred years old, and its ventilation system isn't the greatest. Someone takes a shit in one room, you can likely smell it all the way down the hall.

The only light in the room comes from the street, but that's enough for me to see. Nobody's here. The bed's made, but Dying Man hasn't checked out. On the nightstand are a few magazines, *Car and Driver*, *Wired*, and a *Playboy*. Kind of sad. A fleece vest on the chair. Some empty San Pellegrino bottles by the sink.

Hasn't checked out? Hell, maybe he's in a hospital, dying faster or already dead. I had the impression that nobody's looking out for him, so who'd let the Whitcomb know that 322 won't be coming back?

I no longer think I'm going to trip over a body, but I go into the bathroom just to make sure.

Not much there. An open toilet kit on the back of the sink. I can see a couple prescription bottles in there, and I take them out, thinking maybe there's something I can avail myself of, courtesy of Dying Man. Nothing there says it's for pain, so I put the bottles back. I don't need anything that'll give me the shits.

There's a smell here too. Old Spice. Sadder.

I check the closet. A suitcase and a duffel bag on the floor, and a suit and a white shirt hanging on the rack. Maybe those are what he wants to be buried in.

The room is chilly. I check the window, and it's open a few inches. Probably Dying Man's attempt to air out the room, so he doesn't get caught smoking. On the other hand, what the hell does he care about getting nailed for some petty offense? After all, this is a guy who's willing to murder someone just because someone else wishes him dead.

Outside, the fog has settled in again, and from the third floor it looks like smoke is trying to find its way back inside. I close the window.

I leave Dying Man's room, still wondering where the fuck he might be.

Two days later I have my answer. Sort of. I don't know exactly where he is, but I sure as fuck know what he's been doing.

All the local channels lead off with the story on the nightly news. Professor found dead in parking lot outside his apartment building. Bludgeoned to death. No suspect in custody. No apparent motive. Not a robbery, police say. University releases a statement condemning the act of senseless violence and going on about how respected and well-liked Professor Burch was among colleagues and students. And just in case the locals aren't hip to the fact that a real celebrity lived and died in their midst, the dean of Burch's college blathers on about how the professor's fiction has won a boatload of awards and how his reputation is not only national but international. Blah-blah-fucking-blah. And nothing a news anchor, cop, or colleague says is anything but a cliché, something I could have tossed off at a minute's notice. Except I could add that I know who did the deed.

Dying Man. Jesus fucking Christ. Now I hope his room is empty, and he's gone for good. Either out of Milwaukee or out of this life. I don't care. Just don't let me see you walk out of that elevator again. Though I'd sure as hell like to know what he did the bludgeoning with. Tire iron? Wrench? Golf club? Baseball bat? I personally like the idea of athletic equipment over tools.

Now, ordinarily, a story like Burch's would last through a few news cycles. Not because he was a murder victim. Shit, people are murdered in Milwaukee every day. But this victim was white, an East Sider, a university professor, for Christ's sake. They never get themselves killed, no matter how much they might deserve it. You can almost see the drool as the reporters give us details about the tragedy. Yeah, a real fucking tragedy. You never hear that word when the victim is Devonte over on the northwest side. But then Burch gets elbowed off the news after only a day by just about the only story that could give the media a bigger hard-on than the good professor's: murder and sex. A local cop busted into a motel room and shot his wife and her lover right in the middle of the act. And the wife was a mother too. Sordid *and* tragic. An unbeatable combo. Officer is now in custody.

That night I go up to Dying Man's room again. Nothing seems changed from my previous visit. Open toilet kit and prescription bottles. Smell of cigarettes and Old Spice. Fleece vest. The bastard is either in hiding somewhere or dead, and at this point I don't much give a shit.

When I come back down, I walk out of the elevator and see two men standing at the desk. One of them has my little *Back in a Minute* sign in his hand, and he's examining it like it's some sacred fucking text. They're cops. I spot that right away. What other men go around in pairs, both of them wearing ugly sport coats that don't fit and ugly ties that look like they're choking them? (And don't say Mormons.) I'm willing to bet that the white shirts under those jackets are short sleeved.

"What can I help you with?" I ask. "Officer," I add, so they don't think I'm just some vampire stooge who can't do anything but a night shift.

But, of course, I know why they're here. Dying Man fucked up somehow. A witness saw him, or he dropped his fucking driver's license at the crime scene, or he left his fingerprints all over the lead pipe he used to bash Burch's head in, and the cops traced him back to the Whitcomb. But what the hell am

I supposed to do? *Sorry, Dying Man, your name's on the register.*

It takes me about two seconds to suss out the cops' play. It's not good cop, bad cop; it's yakky cop and silent cop. The one who won't shut up is short, bald, and has a little head that looks like a tennis ball balanced on a bowling ball. The tall dude has a Lurch-like jaw.

After all the *Hey, how's it going, isn't that fog something, they've really kept this old place up, haven't they?* bullshit, the short cop gets to it. He takes an index card out of his shirt pocket, looks at it longer than he looked at my hand-lettered sign, and peers up at me. He pronounces my name slowly and then smiles like he just solved Fermat's fucking theorem.

"That's me," I say.

"We'd like you to come down to our place," he says. "Have a little chat."

Our place. Cute. But I'm not having it. "Sorry," I say. "I'm the only one on duty here. I can't leave the desk. But I can stop in tomorrow." I straighten a few card keys on the desk. "If you tell me what this is about."

"No worries," the short cop says. "We got it covered. Your manager will be here any minute, and he'll watch the store for you."

Walters? Walters is coming in? What the *fuck?* "Maybe," I say, "maybe you better tell me what you want to talk about."

Lurch has a manila envelope, and he reaches inside and pulls out a baggy. He holds it up carefully, like dog owners hold their plastic bags of dog shit. His voice is nothing like what you think it'd be. It's high and flutey. "This your handwriting?" he asks.

Even through the plastic, I can tell what's inside the bag. It's a sheet torn off one of the Whitcomb's notepads. And written across the top is J.G. Burch's name . . .

Fuck! Dying Man, what have you done?

Just then, Al Walters, the Whitcomb's manager, comes rushing through the front door, shaking his head all the way. He's got his suit on but no tie, and his hair is pointing north and south. He needs a shave. The cops got him out of bed.

"Come on out of there, big guy," the short cop says sweetly, a remark that doesn't have a goddamn thing to do with my size. "We'll go somewhere quiet and talk."

Even if I want to run, there's nowhere to go. I'm trapped behind the desk. Besides, Lurch has already got the cuffs out.

Mr. Walters and I brush past each other. I'm going, he's coming. He doesn't look at me or say a fucking word as we pass.

If you have to be arrested, try to have it happen at three o'clock in the morning in the lobby of the Whitcomb. Nobody's standing around staring. Nobody's saying, *Isn't that—? No, it couldn't be . . .*

The police have their car parked right out front in the loading/unloading zone. Well, fuck, why not? They haven't been more than ten minutes in the hotel, and they could have cut it shorter without the goddamn small talk.

The night's cool and clear. The fog that's been wrapped around this part of the city like gray cotton candy has lifted. Nothing to keep you from seeing for miles.

But I'm only looking across the street. Someone's standing there, right where he can see the whole fucking show coming out of the Whitcomb.

The short cop has his hand on my arm, but barely, like I'm the controller for a video game, and it takes just a light touch to make things move the way he wants them to. Hell, I know where we're going.

Lurch has the back door open, but just before I duck inside, I ask the short cop, "Hey, can you take these cuffs off me for a second? There's something I need to do."

"No can do, big guy. Sorry. No can do."

"Can you do me a favor then? See that guy across the street? The smoker in the fleece vest? Would you give him the finger? Please?"

The short cop laughs. "Yeah," he says, "I can do that."

And he snaps off a bird like he's flipping a cigarette into the street.

THE CLEM

BY JAMES E. CAUSEY

Lincoln Creek

"What the hell happened to Becky?" Lou said to his best friend Jay.

"What are you talking about, Lou?"

"I had to get to school early because I couldn't make up detention, so Ms. Reed let me do detention this morning, and I saw Becky go to the principal's office, and it looked like she was in a fight or something."

"Not Becky, she's not a fighter."

"Exactly. Maybe that's why she looks the way she does," Lou said. "I know you like her and all, Jay, but she looked like she went fifteen rounds with Muhammad Ali."

All the excitement with whatever was going on with Becky had the kids riled up. Papers were strewn about their laminated school chair desks, paper airplanes whizzed past Ms. Reed's perfectly coifed Afro. Lou popped a green husky pencil against Jay's #2 blue rubber special.

"Class, I need for you to be quiet," Ms. Reed said. "Lou, turn around in your seat before I add another twenty minutes to your detention. Or do you want me to call your mom?"

"I was just . . ."

"You were just what, Lou?" Ms. Reed said. "Remember what got you detention before?"

The fifth grade homeroom at Samuel Clemens Elementary School burst out in laughter because they'd all heard Lou bragging for a week about how he accidentally saw Vel's mother in just a short robe when she was coming out of the shower. She'd had no idea Lou was in the living room waiting for Vel to find his homework assignment.

What had started as an innocent mistake quickly turned into Ms. Vel giving Lou the eyes and even blowing him a kiss and opening her robe to give Lou a full show. Of course, everyone knew this didn't happen, but it didn't stop Lou from making up the story anyway.

"I was talking about Vel's mama," Lou said. "I apologized, Ms. Reed. Vel knew I was playing."

When Ms. Reed had heard Lou telling the story to several sixth graders, she quickly gave him ten hours of detention and made him write on the wall five hundred times: *I will not lie about my classmate's mother*. Even worse, she made Lou apologize to Vel's mom.

Vel interjected: "You called my mama a ho. And you said—"

"Vel! We don't have to go there again!"

None of this mattered to Jay. He was worried about his crush, Becky. Who did she get into a fight with, and did she really get her pretty little face messed up? Jay loved how Becky's freckles scattered perfectly across her rounded cheeks and the slope of her symmetrical nose. Her eyes, a piercing brown, were amplified by the curliness of her hair. One tendril in particular always found its way into her eyes. Jay found himself lost in them whenever he and Becky were around each other. Jay had had a crush on Becky since third grade. Becky had played the role of Pocahontas in the school play, and Jay had played the role of her love interest, John Smith.

When classmates teased them about being a couple, Becky would frown and say, "I don't like that bucktoothed boy."

Jay's feelings were hurt, but it didn't stop his burning desire.

"Ms. Reed, can I go to the bathroom?" he asked.

"Jay, you know I'm about to start class."

"Please, Ms. Reed. I really have to go."

"Can I go too, Ms. Reed?" Vel asked.

"Let me guess, you have to go really bad too?"

"No, I have to throw up," Vel said.

"Okay, both of you have five minutes," Ms. Reed said.

The boys headed into the hallway. They walked quickly past the bathroom and toward the principal's office to see what had happened to Becky. There were two police officers—one man, one woman—standing in front of the door with their arms folded. The boss could see Becky crying and shaking her head behind the big glass window. She talked to a petite dark-haired officer and Principal Carl. The officer appeared to be comforting Becky; her hand was draped around Becky's quivering shoulder. Principal Carl stood to the side of the officers, rounded at the shoulders, his large hands clasped in front. The frown flanked by his thick, dark goatee couldn't hide the troubled look on his face.

Becky had suffered many misfortunes as of late. Her parents had recently split up, and her dad had relocated to California. Classmates acted like they didn't notice, but Becky's mom began to drink heavily after the separation. They also noticed when Becky's hygiene started to slip, and her normally gorgeous curls had become dry and tangled. But Jay had on rose-colored glasses; none of that mattered to him.

As Jay tried to crane his neck to look past the imposing male officer, the man asked, "Can we help you?"

Vel nervously said no, but Jay asked what had happened to Becky.

"That is none of your business, young man. Shouldn't you be in class?"

Before Jay could say another word, Vel grabbed his arm. "We are leaving right now, officer."

Walking back to class, both boys could not believe how rough Becky looked. "I guess Lou was right," Jay said. "I wonder who she got into a fight with."

"Are you crazy, Jay? That's more than a fight."

Vel had a wild imagination. He was fascinated with movies, mostly horror. He loved *Halloween* so much that he went to see it three times but hid his face during all the scary parts. Jay preferred martial arts films, like Bruce Lee's *Game of Death* or Jackie Chan's *Spiritual Kung Fu*.

"They never have the police come up to the school unless someone got killed or something. I'm guessing she got beaten up by an adult, or maybe she got attacked by a wild dog."

"I don't think there are any wild dogs on 38th and Hope, Vel," Jay said.

"Maybe not, but something got her."

As they opened the door to Ms. Reed's class, Lou was at the board writing, *I will not talk in class.*

Vel smiled and took his seat. Jay silently mouthed to Lou, *What did you do now?* Lou motioned his head toward Rachell, who was known for cracking on classmates and pulling just as many pranks as Lou.

Before Ms. Reed could tell Jay what he'd missed, the classroom phone rang. She took the phone and walked out into the hallway. While some of the kids tried to hear what Ms. Reed was saying, Lou started dancing wildly at the chalkboard while Rachell popped rubber bands at his head.

"Class, be quiet, please," Ms. Reed said, ducking her head in the room. "Lou, sit your . . . down!"

When Ms. Reed came back into class, her smile was gone. "Class, I need you to please pay attention. Becky was hurt today on her way to school this morning. Her mother is up here now."

"Who beat her up, Ms. Reed?" Lou asked.

"She wasn't beaten up, Lou. A man in a black ski mask grabbed her."

"Was he white or black, Ms. Reed?"

"I don't know, Lou, and what difference does it make?"

"Well, I need to know who I need to be worried about on my way home. Was he a creepy black dude? A creepy white dude? A creepy Indian dude? A creepy African dude? A creepy—"

"That's enough, Lou," Ms. Reed said. "A letter is being drafted to go home with you tonight to give to your parents."

Jay raised his hand. "Ms. Reed, is Becky going to be all right?"

"I hope so. But this is where we need you. All of you. To be a friend to her. I know that some of you have known Becky since she started going to school here in kindergarten—"

Ms. Reed was interrupted by the sound of the chime for the school announcements. Today wasn't a second grader reading off the school lunch menu. Instead, Principal Carl came on.

The class looked up toward the dusty brown loudspeaker hanging in the right corner of the room. Principal Carl's gruff voice instructed all students to walk in pairs to and from school and to pay attention to anyone and anything that seemed suspicious. He assured everyone that the police were confident about locating the perpetrator quickly and that there would be extra patrols in their neighborhoods until further notice. He firmly told them not to speak with media and to direct them to him.

"Ah, man, I want to be on TV," Lou blurted out.

"Do you want to go see Principal Carl, Lou?" Ms. Reed said. "Before you leave here today, I want all of you in pairs. So please start partnering up now, because it doesn't look like we are going to get any work done today."

The students moved around in class like worker ants; Lou, Jay, and Vel linked up. Rachell tried to join, but Lou put a stop to that. "Where do you think you're going?" he said to her, standing in front of the other two boys.

"I'm joining your group. Jay lives two houses down from me."

"I don't care. There are no girls in this group. Especially ugly ones like you," Lou said, patting himself on his big belly. "On second thought, maybe you can join the group and scare him away if he comes after us."

Rachell put her hands on her hips and made a loud smacking noise. "If some crazy man starts chasing us, you'll be the first sacrifice since you're fat and slow."

Vel laughed and Jay told Rachell that she could join the group.

"Look, y'all, this is serious. I saw Becky, and she didn't look good. We have to watch out for one another, and that goes for you too, Lou," Jay said.

"Man, she started it. Because of her, I had detention added on top of my other two detentions," Lou said.

"You got detention because you are always trying to rank on somebody. You need to stop with your tight shirt on. Your shirt is so tight that the General Lee car is stretched into a limo," Rachell cracked.

"Forget you, girl, with your egghead," Lou fired back.

"See, that's what I'm talking about. I swear, you two crack on each other like an old married couple," Jay said.

"That's because they like each other," Vel added.

"Like your mama likes me."

Vel raised his hand and announced, "Ms. Reed, Lou is over here talking about my mama again."

"Man, stop being a tattletale."

"Lou, this is your lucky day. Due to the unfortunate cir-cumstances, I'm going to have to suspend your detention. But you will be making that time up when this situation is rectified."

Lou put on a sad face and then turned to Vel. "You see, crime does pay."

"You are such a punk," Vel said under his breath.

"But your mama loves this punk."

Several parents came up to the school to pick up their chil-dren. Riding home in a warm car was a welcome treat for many children who otherwise would have had to walk home in twenty-five-degree weather. The North Side neighborhood of short ranch-style homes did little to shield them from the swift winds. When the weather was warm, though, the tall trees on both sides of the streets high-fived each other, shad-ing their mischievous walks home.

Although it was a blended neighborhood, the whites and Germans didn't like blacks moving into the area. They feared that their property values would go down, so they only talked to other whites. Becky's parents were the exception. She was the first kid Jay ever met with a black mother and white father. Most of the kids at school didn't have a problem with it, but many of the black parents did. Often, they referred to Becky as the "biracial girl" or "half-breed." Jay's parents spoke this way too. The only difference was they'd add the word "cute" in front of it, like that made it better.

When Rachell's mother picked her up, she offered a ride

to Jay, but he passed, electing to walk home with his friends.

"I can't get a ride?" Lou said.

"We would give you a ride, but my mother said you need the exercise," Rachell told him.

"Man, I hate that girl," Lou said.

Walking home, the boys noticed police cars on nearly every other block. When they started passing the football around, an officer in one car honked his horn and told the boys to quit monkeying around and get home.

"Dangit! My mom's probably going to keep me in the house all weekend," Vel said.

"What you complaining about?" Lou said. "At least you're an only child. You won't be trapped inside with four older brothers and sisters bossing you around."

"What about you, Jay?" Lou asked. "What are you going to do?"

"I don't know. I'll probably catch up on my homework, and if my parents let me, I may go to Becky's house and see how she's doing."

"Look at you," Lou said. "You hoping that you can comfort her and protect her from the boogeyman and maybe get a kiss or something."

Jay just shook his head and kept his mouth quiet until he got to his block.

"I have it from here," he said while reaching for his house key tied around his neck. "No need for you guys to come out of the way."

"Nah, we should at least make sure that you make it home," Vel replied.

"Man, forget that. It's cold out here, let's go," Lou said, blowing hot breath on his cold hands.

"I'll be fine," Jay assured. "I'll call you over the weekend."

As the boys went in their separate directions, Jay detoured toward Becky's block. There were three squad cars in front of her house. He hoped Becky would be okay. She'd been through so much lately.

When Jay reached home, he grabbed the bills out of the mailbox, then unlocked the door. He dropped his book bag on the floor, turned on the floor-model television set for background noise, and headed to the fridge. He pulled the red plastic ring from around the bologna before placing two slices in the skillet and coming into the front room to see what was on.

"We interrupt your program to bring you a special report. A Milwaukee public school student was attacked on her way to school this morning by a man wearing a black ski mask. The youngster, who attends a school on the North Side, escaped her captor by fighting and clawing herself to freedom. We will bring you more when information is available. Now, back to your regularly scheduled program."

This is serious, Jay thought. The chime of the fire alarm snapped him from his trance. Jay rushed to the kitchen in time to salvage his burned bologna when the house phone rang.

"Hey, Jay, this is Mama. I heard that something happened at school today. Are you all right?"

"Yeah, Mom, I'm fine. It was Becky."

"Are you talking about that cute little biracial girl around the corner? Oh Lord! Is she okay?"

Word around the neighborhood was that Becky's father had left home to be with a younger woman. A white one. Becky's mom was taking it hard from the looks of things. She was usually drunk on the rare occasion kids saw her getting mail out of the mailbox.

"She's pretty shaken up, Mom, but I think she'll be fine. At least, I hope so."

"Anyway, I just wanted to tell you to be good. You father is working a double shift tonight, and I will be home after six. I need to stop by JCPenney on the way home. There's bologna in the fridge."

"I know. I'm making a sandwich now."

"Okay, well, don't be all up in that TV and burn the house down."

"I'm not." He opened the windows to let the smoke out.

"I love you, Jay."

"Love you too, Mom."

"Gotta get back to this assembly line now."

"Over the weekend, Milwaukee police arrested eight men who they believe could be possibly connected to the attempted rape and abduction in Lincoln Creek. We will have more details during our noon broadcast," a news announcer reported, breaking into Monday-morning cartoons.

"Well, I guess that's good news," Jay said while eating generic cornflakes in front of the TV.

"Jay, I'm going to drop you off at school this morning, because I don't know if they got this guy yet," Jay's mother Ruth said as she was getting dressed for work. Jay couldn't turn his attention from the TV. He was worried that this masked rapist was still on the loose. "Rachell's mom told me that Becky was down at the police station this weekend and couldn't identify any of those men they brought into custody."

Over the weekend, Lou and Vel had stopped by Jay's house. They all had their own conspiracy theories on what had happened. Lou heard that the man was preying on little kids because he was an escapee from the mental institution.

His oldest brother had told him that the guy's goal was to catch little kids, behead them, and place their skulls as trophies on his mantel made from human bones.

"I heard she's coming back to school today," Ruth said. "I sure would like to know why she was over by Lincoln Creek anyway. That's five blocks out of her way to go to school."

Vel had heard that the masked man was a former Clemens student who drowned at the school, but his ghost was reaping revenge on anyone who went down by the creek all alone on the first day of winter.

"Jay, are you listening to me?"

He stared at the TV, not really paying it any mind. He was a million miles away, thinking about Becky. Wondering if this assault gave her nightmares. Had she been able to sleep?

"Well, what did I say?" Ruth asked.

"You asked me if I finished my homework."

"Boy, that's not what I said. Go in there and get ready so I can drop you off at school," Ruth repeated.

"Mom, I really don't need a ride to school. My friends are coming this way, and we're going to walk to school together."

"Are you sure?"

"Yeah, and I know you don't want Vel and Lou in the car."

"Vel I don't mind, but that Lou is always eating chocolates or has something sticky on his hands. I wish you would stop hanging out with him."

"But Mom, he's my friend."

"A friend that stays in trouble."

"I know, Mom."

"Well, call them and see when they're going to get here." She motioned toward the phone before grabbing her car keys and hurrying out the door.

When Vel and Lou rang the doorbell, Ruth had barely made it down the block. Jay was ready to head out the door when both pushed past him into the house.

"What the—" Jay exclaimed.

"This man was chasing us!" Vel said.

"Stop lying," Jay said.

"We're not lying." Lou braced his hands against his knees as he tried to catch his breath. "He had on a ski mask and overalls."

After a few minutes, the boys saw him running past the house. They peeked through the curtains at the man, who carried a lunchbox and thermos. When he got to the corner of the block, he flagged down a city bus.

"Look at you two scaredy cats. He's catching the bus for work. He's probably going to A. O. Smith."

"Come on, man, we're already late for school," Jay said. "We gotta go."

"Look, the way we got it right now with this masked guy on the loose, the teachers don't care about us being late for school. We can just say we took a different route because we were scared. Or we can say we saw the Ski Mask Rapist," Lou said. "As far as I'm concerned, I plan on milking this all the way to the bank."

"I don't think this is anything we need to be playing around with," Jay said.

"Who's playing? Shouldn't we try to benefit from this?" Lou replied. "It already got me out of detention. Maybe it can get me a double lunch at school too."

"All right, guys, let's get out of here," Jay said, forcing Lou to get up off the couch.

"Before we leave . . ." Vel started.

"What is it?"

"Don't show him," Lou said, as Vel took a hammer out of his backpack.

"Man, what is that for?" Jay asked. "You know we can't bring weapons to school."

"It's for the Ski Mask Rapist," Vel said. "I'm not letting anybody take my bootie."

Lou opened his backpack and showed them a blue-handled switchblade. Jay's eyes widened. "I took this from my brother's room. He doesn't need it anyway."

"You know your brother is going to kick your butt when he finds out that you took it," Jay said.

"Jay, you need to bring something. Just in case."

"I don't have anything."

"Don't your daddy have a gun? I know he has a gun around here someplace," Lou said, running to Jay's parents' room and dropping on his knees to look under the bed.

"Man, get up," Jay said, trailing him.

"There's a box right there. I can't reach it," Lou said. "Vel, you're smaller."

Vel crawled all the way under the queen-sized bed and came out on the other side covered with dust bunnies.

"Man, your parents need a maid," Lou said.

When the boys opened the shoebox and removed some old rags, they saw a gun.

"What kind of pistol is it?" Vel said. "Is it a .38?"

"Naw, don't be stupid. It's too small to be a .38. This is a Saturday Night Special," Lou said, holding the gun in his hand. He acted like it was a toy and not a weapon capable of killing them all. "My Uncle Kenny had one just like it."

"Man, put it back," Jay said.

As he tried to get the gun from Lou, Vel stepped in the way. "Jay, stop it. We need to take this gun for our protection.

Becky is going to be coming back to school this week. Maybe, just maybe, you can walk her home and be her knight in shining armor with this in your backpack."

"Where did you get that corny line from?" Lou teased, still holding onto the gun.

After further pestering to get the gun back, Jay finally agreed to put it in his backpack so they could leave. Beads of sweat had formed on his brow. He didn't like guns and knew his mom would bury them all if she knew one had been found in her house.

On the walk to school, the boys passed several squad cars. Each time, Jay felt like he was about to get arrested.

"Man, stop being so nervous," Lou said. "We are the only ones who know you got it. Remember, we are The Clem, and we ain't gonna let anyone mess with us."

"The Clem?" Vel said.

"Yeah, The Clem."

"How did you come up with that?"

"I don't know. Every gang needs a name," Lou said.

"So now we're a gang?" Jay said.

"Well, kinda. We hang out together, and we watch each other's back. That kinda makes us cool, and a gang. Now watch us get mad respect."

As the boys arrived at school, Rachell's mother pulled up next to them in her maroon Cadillac and dropped off her daughter.

"Hey Jay, hey Vel, hey Fat Albert," Rachell said before heading inside to get out of the cold.

"So much for respect," Jay said under his breath.

After two weeks, the news of the Ski Mask Rapist intensified. There were more sightings and rumors of possible attacks, but nothing confirmed.

Becky was back in school, though she still refused to talk about the incident. Meanwhile, Lou was back in detention, so things seemed to be returning to normal. More students resumed walking to school, and the heavy police presence tapered off.

That didn't stop the boys from carrying their weapons. Jay had become so comfortable with the gun in his G.I. Joe backpack that he almost forgot it was there. Being a member of The Clem even gave him a bit more confidence to talk to Becky.

"Okay, class, your assignment this weekend is to write a report on your favorite holiday and what makes it special to you," Ms. Reed said. "I will even let some of you team up to work on the project together, but together means *together*. That means I don't want to hear about one person doing all the work and two people putting their names on it. Is that understood?"

Lou raised his hand.

"Yes, Lou?"

"That's not fair!"

"What's not fair?"

"It's not fair that one person can't kick back and let the other person do all the work. My mama said that's what the presidents of companies do all the time."

"That's observant of you, Lou," Ms. Reed said. "That's why you will be doing your assignment by yourself."

Rachell started laughing.

"Is there something funny, Rachell?"

"No, Ms. Reed."

Over lunch break, Lou, Vel, and Jay sat at the end of their lunch table while Jay glanced down at Becky, who was at the cool table.

"Man, don't do it," Vel said.

"Do what?"

"Remember when she called you bucktoothed?"

"That was a long time ago, and I've grown into my teeth," Jay said.

"But you haven't grown into that gap," Lou said.

"I'm going to go over there and ask her if she wants to work on the project with me."

"Wait, I thought we were going to work on the project together," Vel said.

"If she says no, we will." Jay got up from the table and walked toward Becky.

After a few minutes of chatting and laughing, Jay came back to his friends with a frown on his face.

"Man, I told you she thinks she's better than everybody else because she has good hair and a nice body," Lou said.

"So when do you want to get together to work on this paper?" Vel asked.

"She said yes."

"Wait, what?" Lou said.

"She said we can work on the paper together," Jay said, revealing the gap-toothed grin.

"My boy! I knew you could do it," Lou said. "She heard about The Clem."

"I'm going to walk her home from school today."

"No fair! She's not part of The Clem," Lou said.

"Guys, I want to walk her alone."

His friends gave him five as the bell sounded, ending lunch.

Saturday morning, Jay walked over to Becky's house to work on the project. The house was clean but mostly empty.

When they sat down at the kitchen table, Becky told him they needed to keep their voices down because her mother was still sleeping.

"But it's eleven," Jay said.

"Since my father left, she doesn't get up until noon, and sometimes it's later than that."

The two worked on the paper and finished quickly.

"I know you don't want to talk about what happened, but—"

"I really don't want to talk about it," Becky said.

When her mother finally came downstairs in her half-opened housecoat, she looked in the fridge without acknowledging Jay. "Damn, there ain't shit here to eat," she said. "Becky, I need you to go to the Capitol Foods up the street and pick up a few things."

Jay cleared his throat, startling her.

"Aren't you Ruth's son?" she asked.

"Yes, yes, I am. My name's—"

"Your mom has a big mouth," Becky's mother cut him off, lighting a cigarette. She poured herself some liquor. "Her and all those other cackling women on 42nd Street. Tell your mom to mind her own damn business."

"Okay," Jay said, a bit scared.

"Becky, get your ass up now. I need you to go to the store," the woman said, handing Becky a twenty-dollar bill before heading back to bed.

Becky started getting up to put on her shoes.

"You want me to go with you?" Jay asked. "I mean, that guy is still out there."

"You can if you want," Becky said while she put on her gloves and scarf.

As the two headed toward the door, Jay grabbed his backpack.

"You're not coming back?" she asked.

"I will, but I just like taking my bag."

As they walked the six blocks to the store, it started to snow. Becky didn't say anything. There was an awkward silence and Jay broke first.

"I hate gray days," he said.

"Yeah, I do too. Look, I'm sorry about what my mom said. She runs everyone away. Including my dad."

"Have you talked to him, you know, since he left?"

"No. He just left without any explanation . . . Did I do something to upset him? How could he leave me? My mom? Does he even care? You'd think after what happened, he'd be rushing home."

Jay remained quiet but took Becky's hand. She accepted.

At the store, Becky stretched the twenty dollars and bought enough for both to have bags to carry back to the house.

The two had just made it to the sidewalk in front of Becky's place when they spotted a man in a black ski mask next to the house. The guy came up on the porch and twisted the lock. Jay handed Becky his bag of groceries and reached into his backpack.

"Who is that?" he asked.

"I don't know," Becky said.

They cut down an alley around the side of the house. Becky held onto Jay's coat, while he kept his hand in his bag. The man was now beating on the door.

Jay approached on the right side of the porch, and the masked man turned toward him.

"Who are you?" the guy asked.

"Stay back."

Suddenly, the door opened and Becky's mother shrieked.

The man moved forward. Jay pulled his hand from the bag and heard a loud pop.

"Call the police!" Becky's mother slurred, a small pistol shaking in her hand. The man fell off the porch.

Everything went silent except for Jay's heartbeat. He willed his feet to move, but everything felt like it was going in slow motion. He walked slowly up to the man, who wasn't moving. Blood pooled out from under him.

Jay reached for the man's mask, and when he pulled it off, Becky screamed, "Daddy!" She pushed past Jay and lifted her father's head.

Becky's mom stumbled slowly to her husband and put another bullet in his chest.

THE NEIGHBOR

BY NICK PETRIE

West Allis

For Gordon Myles, Easter Saturday is the first Saturday of the year for lawn care. The snow has almost certainly gone until next winter, although in Wisconsin you never know for sure. But the ground has drained enough not to sink underfoot, and the grass has just begun to turn from brown to green.

Newly sixty, wearing faded khakis that bag in the knee but have not yet begun to fray at the cuff, Gordon opens the garage and removes his tools one by one from their designated hooks, their labeled shelves and racks and bins. He sharpens his edging shovel and shears with a file. He fills the mower with the proper mix of oil and gas, then pulls the cord until the welcome roar echoes down the street, trailing the sweet smell of two-stroke engine exhaust. He drinks his first two outdoor beers of the new year.

While Gordon puffs and pants and otherwise embraces his agricultural heritage, Milner, his next door neighbor, slouches on his unpainted front porch in a ratty folding chair with his feet up on the railing, reading a magazine whose name Gordon can't make out. Milner's lawn lies lumpy and brown and full of thistles, dandelions, and creeping Charlie, but there he sits, reading while weeds grow. As with a car accident or any other man-made disaster, Gordon cannot look, but he must. Just the sight of it gives him chest pains.

In May, Gordon rents an aerator for anyone on the block to use. He picks it up in his minivan and fills the barrel with water from his hose. It passes from neighbor to neighbor, and Gordon makes sure to do the older ladies' yards as well. He rolls it across each green lawn in turn, the machine's hollow spikes plucking neat cylinders of dirt and root mat from the compacted earth, leaving the tubular deposits to break apart and disperse into the rich grass. Milner just sits on his porch and reads.

"Aeration," Gordon calls out to Milner as he wheels the clunky machine across the driveway. "It gives the worms room to move," he says. "Room to breathe, really. And healthy worms make a healthy lawn."

Milner does not respond.

"I'd be happy to do yours too," says Gordon. "I have to cross it anyway to get to Mrs. Hansen's house."

Milner shrugs in his chair. Scrapes his hand across his stubble. "Fuck the worms," he says. "They can wait until I'm in the ground."

Gordon pushes the aerator across Milner's yard, just one row, then across his driveway to his own yard. At least Milner's worms will have a little breathing room there amid the thick, hairy roots of weeds. Gordon finds himself feeling sorry for Milner's worms. Maybe they've all died. It's that or they've made the long stretch across the driveway to Gordon's own well-watered and fully aerated lawn.

Two weekends later, Gordon is out with the Weed & Feed, rolling the spreader back and forth, the wheel carefully kept in the track made on the previous pass, to ensure an even spread. An even spread is important to Gordon. He has extra in the machine, he tells Milner. He'd be happy to make a pass around his neighbor's yard, just to use it up. It never goes back in the bag very well, always makes a mess.

"It's just Weed & Feed," says Gordon. "I'd be happy to do it."
Milner refuses. "I don't believe in pesticides," he says.

Doesn't believe in them? Gordon shakes his head. Milner might as well say he doesn't believe in the stock market, or gravity. Just look at Gordon's lawn if you want to see the value of chemicals. A shining expanse of emerald perfection.

Late one Saturday night in July, Gordon can't sleep. He gets like that after four or five gin and tonics. Restless. His hands and legs twitch on the couch. He paces in the living room, the old wooden floors squeaking underfoot.

Until a few years ago, when wakeful after midnight, he'd walk across Greenfield Avenue to the county golf course. He'd stride the sculpted fairways and feel the glorious turf beneath his feet. But when budget cuts reduced the maintenance crew, the roughs grew tangled with knotweed and clover. The ponds became clotted with algae. Even the thought of it makes Gordon want to weep, and he is at loose ends again.

Now he paces past the neat stack of mail that Rita has taken from their neighbor's mailbox at Milner's request. Milner has gone away for a week. An opportunity for charity has presented itself. With liquid clarity, Gordon steps outside, shirtless and stealthy in the warm midnight air, and unlocks the side door of the garage. He quietly takes out the spreader and the Weed & Feed. Turns the handle to maximum and makes a double pass across Milner's wasteland tract.

Gordon doubles up his hoses to get his sprinkler over to Milner's lawn, using his own water to give the wasteland a good soaking. He sits on one of the expensive lawn chairs his wife had to have, watching the sprinkler sweep back and forth. Mesmerized by the steady motion. Ice from another gin and tonic rattling in the glass.

He wakes in the chair at first light, back aching, his mouth like a pickle jar. Milner's lawn is a mud pool. He scrambles to collect his hose, hide the evidence. Stays inside all day watching golf. He tells Rita he's sick.

"A hangover is not sick," she says. "It's your own damn fault."

Gordon's neighborhood has bigger homes on bigger lots, but West Allis is mostly a working-class area, a series of narrow rectangles laid side by side, end to end. A place to get a foothold for the climb up. Or dig in your fingernails against the slide down.

Gordon laid out a good sum for his new roof, three years back, which included an unexpected chimney rebuild that took the vacation savings too. So, instead of their week up north, Gordon repainted his windows. Rita complained, of course. "Eternal vigilance," Gordon reminded her, "is the price of freedom." But where Gordon used to love these chores, the endless painting and caulking and glazing, in the last few years he's noticed that he mostly just enjoys having finished them. That, and the gin and tonic afterward.

Rita always thinks they should just hire somebody. Rita's not much of a saver, and Gordon has a hard time conveying to her the reality of their situation. Which is that machine tool sales is not what it used to be, and never will be again, especially not for a man just turned sixty who never truly had the backslapper's knack. Who now wants nothing more than to never have to manufacture another smile again.

Still, the house is perfect, no expense spared. The kitchen gleams with steel and polished granite, and in the bathroom, three kinds of Italian tile. The tile-setter's minivan was newer than Rita's, with heated leather seats, he said. Gordon saw him flirting with her on two separate occasions. Gordon didn't say anything at the time. Though he wonders still if he should have.

But now Gordon has a nice clean place to unclench his fisted bowels. His legs still fall asleep when he sits on the throne for too long, that hasn't changed. And when he stands, feet on fire, he has to clutch the spindly but expensive towel bar and try hard not to fall down. To pull the whole thing down with him.

Milner's house, on the other hand, hasn't been painted in over a decade, and the roof looks like one of those West Coast moss gardens. The windowpanes are filthy, some even cracked, and the porch is settling in one corner, a little more each year. Gordon has never been inside, and drawn shades block the sidewalk voyeur's gaze. He imagines tomato plants sprouting from the dirt on the unswept floors. Feral cats hissing on the mantel.

Gordon and Rita have lived on the block for nearly twenty years. It is a sociable block, with much visiting back and forth, and Gordon especially is often consulted on matters of lawn care. But Milner does not join in the streetside conversations, does not attend the impromptu cocktail hours. He does not discuss his personal life. Nobody knows what, if anything, he does for a living. He's either unemployed or works at home, for he comes and goes at all hours, day and night. Nobody now living on the block has ever been past the front door. He's fifteen or twenty years younger than Gordon, never clean-shaven, always wears torn jeans and a shirt with the tails hanging out. And clean white jogging shoes, though Gordon has never seen him move faster than a slow shamble. He owns a rusty out-of-date BMW but is rarely seen driving it. Instead, he rides his bicycle, a shiny intricate mystery, in almost any weather, even January if the streets are free of ice. He has an old wooden crate strapped to the back and fills it with groceries and library books and God knows what else. He wears a tiny blue plastic helmet when he rides.

When Milner returns from his July trip, he doesn't seem to notice the apocalyptic wasteland that is his overwatered yard. At least he does not mention it, even in passing, to his neighbors. Several times Gordon has to bite back a comment, restrain himself from pointing it out to the man. Or reminding him that if he'd let Gordon aerate his yard, the drainage would have been much better. But Gordon can't decide whether it would incriminate him or absolve him from suspicion. In the end, he says nothing.

Oddly, the weeds and scrub grass that constitute Milner's lawn do not seem to suffer from the flooding or the pesticides, but take it in stride. The weeds especially seem to profit from the fertilizer. By the end of the month, the dandelions are up to Gordon's knees, and full-grown thistles shake their spiky purple heads at him like the insolent teenagers who gather outside the convenience store where he gets his gas.

Gordon and Rita's own four children are gone, long out of college now, though the loan payments still linger. They live in the four corners of the country, as if to get as far as possible from their parents and each other. Rita insists on visiting each of them once per year and insists that Gordon accompany her. Gordon rolls his eyes but does not complain. Even such an obtuse specimen of his generation knows that there is more to these trips than a visit to the children, though it must be discussed in this way. Undisturbed, the marriage would settle to the floorboards of the house like dust, and Rita fusses over their travel details for months. It's unending, really.

As part of this ongoing program, Rita plans a trip to Atlanta over Labor Day weekend to visit their youngest son, Mark. She sends for golf course layouts, restaurant menus, and museum exhibition brochures. She even buys new underwear. Gordon flips through the folders at dinner, picking a golf course at random. Any museum is fine as long as it has a headphone tour and he can leave before happy hour.

Mark meets them at baggage claim. He is twenty-seven, smiling, bouncing on the tips of his sneakers. His dark hair falls past his shoulders, and he has clearly not shaved for several days. He wears a small silver hoop in each ear, ancient paint-spattered blue jeans with holes in the knees, and the most beautiful black sport coat Gordon has ever seen. Rita takes the sleeve between her thumb and fingers, feels the fabric with an appraising rub, and raises her eyebrows at Gordon.

Mark carries their bags out to his car, a new European station wagon with power everything and paint smears on the leather upholstery. The boy has never done a real day's work in his life, having squandered his out-of-state education on an art degree. Gordon despaired for him, he really did. Then Mark sold a painting of a coffee cup to a national chain of coffee shops, which turned into a commission, which started the avalanche of money that makes Gordon embarrassed, proud, and jealous all at the same time.

Rita loves to talk about her son, the successful artist. But the whole thing makes Gordon feel like he's been thrown from the Tilt-A-Whirl. If Mark could make that kind of money with a single sale, more than Gordon will ever again make in a year's time, what has Gordon been doing his entire life? What about the long chain of decisions that has left him adrift in this place he now finds himself? And which was the choice that would have made the difference? In 1967, Gordon wanted to be a bossa nova sax player. He was going to move to Brazil after graduation. Share his bed with a dancer, a long-limbed, brown-skinned cabaret girl he would meet on the beach. He took a part-time job stocking a warehouse to save money for the plane ticket. But he never got on the plane. Here he is, almost forty years later, stuck in an unraveling suburb, sales manager to a dying industry.

Mark was sweet and dreamy as a boy, either staring out the window or finger painting on the kitchen floor. Now he has a website and an assistant and an airy loft apartment larger than Gordon's house. Gordon watches his son deftly scoop up the dinner check at a restaurant Gordon himself can't afford; his youngest son has somehow become a wide-shouldered man of the world. And Gordon knows that his son no longer has need of any help he might actually be able to offer.

Then there is the matter of Britta, Mark's girlfriend. She is Swiss, speaks English, French, German, and Italian, wears a crisp and cool white blouse and a short black skirt, and looks like Ingrid Bergman. Rita adores her, asks for translations from the menu. Gordon can't look away from her legs. He is so glad to be heading home.

When they pull into the driveway, Gordon sees the fragments of brick on the cement. He doesn't even take the suitcases from the minivan, he just runs up the stairs to the bathroom window, which looks out on Milner's chimney. He can see the gaps where the brick has calved off like an iceberg in warm weather. Shrapnel in a scatter on the shingles. Rita stands below in the driveway, struggling alone with the luggage, calling out to her husband, but Gordon does not hear.

He has talked to Milner about this before. Told the man that his damn chimney needs tuck-pointing, even rebuilding.

And now the proof is here on his driveway, plain as day. What would it take, the minivan crushed under the fallen chimney? Or just Gordon, prone on the driveway, a brick-shaped dent in his head?

He pounds on Milner's door, but there is no answer. Rita has thrown up her hands and gone inside, leaving the luggage where it lies. Gordon hesitates for only a moment before stomping down Milner's driveway, in gross violation of accepted protocols, to look through the side-door glass, which gains him nothing. He sees clean carpet, a bathroom door half open, the toilet lid down. No mounds of filth, no feral cats. A surprise, really.

In Milner's backyard, he stands precariously on a cheap aluminum lawn chair to peer through the windows, shading his face with his hands. The kitchen counter shines, not a dish out of place. The rectangular dining table is taken up with unfathomable computer equipment, wires arranged in tidy bundles. The hardwood floor gleams with polish. A brassiere hangs from the chandelier.

This last detail lies somewhere beyond comprehension. Gordon imagines Milner in women's clothes, performing a striptease for himself before his computer. He has heard about these things, and what people can do on the Internet, though he is not a computer person himself. Or is the brassiere simply a bachelor's decoration, a relic from his younger life, when women's underthings were exotic rather than a nuisance of laundry? Rita hangs hers from the shower door to dry twice a week, and Gordon, who is invariably first in the bathroom each morning, must take them down and tuck their gauzy folds into Rita's dresser, a task he now realizes that a) he resents, and b) has long ago removed the last pale shreds of mystery from his wife's underclothes.

Rather than dwell on this, his own shriveled life, he wonders what size the hanging brassiere might be, and if it would fit Milner's frame. But recognizing this thought in progress and its logical outcome, in which he might find himself actually picturing his neighbor Milner dressed in women's underwear, he tries desperately to halt this process but, shifting his weight on the lawn chair, feels his foot slip through the elastic bands of the seat.

He falls. Arms spinning like a cheap garden windmill, he falls.

He lands flat on his back on the hardpan that is Milner's yard, *woof*, the air somehow vanished from his lungs. Lost behind a wild, unpruned shrub, foot still tangled in the chair, his shoulder on fire, he kicks to free himself, but the chair does not come off. The clouds float overhead. His legs tire so easily. He feels like a turtle that some child has flipped onto its shell. A cartoon turtle wearing glasses and a tweed coat with elbow patches, weakly waving his extremities rather than taking real action to right himself.

His heart thuds in his chest. Rita has been after him to exercise. He should exercise, he should. He'll join a gym. He'll take up racquetball or something. He looks up through the leaves of the unpruned shrub he cannot name. It is an autumn bloomer with shocking yellow flowers. Lovely, really.

He lies there for a while, resting. It's not so bad down there. He's starting to get used to it. Then he hears an engine in Milner's driveway. Straining, he peers up from his place on the ground as the car noses past the house toward the moldering garage. It is a convertible, old and layered with dust, and though at first Gordon is not sure because he is upside down, he does know the car. It is a 1967 Mustang. He had a color poster of this car, a beautiful car, hanging in his own garage as a young man, a car he once planned to buy. When Rita got pregnant they got a used station wagon instead.

The convertible top is down. Milner lounges in the passenger seat, arm hanging loose over the top of the door, his head back, laughing. On the seat beside him is a woman, dark hair and a white shirt with creamy skin showing at the vee. Deep lines bracket her mouth as she talks. Her teeth are a little crooked, but that makes him simply want to touch them with his tongue. There is no mistaking the brilliant smile, the brightness of her eyes, the new shine held aloft there between Milner and this luminous dark-haired woman.

And at that moment, still mostly hidden, his foot entangled in the webbing of the overturned chair, Gordon Myles finally feels something. A sympathetic understanding at the rage of a dumb machine, rusted in place. *He* is rusted in place. A blue flame ignites in his mind. He wants to burn down Milner's house. Set fire to that beautiful car. Call in an air strike on the whole goddamn block.

No. Burn down his *own* house, with Rita and her enormous underwear still in it. Move to Brazil, find a big loft apartment. Buy another saxophone.

He will do anything.

He will change! He will change! He will change!

WONDERLAND

BY MARY THORSON

Cambridge Woods

Nancy knew that the river had always been dirty. She didn't know what was underneath. She didn't know about the junked rides from the old amusement park. How the rails of the Milwaukee Motorway twisted through the mud and would occasionally disappear underneath the layer of shifting sediment. How the Ferris wheel lay out broken on its side, and how the river bottom grew up around it, making six muck caves out of the cars where things could hide. She didn't know about the electrical tower, fallen over and studded with shattered lightbulbs, cutting through the bend of the river like a broken bone.

As Nancy watched a police officer zip into a black rubber wetsuit, she couldn't help but feel filthy and polluted. She had never really been friends with the Kings, but she wondered if they thought the same. She had the occasional glass of wine on their back porch, and they invited her for dinner, but she often denied them. Nancy wasn't the only person down by the river, but she tried to stick close to the trail in case she needed to hop on and start walking. She wasn't as brazen as the people who were right up on the yellow tape, she thought. But that wasn't true. She had seen the police moving quickly down the trail behind her house, and she had followed them as if it were any of her business.

It was close, which surprised her, even though she knew she shouldn't be surprised. If it really was Jessica, she wouldn't have gone far—that's what the Kings had said at the press conference where Melissa smiled so much. That had been noticed. Could a four-year-old know about running away? Did they remember how to get places?

A few people there had come from the beer garden holding half-filled liters. They were the generally curious, naturally responding to some activity near them. The way Nancy waited by the trail was pretend. If anyone asked her what was going on, she would lie and say, *I don't know, I was just walking by.* She imagined Jessica's red hair and how it would float underwater, away from her, reaching out like strands of pale fiberglass lights dimmed by the dark. The river was good at hiding things.

The morning that Jessica had gone missing, Melissa showed up at Nancy's door.

Nancy had gone out the night before, and a man she couldn't quite remember meeting was sleeping in her bed. He had black hair all over his back, and she was afraid it might stain her sheets. She wasn't thinking clearly. She prepared herself to be yelled at. Their houses were unfortunately close, with the Kings' kitchen window lining up perfectly with her bedroom window. Had they been too loud? What things did she scream when the man fucked her? She thought of Linda Blair in *The Exorcist*, and she squinted her eyes even though the sun didn't hit her face. But then Melissa smiled.

"I'm sorry," Melissa said. "I'm sorry to bother you, but we can't find her."

"Who?"

"Jessica. She's not inside. You haven't seen her? Or maybe she stopped by?"

The suggestion was farfetched; Nancy only ever waved at her when Jessica screamed "Hi!" from the front lawn. Jessica seemed frustrated when she did it. Indignant, attention-seeking—Nancy could relate. But this had only happened when Nancy and Jessica were awake and moving in the world at the same time, so once or twice. They had never formally met. Suddenly, Nancy heard a man scream somewhere close, and she thought it might be the strange man in her bedroom, but it was Joe, calling out Jessica's full name. Her middle name was Joy, and it was strange hearing that word shouted in desperation.

"Oh," Nancy said. "No, I haven't seen her. I've been asleep."

"She was in her room, and I took a shower. I thought Joe was up, but he fell asleep on the couch. He's been sick."

"Right."

"Anyway, she was gone when I came back in."

The zipper on Nancy's sweatshirt hit her bare skin, and the cold startled her. "Here, let me get a coat on, and I'll come help you look. I'm sure she just went to a friend's house."

"Thank you so much," Melissa said. "We'll be in back of the house, or near it. If you want to walk up and down the block and knock on a few doors, that would be great."

Nancy didn't want to do that.

She went back into the house and stood at her kitchen window that overlooked the trail. She stared at the dark pavement, then into the trees and bushes, until she forced herself to go into her bedroom. She opened the door slowly, though he was already sitting up and rubbing his neck as he faced her closet. He still had his clothes off, and she couldn't stop staring at his back.

"Hi," she said.

"Oh, hey," he said, turning to look at her. She wished he wouldn't.

"So, my neighbors can't find their kid."

"Huh."

"I was going to help them look for a bit," she said.

"Let me just get some clothes on, and I'll go with you."

"No, you don't have to."

"It's fine, can't hurt to have more people out there. What's her name?"

Nancy thought for a moment, but there was no good way she could tell him to go home, that their transgression had ended. They went outside together, one going north and the other south.

"Skip the pink house," she called out to him, and he nodded, scanning the rest of the houses as if he were counting them. She wondered what he did for work.

She finished before him. At first, she believed this was a good thing—efficient. But while she waited on her cement steps, getting more uncomfortable as her jeans let in the cold from the ground, she felt nervous. Did her strange man find the girl? Did he meet up with Melissa or Joe and rejoin them already? Had she missed it? Finally, she saw him, walking back with his hands stuffed into the pocket of his hoodie. He looked defeated.

"Nothing," he said.

Before he left, he asked her to let him know what happened. If they found Jessica, he said. Her name came out of his mouth without any hesitation, which put Nancy off. He was just a stranger, after all.

The police came later, around dusk. One parked in the Kings' driveway, and the other drove around the neighborhood, slowly. They both had their lights on but left their sirens off, and it looked very strange, as if they had been muted. One of the officers showed up at her door, asking again if she had seen Jessica. Nancy told them no, but that she had helped search for a while that morning.

"And did anything come from that?"

She was embarrassed. "No," she said.

"Well, if you see her, or think of anything, give us a call." He handed her a card and walked to the next house, where the couple she had met earlier, and still couldn't name, waited at the door.

The neighbors gathered in front of the Kings' house that night. They had flashlights that kept sweeping into Nancy's house. She watched as they went to the trail and then back into the woods and brush, their lights streaming and blinking in and out. Nancy didn't think she had a flashlight.

She showed up to the first official daytime search party. They met in the middle of the street; this way, Melissa said, if people wanted to get through they would have to ask what was going on. As if they didn't know already. Jessica's picture was somehow already everywhere, printed with the concrete details of her person, everything she could have possibly been: *Age 4, strawberry-blond hair, blue eyes, 40 inches tall, 39 pounds. Last seen in her room.* They ran her face on the news, with Melissa still smiling and talking beside it. "She loves animals," she had said.

"Okay, everyone!" Melissa shouted to the crowd. Nancy didn't know how many people were there, she was never very good at guessing how many gumballs were in the jar, but the crowd was large. "These are the places that Jessica knows!"

She handed out maps with playgrounds and the grocery store highlighted in fluorescent pink. Her handwriting was perfect as if she were replying to a wedding invitation instead of writing down the spots her missing daughter had frequented. *Jessica liked to watch the dogs here,* with a beautiful X crossing over the dog park. It took a moment before Nancy realized that Melissa was giving directions. She talked too fast and then trailed off. As Nancy watched her, she noticed that one of Melissa's eyes kept drifting. When Melissa finished, she clapped her hands together, and Nancy expected her to jump in the air.

"Let's go, everyone! Let's find our girl!" But Jessica wasn't their girl.

The search party numbers rapidly declined. The news conference had changed things. Nancy woke up to the noises that morning, the loud murmuring outside of her small house. She half opened her eyes, squinting as her contacts squeezed them tightly. Her TV was on, but the volume was low, too low to be the source of the sound. Then she saw the side of her house on the screen and instinctively put a hand over her face.

She went to her front window and spread the blinds with her fingers. A massive crowd spilled over onto her lawn from the Kings' front porch, where Melissa was holding a piece of paper and a cupcake, and Joe stood behind her, looking down. Nancy ran back to her room and watched.

"Hey, everyone! Thank you so much for coming today because it's a very special day today. Wow, I'm saying that word a lot." Melissa laughed. "But today is Jessica's fifth birthday, and we just wanted to let everyone know that we haven't forgotten, and we want to celebrate with you all."

She started singing and held the cupcake out in front of her. She interrupted herself after the first "Happy birthday to you," and said, "Come on, help me out." That's when Nancy could hear them from her bedroom, a slow and awkward song that sounded more like people talking at once than singing. Joe kept his mouth closed, though he started swaying back and forth a little. There was a two-second delay, and at the end, she heard a few of them clap before she saw Melissa blow out the candle.

"Take a bite," Melissa said, handing it to Joe.

He waved it away without even glancing at it.

She laughed, then said, "Does anyone else want it?"

Nobody said a word, and most of them turned their heads away.

"Well, can't let it go to waste," she said. She took a big bite, without restraint. The frosting stained her teeth instantly.

The first snow came just before Christmas, and the flyer taped to the cement light pole outside Nancy's work was slipping. Jessica's face had started to warp. The top of her head was protected under the layers of scotch tape, and you could see the part in her hair, but her cheeks and nose had melted. You could still see the row of baby teeth between her lips. Nancy thought about taking it down and replacing it later, but the idea of touching it made her wipe her hand down her coat.

The restaurant was small, and the smell of garlic hit her first thing as she walked in the door. She hated it now. There were only a handful of people dining, which was as many as there ever were. Inside the glass menu case at the front was another flyer, this one well-preserved and hanging perfectly straight. On it, you could see that the sundress Jessica was wearing had red and yellow balloons on it, floating up toward her neck.

Nancy took a basket of bread over to a two-top and set it down. While she arranged the oil and vinegar and placed the small plates in front of two faceless people, she half listened to their conversation about how much homework their kids had. In the beginning, any mention of children would dredge up Jessica's name. "Those poor parents," and, "I can't imagine." The phrases that flow out of people's mouths when they're automatically responding to something while thinking about something else. *You can imagine, of course you can*, Nancy would think. *It's not difficult.*

Once, a woman had told the other woman she was with that she would never have bought a house so close to the river. "It's like living on a busy street," she said.

"I live next to the river, and it's fine. Beautiful," Nancy had said.

The woman was taken aback and leaned away from her. "Do you have kids?" she asked.

"Sure," Nancy said. They didn't leave a tip.

By mid-December, a month after Jessica disappeared, the conversations had changed, and the phrases were altered. "But those parents," and, "Can you imagine?" They didn't whisper this like they had before. They didn't treat their words carefully.

When she got home one night, she pulled into her driveway and her lights caught something in the distance. Melissa was walking away from her house, and Nancy could only see the pale skin of her back as she disappeared down the small hill. It was like seeing a ghost. Nancy got out of her car and ran over to the edge of her backyard, but she couldn't see Melissa. She shouted her name, but the sound of it reminded her of Joe's "Joy!" and she clapped a hand over her mouth. She stood as the snow fell over the tops of her shoes, hitting her socks and skin.

She had forgotten how she met the strange man, but he was apparently a bartender working a few blocks away from her house, and that made sense—Nancy didn't like to go too far. She hadn't gone out in a while; the winter forced her inside like a mouse. He was playing bar dice when she walked in, and he slammed the shaker down hard enough that the sound bounced off the door that had closed behind her. He saw her before she could turn around, and he smiled. She gave him a small wave and walked up to the bar.

"Hey there," he said, coming over to her.

"Hi," she said. "How are you?"

"Good. What can I get you?"

"A PBR is fine, thanks."

"Tallboy?"

"Sure."

He turned and bent over to get in the fridge. His shirt lifted up, showing the small of his back, and Nancy closed her eyes.

"Your friend's playing pool," he said.

"Sorry?"

"Your neighbor, you know . . ."

Then she saw her.

Melissa smiled and threw her head back as she touched the arm of the man at the pool table with her. He was barely a man—he looked young. The two of them together made it seem like Melissa was a young mother with her adult son.

"I called you a few times." He smiled.

"I got a new phone," Nancy said. She never answered numbers she didn't know, though she wouldn't have answered if she did. She dug her nails under the tab and kept watching her neighbor.

Finally, Melissa saw her, and she waved before running over. She smelled like hard alcohol and perfume. "Nancy!" she said. "How are you? I haven't seen you in a long time."

"Melissa, are you okay?"

"Actually, I'm thirsty. Let's have my friend get us some drinks." She waved him over, furiously. "Nancy, this is my friend Zak. He's an art student like I was. Look at his hands!" She grabbed them and pushed them into Nancy's face. They were stained with blue paint in the nail beds and the creases between his fingers. His hair was long and brown; he had an unkempt beard and muddy eyes.

"I was thinking we could head back soon." He leaned over Melissa, saying it into the top of her hair.

"He's going to show me something he's working on. Do you want to come?"

"Melissa, do you think that's a good idea? I mean, wouldn't Joe worry about where you are?"

"It won't take too long."

"Why don't you stay for a while?"

"The building's going to close soon," Zak said.

"I think we're going to go now. But it was good seeing you." Melissa said the last part as if she were leaving a party at someone's house because she was tired.

"No, wait." But before Nancy could get off her stool, Melissa was already at the door. When she got outside, she saw Melissa running, a block down, holding her shoes in her hands and laughing as her breath steamed out of her mouth.

Nancy went home with the strange man whose name was Rob. This time, things were clearer, though she was good and drunk. There were no animal noises, no demonic screams, and they both kept their shirts on. Rob, the strange man, left before she woke up.

When spring came, everyone waited. If someone went in while it was cold, the river held onto the body until the temperature rose. The gasses expanded, causing it to become buoyant and float up to the top like a dead fish. Nancy looked through her blinds when she woke up and went to sleep as if she were checking an alarm. Yet nothing changed. After the grass had grown to an embarrassing height, Nancy rolled out her lawn mower one afternoon but couldn't get it started.

"It's out of gas," Joe said. He stood behind her on his side of the dip between their lawns.

"Right," she said. "Shit."

"I have some in mine. I'll bring it over and take care of it."

"No, no, don't worry about it. I'll run over to the gas station and fill the thing up."

"I'll be right back."

Joe's arms shook as he cut the yard. He started sweating around the collar of his shirt and in his armpits, even though the lawn was small. Finally, when he finished, he let the bar snap back from his hands, keeping them rested on the handle.

"Thank you," Nancy said from her seat on the steps. She was apprehensive about going up to him.

He nodded, breathing deeply. "Melissa's been acting strange," he said abruptly.

Nancy stared at him. He wasn't looking back; he narrowed his eyes at his house.

"I'm sure it's hard," Nancy said.

"She walks around the house at night, she can't sleep. I can't sleep either, but she's talking to herself. She comes back to bed in the morning, and she's not wearing anything, but when I look, I can't find her clothes. I don't know where she's putting them . . . You should see her sometime. She could use a little, I don't know, distraction. Maybe you could take her out? The house is hard for her. She doesn't like to be around here." He twirled his finger around.

"Okay. Sure," Nancy said.

After they brought Jessica up, the police gave an update. They said there was no indication of foul play, and she had died from drowning brought on by hypothermia. They didn't say that her muscles tore after twisting in the cold. They said her body had gotten stuck down there, but didn't elaborate. There was no mention of the Ferris wheel.

Nancy fell asleep early that night, but she slept fitfully as she dreamed of being underwater for too long. When she snapped her eyes open, she was facing the wall and noticed a rectangle of light cut up in lines. She turned and saw Melissa in her kitchen, sitting at a table with a drawing in her hand. She wasn't looking at the drawing, but instead stared out the sliding glass doors into the dark. It was a messy picture, on a piece of tan coloring-book paper. A pair of blue and green horses stood side by side. Jessica's name was smeared over the top; she had painted it with her fingers, leaving prints all over. Nancy suddenly wanted to call the man from the bar and tell him that they'd found her, but she didn't know his number.

The next morning, she woke up and saw Melissa with her head down on the table and her arms spread out in front of her, almost unnaturally long. It scared Nancy, and she hit the glass with her palm. Melissa didn't move, and so she did it again—in rapid succession like a large bird trying to get into her house, or out of it. Melissa shot up in the chair, her face red on one side with the crease from the table leaf cutting through her cheek. They stared at one another until Melissa got up and walked to the sliding doors. Nancy crawled out of bed and walked to the back door. Melissa stood in her yard, looking toward the river.

"I'm sorry I scared you," Melissa said.

"No, it's fine. I just thought . . ."

"I know. I think I scare everybody, all the time."

"I'm sorry," Nancy said, and before she could stop herself, she added, "I can't imagine."

"Do you want to take a walk with me?"

Nancy walked with her down the Oak Leaf Trail; they went slowly and started drifting closer together. Melissa stopped and turned left into the woods on a smaller, unmarked dirt trail that took them both down to the river. There, a long pile of rocks reached out into the water like a makeshift pier.

"It's like dying but staying alive, even though you're all dead, every part of you," Melissa said.

"I'm sorry," Nancy said again.

"They found her underneath a Ferris wheel. There's old rides down there from an amusement park that used to be nearby. They just threw them in the river when they closed the park. I wish they'd kept it. It would have been nice to have that kind of thing close."

Nancy thought of wet and rotting roller coasters, all of the cars sloshing with mud as they jerked along the track.

"We never even took her to the fair. Is that funny? I took her here, to this spot. She named it, but then kept renaming it. I don't know what it was last," Melissa said.

"I'm sure she loved it."

"She must have been so cold. I tried to understand," Melissa said. She picked up a small rock from the water and held it in her hand before she put in her pocket. "No one's out here. No fishing or kayaking. Seems strange, no?"

"You're right."

Nancy walked to the last rocks, letting the water creep up on her feet. Maybe people were afraid to go in. To fall or get caught up in something they couldn't see. The park was bigger than anything they thought could be beneath them. The rides could float up, dirty and bloated just the same as Jessica. Underneath the muddy brown surface were long, twisting tracks; carousel horses that had once been colorful bared their teeth; and fallen towers covered in shattered light-bulbs rested in wait. Somewhere, too, there was an iron gate that said, *Welcome to Wonderland*. Nancy didn't want to know what was down there. She didn't want to see underneath.

ABOUT THE CONTRIBUTORS

SHAUNA SINGH BALDWIN is a novelist, playwright, and short story writer. Her awards include the Writers' Union of Canada Prize, the CBC Literary Prize, the Friends of American Writers Prize, the Commonwealth Writers' Prize for Best Book (Canada and the Caribbean), and a short-listing for the Giller Prize. Her seventh book is *Reluctant Rebellions.* Baldwin received her MBA from Marquette University, and an MFA from the University of British Columbia.

JAMES E. CAUSEY is an award-winning columnist and special projects reporter for the *Milwaukee Journal Sentinel.* He received his BA in communications from Marquette University in Milwaukee, and his MBA from Cardinal Stritch University in Fox Point, Wisconsin. Causey was also a 2007–08 Neiman Fellow at Harvard University. He is married and has one daughter.

CHRISTI CLANCY grew up in Whitefish Bay and now lives in Madison, Wisconsin, where her yard is woolly, wild, and pesticide-free. Her work has appeared in the *New York Times*, the *Washington Post*, the *Chicago Tribune*, the *Sun Magazine*, and in *Glimmer Train Stories, Hobart, Pleiades, Midwestern Gothic*, and elsewhere. She teaches English at Beloit College.

REED FARREL COLEMAN is the *New York Times* bestselling author of twenty-eight novels including stand-alones and those in his Moe Prager and Gus Murphy series. He is also the current author of Robert B. Parker's Jesse Stone novels. He is a four-time recipient of the Shamus Award and a four-time Edgar Award nominee. He is currently writing the prequel novel to director Michael Mann's movie *Heat.*

VIDA CROSS'S book of poetry *Bronzeville at Night: 1949* was published in 2017. She is a Cave Canem fellow, a 2018 Pushcart Prize nominee, a graduate of the School of the Art Institute's MFAW program, and a Chicago native who teaches and resides in Milwaukee. Her work has appeared in a number of anthologies including *Creativity & Constraint, 1963–2013: A Civil Rights Retrospective, TAB: The Journal of Poetry & Poetics, Cave Canem Anthology XII: 2008–2009*, and the *Journal of Film and Video.*

Leslie Brown

JANE HAMILTON'S novels have won literary prizes, been made into films, have been international best sellers, and two of them, *The Book of Ruth* and *A Map of the World*, were selections of Oprah's Book Club. Her nonfiction has appeared in various magazines and anthologies. She's married to an apple farmer in Wisconsin, and has a relative who lives in an Abbot Row house in Milwaukee.

Gaetano Catelli

DERRICK HARRIELL is the director of the creative writing MFA program and associate professor of English and African American Studies at the University of Mississippi. He is the author of three collections of poetry: *Cotton*, *Ropes*, and *Stripper in Wonderland*. His essays and book reviews have been published widely.

Lucien Knuteson

TIM HENNESSY is a bookseller and writer who lives in Milwaukee with his wife and son. His work has appeared in *Midwestern Gothic*, *Tough*, *Crimespree Magazine*, and the *Milwaukee Journal Sentinel*, among other places.

Jaci Ruben

VALERIE LAKEN is the author of the novel *Dream House* and the story collection *Separate Kingdoms*. She teaches creative writing at the University of Wisconsin–Milwaukee, and at Pacific University's low-residency MFA program.

Jennifer Morales

JENNIFER MORALES is a poet, fiction writer, and performance artist based in rural Wisconsin. She lived in Milwaukee, including a stint in the Silver City neighborhood, for twenty-three years, and served as the city's first elected Latinx school board member. Her short story collection *Meet Me Halfway: Milwaukee Stories* was the Wisconsin Center for the Book's 2016 "Book of the Year." She serves on the board of the Driftless Writing Center.

Troye Fox

NICK PETRIE'S first novel, *The Drifter*, won the 2016 Thriller Award, the 2016 Barry Award for Best First Novel, and was nominated for Edgar and Anthony awards, as well as the Hammett Prize. He was named one of Apple's "10 Writers to Read" in 2017. His Peter Ash novels include *The Drifter*, *Burning Bright*, *Light It Up*, and *Tear It Down*. A husband and father, he lives in Milwaukee.

Elis Ramos Garcia

MATTHEW J. PRIGGE is a writer and historian. He is the author of three books, with a fourth due out in 2019. His book *Outlaws, Rebels, & Vixens: Motion Picture Censorship in Milwaukee, 1914–1971* won the Milwaukee County Historical Society's Gambrinus Prize for best local history book of 2016. He lives on Milwaukee's East Side with his wife Erika and their three rats, Mavis, Penguin, and Pinecone.

Katrice Battle

MARY THORSON was born and raised in Milwaukee. She received her BA in creative writing from the University of Wisconsin, Milwaukee, and her MFA from Pacific University. She has been published in various literary journals and has been nominated for a Pushcart Prize. She lives in Shorewood with her husband, daughter, and loud dog.

Susan Watson

LARRY WATSON is the author of *Montana 1948*, *Orchard*, *Let Him Go*, *As Good As Gone*, and other novels, as well the story collection *Justice*. His short stories and poems have appeared in *Gettysburg Review*, *New England Review*, *North American Review*, *Mississippi Review*, and other literary magazines. His essays and book reviews have been published in the *Los Angeles Times*, the *Chicago Sun-Times*, the *Washington Post*, the *Milwaukee Journal Sentinel*, and elsewhere.

Marie A. Wheeler

FRANK WHEELER JR. is the author of *The Wowzer* and *The Good Life*, which was published in France as *L'ordre des choses*. He is a graduate of both a police academy and a master's program in English. He works as a global security analyst and lives in Wisconsin with his wife Marie.

Acknowledgments

Special thanks to Scott Phillips, Erica Ruth Neubauer, Kate Hofmeister, Bryan and Jenny Veldboom, Daniel Goldin, Jon and Ruth Jordan, and my coworkers at Half Price Books Brookfield for their support. Thanks to Johnny Temple and the Akashic staff for this opportunity.